THE
NIGHT
SHIFT

ALSO BY ALEX FINLAY

Every Last Fear

Praise for
THE NIGHT SHIFT

"*The Night Shift* is a masterpiece of misdirection and misplaced motivation, further establishing Finlay as a literary force to be reckoned with."
—*Providence Sunday Journal*

"A suspenseful tale of vengeance, brotherly love, teenage romance, and the perils of jumping to conclusions. Finlay spins it at a rapid pace, his characters well-drawn and his tangled plot expertly developed. The twists arrive at a dizzying pace, and when the killer is finally revealed, few readers are likely to see it coming."
—Associated Press

"Encompassing the genres of thriller, mystery, and horror, *The Night Shift* is a novel that will stick with you."
—*Reader's Digest*

"[Finlay] has outdone himself with this latest. . . . [He] grabs readers from the very first line and keeps them propulsively turning pages with absolutely thrilling cliffhangers."
—*Newsweek*

"Fans of dual-timeline thrillers with intricately connected characters will love Finlay's fast-paced tale that delivers one stunning surprise after another."
—*Library Journal* (starred review)

whose intertwining fates—and secrets—will keep you hooked from the book's first page to its very last."
—*Crime by the Book*

"Instead of succumbing to the pressure that comes with a sophomore release (following last year's highly anticipated *Every Last Fear*), Finlay embraces that buzz and tension with his latest release, *The Night Shift*, and transfers all that potential angst onto his characters. From the book's opening scene, the tension never lets up."
—*The Big Thrill*

"Highly recommended for readers looking for fast-paced, twisty thrillers."   —*Mystery Tribune*

"Wow, this is crime fiction at its best. Instantly immersive, pacy and propulsive, and full of surprises. Alex Finlay is the real deal, believe me."
—Lee Child, #1 *New York Times* bestselling author

"*The Night Shift* weaves together two crimes, past and present, into a fast-paced, page-turning, slam dunk of a thriller. An exciting, entertaining read that I couldn't put down!"   —Samantha Downing, #1 international bestselling author of *My Lovely Wife* and *For Your Own Good*

THE
NIGHT
SHIFT

ALEX FINLAY

St. Martin's Paperbacks

Published in the United States by St. Martin's Paperbacks, an imprint of St. Martin's Publishing Group

THE NIGHT SHIFT

Copyright © 2022 by Alex Finlay.
Excerpt from *What Have We Done* copyright © 2022 by Alex Finlay.

For information, address St. Martin's Publishing Group, 120 Broadway, New York, NY 10271.

www.stmartins.com

Library of Congress Catalog Card Number: 2021044953

ISBN: 978-1-250-85038-6

Our books may be purchased in bulk for promotional, educational, or business use. Please contact your local bookseller or the Macmillan Corporate and Premium Sales Department at 1-800-221-7945, ext. 5442, or by email at MacmillanSpecialMarkets@macmillan.com.

Printed in the United States of America

Minotaur hardcover edition published 2022
St. Martin's Paperbacks edition / December 2022

10 9 8 7 6 5 4 3 2 1

For Trace

The world breaks everyone and afterward many are strong at the broken places.

—ERNEST HEMINGWAY, *A Farewell to Arms*

PROLOGUE

The night was expected to bring tragedy.

Planes falling from the sky. Elevators plunging to earth. World markets collapsing.

A digital apocalypse.

But Y2K was an otherwise typical Friday night at the Blockbuster Video in Linden, New Jersey. Steve had been store manager for six months now, and it was sure as shit a step up from his last job at the Taco Bell. Where his clothes always smelled of cooked meat and grease, and where cadres of drunken teens arrived loudly around eleven until he kicked them out at 2 a.m.

Here, they closed at ten, sharp. The customers were polite. Tonight, mostly couples looking for a rom-com or "something scary."

They didn't call Steve "pizza face," on account of his acne; didn't mock his uniform or leave smashed enchiritos all over the floor. His employees were better here too, more or less. The night shift included four sweet, albeit mischievous, teenage girls. All juniors or seniors, like the Taco Bell hooligans. Hell, like Steve himself only a few years ago, but somehow the girls treated him like he was their embarrassing dad. After only a few months on the job, he truly felt for their real fathers.

"Can I go on break?" Mandy said, shoving a VHS cartridge into the store's machine. It was the bane of the job, proof that nobody read the BE KIND, PLEASE REWIND stickers on the tapes.

Steve studied the long checkout line, the new girl, Ella, fumbling at the register next to him. "We close in half an hour," he said, exasperated. "Can't you wait? I need you to take register three."

"But *Steeevie*," Mandy said, lowering her voice to a whisper, "I have *girl* issues."

Steve blew out a loud breath. Unless he'd missed something in Sex Ed, it was impossible to have *girl* issues every single weekend, but what could he do?

"I can cover for her," Katie said, coming in from the cold, snowflakes in her hair, a pile of videos stacked in her arms from emptying the metal return receptacle stationed in the parking lot. She was the most responsible of the group, a Catholic school kid, a rule-follower. But even she was a pain in the neck. Just an hour ago, he'd had to remind all the girls not to venture out to the parking lot alone. The buddy system—was that so friggin' hard to grasp?

"Make it fast," Steve said to Mandy. "And where's Candy?"

Candy O'Shaughnessy was Mandy's partner in crime,

the other perpetrator of what the Blockbuster, Inc. Employee Handbook called "Class A violations." Though the store was four thousand square feet of open space, Candy always managed to disappear. She constantly gave him attitude, and once smuggled wine coolers into the break room. And Steve remained convinced that *she* was the one who put *Friday the 13th* inside the box for *101 Dalmatians*. Those parents had given him an earful. Said their kid would need therapy.

Join the club.

"I think she was in the kids' section," Mandy said with a smirk as she sauntered off to the break room.

Steve shook his head as he reached around the theft censors at the door and handed the customer the small plastic bag full of movies.

By closing time, neither Candy nor Mandy had emerged. They'd be hearing about this. For sure. Not cool.

Steve instructed Ella to work the door, unlocking and locking the dead bolt to let customers out but ensuring no one got in. She could handle that much, he thought. He told Katie to close out the registers. He'd go deal with the other two. Always something. He just wanted to get out of there, stop by Dad's house for a Pabst to celebrate surviving another year before the old man fell asleep. Then maybe catch more beers at Corky's Tavern, watch the ball drop on the TV behind the bar, see if there'd been any real chaos from the computer bug the news wouldn't shut up about. Not exactly "party like it's 1999"—if he never heard that song again it would be too soon—but it beat being alone at his crap apartment.

He navigated through the shelves of tapes, past the newer section with DVDs, and to the break room. It was cold as hell in there.

"Dammit, girls," he said to nobody, as he noticed the back door was open, the wind howling. If they were smoking out there, he swore to God . . . He'd told them a million times that for security they weren't supposed to open the back door. Steve could get in big trouble with Corporate if somebody—

He froze when he saw two sets of legs on the floor jutting out from behind the break room table.

As fear shredded through him, Steve felt someone grab a fistful of his hair and yank his head back. Then a strange coldness at his throat.

He was on the floor now, an ugly gurgle emanating from his neck. He watched as the figure turned out the break room lights. It felt like a small eternity before the door flew open, a burst of light filling the room. The sound of teenage chatter abruptly dying.

Steve wanted to call out, to warn them. But he felt his body convulsing and the world turning dark.

The last thing he heard was the screams.

DAY 1

FIFTEEN YEARS LATER

CHAPTER 1
ELLA

APRIL 2015

Ella pops a Xanax as she waits for the valet to take her keys. Driving into Manhattan always stresses her out. The frenetic confluence of cabbies rage-driving, cops jetting by with sirens blaring, pedestrians all but challenging you to run them over as they step defiantly into the street.

What the fuck is she doing here?

Last time, she'd promised herself that it would be the *last time*.

A young guy in a bellhop uniform stands at her window now. She hums down the glass.

"Checking in?" he asks. He's in his twenties and gives her the once-over.

"No, just meeting a friend."

He nods as if enjoying the euphemism. Sure, in that outfit, *a friend*.

Ella slips out of the car and palms the kid a five. She catches him stealing a look at the bill, unimpressed.

Give her a break. She's a therapist making $30K a

year, for fuck's sake, not some businessman on an expense account.

Inside the marble lobby of the Carlyle hotel, she makes a beeline for the bar. Against all sound medical judgment—she'd taken a pharmacology class at Wellesley—she pops another tiny blue pill.

She feels eyes on her as she enters the mahogany room. Faux old-money decor and the din of Franz Liszt from the gray-haired pianist trying not to look defeated at the culmination of his music career.

Ella should talk. She's barely making her half of the rent, coming into the city so she won't bump into one of her fiancé's friends. Or a client from her fledgling practice. She thinks about sixteen-year-old Layla from their session that morning. She's cutting herself again. Layla didn't need to explain why. Ella understands.

Surveying the bar, Ella snags the look of a man in an expensive suit holding a tumbler of Scotch. They always drink Scotch. And love to talk about it. The special barrels this, the unique region that. Beyond the Scotch prattle, most tend to have a pale band of skin on their left ring finger. Ella doesn't bother to take off her engagement ring. The Scotch guys don't care.

The man smiles at her.

He'll do.

Ella is always surprised how easy it is. She doesn't need Tinder when she has this black dress.

So she goes to meet her new friend.

A few hours later, her phone chimes. She's in a hotel room now, the only light from under the door. On these frolics, she always sets the alarm for 5 a.m. It avoids awkward morning-after talk.

But it isn't the sound of the alarm. It's an incoming call. She extracts herself from under Rick's hairy arm. She wonders if that's his real name. He looks like a Rick. Though he probably thought she looks like a Candy. Something sweet but bad for you. Much like her old friend, whose name she borrowed. She always uses their names. Candy, Mandy, Katie. She has no idea why.

"Hello," she whispers into the phone. She scuttles quietly to the bathroom, scooping up the black dress off the floor. The marble is cool under her feet.

"Ella, I'm sorry to call this late. It's Dale."

"Mr. Steadman?" After all these years she can't bring herself to call him by his first name. You're always a kid to the teachers in your life. She hasn't spoken to him in a year, not since her former teacher and now principal at her old high school had her meet with students in the wake of a school shooting in a neighboring township. "Is everything okay?" She feels drumbeats in her chest. *Why would he be calling at this hour? Could it be? Could they finally have caught him? No, good news rarely arrives in a wee-hours call.*

"Something awful has happened. I know it's asking a lot. But can you come to RWJ?"

Come to the hospital? Now?

Before she can ask, Mr. Steadman says, "There's been a—one of my students needs your help."

She wants to protest. Wants to make an excuse. But she can't. Not after everything Mr. Steadman has done for her.

"Sure, of course," she says. "I'm visiting a friend in the city. I can get there in about an hour."

"I wouldn't drag you out here if I thought there was someone else who could . . ." He trails off.

Ella's head is swirling. She's exhausted. Still tipsy. Confused. She composes herself. "Can you tell me what this is about?"

Mr. Steadman's voice catches. "Four girls were attacked at an ice cream shop in Linden. Only one survived. She needs someone who understands, who can—"

"I'm on my way," Ella says killing the line, knowing she's uniquely qualified to help this girl.

Knowing what it's like to be the only one who made it out alive.

CHAPTER 2

The parking lot of the Robert Wood Johnson University Hospital is covered in a spring fog. The lot is nearly empty save for a gathering of police cars. A woman in scrubs paces outside the front doors, talking on a cell phone.

Ella grips the steering wheel even though she's parked, and looks down at her pale, bare legs. She debates going home to change into something more professional. But Mr. Steadman sounded uncharacteristically rattled. He's usually a rock.

She takes a look at herself in the visor mirror, thumbs her smeared eye makeup. Climbing out of the car, she decides the fuck-me heels are a bit much. She reaches back for her gym bag, pulls out her sneakers.

The woman in scrubs is still pacing out front. Ella sees her discreetly put a fist to her mouth, suck in a deep breath, followed by a plume of vape mist.

We all have our secrets.

The receptionist inside barely gives her a second look. The woman has probably seen it all working the ER night shift. Ella once dated a med student who'd done an ER residency rotation, and he regaled her with tales of the guy with a Barbie stuck up his ass, the PCP fiend who'd eaten two of his own fingers during a bad trip, the construction worker with a nail deep in his brain yet still conscious and talking. A therapist in nightclub attire probably didn't make the Top 10 for weird.

The receptionist says something into the phone, then waves Ella inside the treatment area. The door makes a jarring buzz and Ella walks into a large room bathed in fluorescent light, beeping and voices echoing from behind beds surrounded by blue curtains. At the far end, she sees Mr. Steadman talking to a group of white guys. Three uniformed police officers and a stern-looking man with a mustache whose polo shirt is tucked tight into his jeans. He and Mr. Steadman seem to be having a disagreement.

For a split second, Ella feels a flight instinct. A memory slithers into her head, the procession of cops, doctors, and social workers asking the same questions. *Did you get a look at him? What do you remember? Did he touch you?* She looks at the floor for a moment, trying to collect herself, then catches a glimpse of her bare thighs again and is transported back to the exam room, her legs in stirrups.

Ella had been nonresponsive after the attack. The hospital's psych team was unsuccessful, and Ella's parents were at a loss. The school sent over Mr. Steadman. He wasn't trained in trauma response, he was merely the fill-in for a guidance counselor out on maternity leave. The cool teacher. Young, good-looking. The one the moms fawned over. At the same time, he was capable, no-nonsense, the kind of person who you wanted in charge, which is probably why they later made him the school's principal.

Mr. Steadman sees her and gives a small wave. He doesn't react to the muffled screams coming from a curtained room near the huddle of men. A doctor emerges from the room, grimacing. He says something to the group gathered with Mr. Steadman, shaking his head. Mr. Steadman puts a reassuring hand on the doctor's shoulder, then walks over to Ella.

"Thanks for coming. I'm sorry to interrupt your night," Steadman says, the only acknowledgment of her getup.

He fills her in. After midnight, the teenage employees of the Dairy Creamery were found murdered in the back room of the ice cream shop. The mother of two of the girls, sisters, got worried when they didn't return home from their shift and didn't respond to texts. The mother is sedated now.

"There was a survivor?" Ella knows the answer. It's why she's here.

Mr. Steadman nods. "A student at my school. She didn't work there. We think she was just a customer. Maybe interrupted him." Mr. Steadman takes a cleansing breath. "I was hoping you could talk to her. The doctors and detectives aren't getting anywhere. She's— well, you'll see. The Union County prosecutor called me, since . . ."

He doesn't need to complete the sentence, the reason clear: because it worked for Ella after Blockbuster.

"But she won't talk with me or anyone else or let the doctors examine her. I hoped you could try before they're forced to sedate her."

"I'm not sure I have the—"

"You're our best hope. And I won't be able to hold them off for much longer." Mr. Steadman directs his gaze to the man in the polo and jeans, a detective, she presumes, who undoubtedly is itching to interview the girl. A killer's on the loose.

"What's her name?"

"Jessica Duvall, but she goes by Jesse."

"Where are her parents? Won't she talk to them?"

"She's in foster care. I'm not sure why. She's new to my school, and they don't give us much information."

The murmuring from the huddle of cops grows louder. They're looking at Ella.

She takes a deep breath and steps into the room.

CHAPTER 3
KELLER

Sarah Keller reaches for her phone, which is pinging on the nightstand. Three texts at 5:30 a.m. She's been lying awake for an hour anyway. Feeling the two sets of feet inside her belly kicking wildly, fallout from the Thai food last night. She spent those sixty minutes listening to Bob snore. Worrying about keeping up with her job and money when the twins arrive. In their five-year marriage, she's never known Bob to lie awake about anything. Not a worrier, her husband.

She reads the texts from her boss.

Locals need assistance.
Union County.

That's unusual. The FBI usually doesn't get involved with local law enforcement unless it's something big—terrorism, kidnapping, or the like—and Keller's still a relatively junior agent.

Another text pings. A link to a news story. She feels

a flutter in her chest as she reads the details, which are still sketchy. A mass killing at an ice cream store in Linden, three dead. A possible survivor.

She taps out a return text.

Sure, need me there right now?

There's a long delay as the dots pulse while he types. He likely thumbed out an annoyed response—*of course, now*—then erased it. A good boss deletes annoyed messages before sending them. And despite his cold, Swiss-banker demeanor, Stan Webb is a good boss.

As she struggles to get her giant, eight-month-pregnant body out of the bed, the text finally arrives.

Yes.

Always an economy of words with Stan. She'll call him from the car.

After showering—a precarious endeavor of stepping into the tub without crashing to the floor—Keller puts on her maternity suit, one of two that still fits. She smells something coming from the kitchen. She's not one to buy into old wives' tales about pregnancy, but her senses really are heightened.

Bob's out of bed and washing a pan in the sink. On the small kitchen table, he's set a plate with scrambled eggs and grilled tomatoes on a bagel. All month he's been preparing recipes from a website catering to pregnant women.

"You didn't have to get up," she says.

"When Clarice Starling gets a text at five in the morning, I know I'd better cook or my bambinos will only get a PowerBar to keep 'em going." He pulls back the chair for her to sit.

"I've gotta run. Stan needs me to—"

"Ah, ah, ah, when Stan has two humans in his belly he can tell you to hurry up." Bob sits across from her. He has bags under his eyes and looks ragged.

"What time did you get home last night?" she asks. He's a soundman at a recording studio, his schedule at the whim of the artists.

"Three or so," he says. "A rowdy polka band," he adds, as if that explains the late night. She doesn't know if he's kidding. It's hard to tell sometimes.

"You shouldn't have gotten up, I can get my own—"

"I almost forgot, I made you something." He jumps out of his chair and retrieves a thermos from the counter.

"Please, not the pregnancy smoothie you've been going on about?"

He raises his eyebrows up and down.

When she finishes the bagel, Bob helps her out of the chair.

"I'm pregnant, not incapacitated, you know."

Bob doesn't reply. He kneels so he's facing her belly. Looking down at his bald head—the dome surrounded by the doughnut of hair that is ironic without him intending it to be—Keller feels a surge of warmth run through her.

"Take care of your mama, little Feebies," Bob tells her tummy.

Keller has never discharged her firearm in the line of duty, yet her husband treats her like she's a serial-killer hunter.

Today, though, maybe she is.

CHAPTER 4
ELLA

The survivor, Jesse Duvall, sits in the corner on the floor, her arms wrapped around her knees, head down.

The room is too bright, the paper covering the exam table wrinkled and ripped.

Without looking up, the teen says, "I already told you *assholes* that I don't need an examination. Now leave me the *fuck* alone."

It's not a yell. She sounds more tired. Matter of fact.

Ella says, "No one's going to touch you without your permission."

Jesse's head pops up. She has a pretty face, large, almond-shaped eyes. A curious expression. "Who are you?"

"My name's Ella. I'm a counselor."

This seems to amuse Jesse. "Where do you counsel— a strip club?"

Humor—even dark humor—is a good sign. Ella's instincts tell her that this girl is strong. Ignoring the jab, she says, "I know right now you want nothing but to be left alone. To go home to your own bed."

"Home." Jesse says the word with derision.

Ella realizes she's already made her first mistake. Mr. Steadman told her that Jesse's a foster kid.

"The thing is," Ella continues, "that whoever hurt you and your friends, he's still out there. We need to make sure he can't hurt anyone else. You may have seen something that can help the police catch—"

Jesse murmurs something; her head's on her knees again.

"What was that?"

Jesse says nothing.

"I know this is hard and—"

Jesse's head snaps up. "How would *you* know? Because you read it in some book? Or because you talk to housewives about their feelings? Or rich kids about their anxiety over getting into a good college? Lady, I've talked to dozens of you people, and the only difference between them and you is that *they* weren't dressed like a ho."

"But I do know, Jesse. I do."

Jesse listens while Ella explains. About coming into the break room on New Year's Eve 1999. About the crushing blow to her head. About not remembering much else until they found her in a ring of red in the snow after she'd come to and run outside. She tries to keep it clinical but she feels the tears filling her eyes. She leaves out the part about awaking to Katie's nearly decapitated head on her lap, as if her friend had crawled to her for help and died there. And she leaves out th recurring nightmare of the figure bending down, sliding the blade into her as he whispered: *"Good night, pretty girl."*

"They weren't my friends," Jesse says when Ella's finished. "I barely knew them." For the first time, her voice breaks.

"You were buying ice cream?"

She shakes her head. "I just needed to use the bathroom. When I came out . . ."

"Did you see who—"

"No. He hit me. It felt like being hit with a baseball bat and everything else is a blur."

Ella tries not to react. It's so familiar, so horrible, so . . . *Stop it.* "Were there any customers in the store when you went inside?"

"No. They were closing up."

Ella swallows a lump in her throat. "Did you see anyone outside around the shop or anything suspicious?"

Jesse shakes her head again.

"Did he touch you?" Ella can't bring herself to say more; she clasps her hands behind her back to hide the trembling.

"No," Jesse says with too much conviction.

"You were unconscious. Are you sure? Because—"

"I've been in group homes since I was fourteen. I know what it feels like to have someone try to touch you in your sleep."

Ella nods, swallows again.

By 6:30 a.m., Jesse's agreed to give them her clothes—for DNA and crime scene analysis. She's also agreed to talk to a doctor—a female doctor. And she'll stay for observation—because of the concussion.

"I'll come back later to check on you," Ella says.

Jesse nods.

Ella considers hugging her. Putting a hand on hers. But decides against it. Jesse Duvall isn't fragile like Ella was. She's in shock, traumatized, but Ella's instincts were right: she's a strong girl. This makes Ella ashamed of herself for some reason.

As Ella reaches the door, Jesse says it. The thing that nearly levels Ella.

"I do remember one thing."

"What's that?"

"I didn't see him, but I have this foggy memory of a figure crouching down and whispering in my ear."

Ella feels heat in her face, the world tilting.

"He said, *'Good night, pretty girl.'*"

CHAPTER 5
CHRIS

Chris examines the man sitting across from him in the filthy conference room of the Union County jail. He has an ogre's teeth and is picking at the scabs on his pale arms. Par for the course for Chris's public-defender clients.

Most are in for drugs. He pities them more than anything. The low-income kids have it the worst, swept up in disproportionate numbers. But he's also seen his share of affluent teenage beauty queens turned to balding, pockmarked monsters. College kids holding up CVS pharmacies to get a fix. Their families devastated and confused. *We're not those kinds of people.* But you don't know that until you get your first taste of crystal meth. Or experience the euphoria of painkillers stolen from your mom's medicine cabinet.

The families usually blame the dealers. But Chris knows better. No one blames the liquor store clerk for your aunt being in AA. And his own brother had been a small-time dealer. Not because he was a bad person, but for the simple reason that they needed food on the table.

"If you agree to go to a treatment center," Chris says to his client, "I might be able to convince them to avoid any time."

The genius had tried to pawn a Louis Vuitton hand-bag that still had the snatching victim's ID in it. Even the crooked pawnshop owner couldn't turn a blind eye.

"And who's gonna pay for that?"

"I can try to get you into a state program."

His client thinks about this. Debating life without a fix versus a likely short stint at the jail, where drugs are easier to get than toilet paper.

"I want me a real lawyer. Not some public *pretender*."

Chris no longer takes offense at this. It's a common misperception: that a lawyer dumb enough to work for poverty wages and zero respect probably isn't Clarence Darrow. Maybe not. But Chris passed the bar two years ago and has already first-chaired more jury trials than most private-practice lawyers did during their entire careers. And PDs are the best at working plea deals for lost causes like this one. They know the prosecutors—the hard-asses to avoid, the softies who can be manipulated with sob stories, and the lazy ones you can slip things by.

"You got the money, you can hire any lawyer you want," Chris says. "But if not, you got me."

His client's pupils, saucers even after a night in the can, set on Chris. "Make the deal," he says.

The guard returns and ushers the twitchy man away,

and Chris looks at his phone for the next sad case on his schedule.

On his news feed a headline momentarily causes his heart to trip: TEENAGE EMPLOYEES KILLED AT LINDEN ICE CREAM SHOP, ONLY ONE SURVIVOR.

Chris feels acid crawl up his throat, his head fuzzy, like a contact high from being in close quarters with his client. He reads the opening to the story:

Three employees of a Dairy Creamery in Linden were found brutally slain last night, sending shock waves through the community. The bodies of night manager Beth Ann Hughes, 18, and two other employees, both minors, were found after midnight in the store at 500 Elizabeth Avenue, police said. A fourth victim, a customer, survived the attack and is hospitalized but in stable condition. The crime is reminiscent of a New Year's Eve attack at the Linden Blockbuster Video fifteen years ago . . .

Chris stares absently at the marred table as his mind jumps to that night; Chris sitting at their own marred kitchen table, watching his big brother Vince rushing to finish the Hamburger Helper on the stovetop.

"Where you been?" Chris asks his older brother. It's nearly ten o'clock. Vince has just rushed in and is clanking pans around the kitchen. A block of ground chuck sizzles in the skillet.

Vince turns and cocks an eyebrow.

Chris's eyes flash. "A girl?" At twelve years old, Chris is both fascinated and perplexed by the opposite sex.

Vince dumps the powder and noodles into the pan. "Not just any girl."

"Is she hot?"

Vince whirls around and gives him a hard glare. "What'd I tell you about respect? You wanna be like *him* or like us?" He says this a lot to Chris. A reminder that neither wants to turn out like their dad. The man who punches first, asks questions later, and who'd driven their mother to flee.

Chris frowns. He doesn't like to disappoint Vince, who's filled with teenage wisdom, never mind that he sells dope on the side.

Vince says, "She's— I can't explain it. But you know how we talk about getting out of this shithole life?"

Chris nods. *Nirvana,* Vince calls it. Like the band. That's why Vince puts so much pressure on Chris to get good grades.

"By the way, you get the grade on that book report yet?" Vince says, eyes narrowed.

"Not yet, I will after the break," Chris says.

"Anyway, the new life you're gonna get with that brain of yours? She smells like that."

"Smells?" Chris says, bunching his face.

"It's just a—"

The front door flies open and Vince scurries to put the gray slop on the plate. The smell of booze wafts from the doorway and Dad's face turns dark when he sees that dinner isn't on the table. Their father works at a self-storage company near the Linden sewage plant. His shift is from eight to eight, then he drinks at the bar until he gets hungry, and expects his meal hot and waiting for him or someone's getting the belt. New Year's Eve is no exception.

Their dad takes his seat, the chair scraping loudly on the cracked linoleum. Vince puts the plate in front of him. His brother goes to the sink to fill up a glass with tap water when Dad lobs the full plate at the back of Vince's head. After hitting its target, the plate smashes to the floor, ground beef and oozy gravy spattering all over his big brother and the kitchen.

Vince turns, his eyes wild, but he isn't seriously hurt. "Why'd you—"

But their father is already on his feet. He rams his fist into Vince's gut.

"Too much damn salt!"

Chris starts to rise from his chair to defend his brother, or at least make sure he's okay. But even doubled over, Vince glances up at Chris and gives a small shake of the head. *Don't.*

Their father staggers to his bedroom.

Chris runs over to his big brother. "You all right?"

Vince stands upright, touches the back of his head, then studies the mix of red and brown on his fingers. He gives Chris a wistful smile. "I thought the salt would hide the taste of the spit."

Chris smiles back at him.

Looking Chris in the eyes, Vince says, "Promise me you'll keep those grades up and you'll leave here and never look back. If you let it, the stink of him will cling to you forever. Promise me you won't let it."

"Nirvana," Chris says, "I promise."

Later that night, Chris wakes to the sound of cracking

wood. He hears shouting and heavy footsteps, lots of them. Chris thinks someone is breaking into their house.

He runs out of his bedroom to Vince's room, but his brother isn't there.

Dad's voice booms from the living room. *"I knew you was no good! I swear, I regret the day you was born!"*

Chris musters the courage and heads to the living room. It's filled with men in uniforms. Two of them are standing in front of his father, who's on the sofa, still ranting. Vince is facedown on the floor, a cop's knee drilling into his back, roughly putting on handcuffs.

Vince is hoisted to his feet, one eye nearly swollen shut, his mouth bleeding.

Chris is scared, confused. All *this* for selling pot?

The cops drag Vince out, leaving behind a broken doorframe and their father, who's angry about the damage and will take that out on Chris.

The sound of Chris's phone mercifully pulls him to the present.

It's Ms. May. His adoptive mother, who he still doesn't call *Mom,* but she doesn't mind. He contemplates swiping her to voice mail, but she rarely calls while he's at work. It might be about Clint, his adoptive father, who's been having health problems.

"Christopher, how are you doing, dear?"

"I'm great, Ms. May. I'm actually at the jail for work. Is everything okay?"

"Everything's fine here. I was baking an apple pie and I know how much you love them and just wanted to check in on my favorite person."

Chris puts two and two together and realizes why she's calling. It isn't because of a pie.

"I'm not sure if you've seen the news," she continues, confirming his suspicions, "but there's been an—"

"At the ice cream store," he interrupts, "yes, I saw that. Just awful."

"Oh, you saw it. I thought you might, and I just wanted to make sure you're all right. I thought it might bring back some unpleasant—"

"I'm okay."

She's a kind, sweet woman, Ms. May. In the aftermath of Vince's arrest, one of the prosecutors running the investigation—now the head of the Union County Prosecutor's Office—had questioned Chris. He'd seemed more interested in Chris's bruises and fat lip than the whereabouts of his fugitive big brother. Shortly after, Chris found himself in foster care with Ms. May and Clint. Clint isn't his real name, just what Ms. May and Chris call him ever since Chris had compared him to a cranky character played by Clint Eastwood in a movie they'd watched together.

"Really, I'm fine, but thanks for checking. How's Clint doing? Feeling okay?"

"You know him. The doctor tells him to take it easy, so he's out there building a shed in the garden."

Chris smiles. "You tell him to take it easy."

"I try, dear," she says. "I know you're working, so I'll let you go." She pauses. "Are you sure you're okay?"

"I'm totally fine. I'll see you tomorrow night for dinner." They'd changed his life, adopted him, given him a new name, a new school, a new life. He's Chris Ford now. The guy with supportive parents, a beautiful girlfriend, a law degree from Columbia. The least he can do is dine with them once a week, the only thing Ms. May has ever asked of him.

"I'm looking forward to it," Ms. May says. She disconnects the line.

Chris looks around the bleak conference room.

Are you sure you're okay?

He isn't so sure about that.

CHAPTER 6
KELLER

"The prodigal daughter returns."

Keller smiles at Union County Prosecutor Hal Kowalski, who's stationed behind a mountain of papers on his desk at the Ruotolo Justice Center.

Eyeing Keller's pregnant belly, the county's chief law-enforcement officer smiles broadly. "Holy smokes, you came with a task force."

"How are you, Hal?"

"You know better than to ask someone my age that question." Hal actually doesn't look much older than he had when Keller interned at UCPO during summer breaks from college. Hal's still athletic with a Marine's hair and demeanor. He gestures for her to take the chair opposite his desk.

"When I told Stan we needed help from the Feds, I didn't know he'd send the A Team." Hal's an old friend of her boss, the SAC of the Newark field office. Keller suspects that's how she landed the Newark assignment five years ago, a plum post for a new agent. She also thinks that's why she's here now.

"How is Stan?" Hal asks. "Still got that stick up his keister?"

"No, he's actually started yoga and has us all going to mindfulness seminars."

Hal studies her for a long moment. "Tell me you're kidding."

Keller grins, confirming that she most certainly is.

"Still a smartass, I see. That's good. Don't let them dark suits take that from you."

Requisite small talk out of the way—neither Hal nor Keller cares much for it—Hal gets down to business.

"You've been briefed on the ice cream shop?" he asks.

"Yes. I see there's already media stationed out front. They brought out the tents, so it looks like they're getting comfortable."

Hal sighs, shifts in his chair. "They're gonna go on a feeding frenzy when they find out the perp used a knife."

He doesn't need to say why. In the fifteen years since the Blockbuster slayings, there've been countless mass killings. The world has changed dramatically. But in only a vanishing few cases has the perpetrator used a blade.

"You don't think Vince Whitaker . . ." Keller doesn't finish the question.

"I don't know—that's why I brought you all in. Let your shop shrink some heads, see what *you* think."

"Any leads?"

Hal puts a hand on his temple and massages. "Negatory," he says. "We're trying to get info from the surviving girl. I'm told she's in shock but maybe we'll get a break. If not, I'll give it a week before they're calling for my head."

"And mine."

"Why the hell else would I call in the FBI?" The corners of Hal's lips rise slightly.

"What can we do to help?"

"Rule out Vince Whitaker. I can't imagine he's back. He fell off the face of the earth fifteen years ago. But you have resources we don't. And I'd prefer my team not get pulled sideways chasing a ghost. Stan said you all can handle the Whitaker angle because of the UFAP warrant."

The FBI generally doesn't have jurisdiction over homicides, which are state-law crimes. But here the federal hook is an Unlawful Flight to Avoid Prosecution warrant for Vince Whitaker. Standard operating procedure when a high-profile perp goes on the run. The state and local authorities get the Feds to issue a UFAP warrant, which opens up federal coffers to help track the suspect.

Keller nods. "But the ice cream store . . . what can we do to help with—"

"On that, let's take things a day at a time. My chief detective, a humorless SOB named Joe Arpeggio, is running point. In case you don't watch TV cop shows, the local yokels are never happy to have the Feebies crash the party."

"You know I won't try to—"

"I know you won't. But let him figure that out on his own. Between the two of you, maybe you can solve this thing before they give me my gold watch in June."

"You're retiring?"

"Put in my papers a few months ago," Hal says with zero nostalgia. "Arpeggio will come around, particularly if he gets no leads, but short-term, I want you to focus on Vincent Whitaker. But if Arpeggio needs your lab or anything, I'd appreciate the assist."

Keller nods. It's likely a fool's errand. She pulled the UFAP file on Vince Whitaker that morning; the case is icc-cold, the file razor-thin. The Feds are being brought in for their resources, that's it.

"One of our detectives, the closest we have to an expert on the Blockbuster file, he'll ride shotgun if you don't mind."

Keller frowns.

"Don't worry," Hal says, "he's a good kid, gonna be a helluva detective."

Good kid? Just how old is he? The Union County Prosecutor's Office is unique in that it has more than two hundred employees, including its own squad of detectives. Back in the day, Keller interned with UCPO's Homicide Task Force. She considers arguing against being coupled with a rookie. But she knows Hal well enough to understand that he's not asking permission.

"He's in office four-thirty. You know the way."

Keller's office when she was an intern.

And with that, she knows the meeting is over. She thanks him and heads for the door.

"Sarah," Hal says, his voice softer than before.

She turns.

He motions to her belly. "Congratulations, dear."

CHAPTER 7
ELLA

Ella sits in her car in front of a boarded-up structure with a giant FOR LEASE sign plastered on it. When she was in high school, she'd take the long way to avoid seeing the familiar blue-and-yellow sign shaped like a movie ticket. In college, when she came home on breaks and convinced herself she needed to face her fears and all that nonsense, the old video store building housed a Sizzler steakhouse. The thought of people eating low-end beef on that site felt sacrilegious.

Ella tugs at her dress top. She needs to get home and change. She glances at her cleavage and her mind flashes to Candy. On Ella's first day on the job at Blockbuster, her coworker took scissors to the hideous uniform, the blue polo with the bright yellow collar, so that the front plunged nearly to Candy's belly button. Their manager—Stevie they all called him—nearly fainted when he saw her.

Ella needs to stop. She's twisting her hair again. A habit she once thought was cute that had morphed into a compulsion after that night. She would twist at the roots, leaving tiny bald spots. Her parents sent her to a specialist on trichotillomania. Talk therapy, making fidgets for her hands, habit-reversal training, but the truth was, they had no idea what caused the compulsion or how to stop it. That's what drew Ella to work in the trauma field: how little all the well-meaning therapists understood her. Maybe, just maybe, she hoped, she could unlock the secrets of the mind and help other victims. And maybe even herself.

She looks over to the corner of the lot. That's where a witness saw *His* car. Near the video-return receptacle, long since removed.

She puts her face in her hands, and she weeps.

CHAPTER 8
KELLER

Keller makes her way to the office of Atticus Singh—yes, that's his actual name. He has brown skin, doe eyes, and wears a nice suit with a skinny tie over expensive shoes. Like Hal said, Atticus is young—he has to be just out of college. No degrees hang on the wall but she notices a coffee mug inscribed with a single, powerful word in blue: YALE.

"Special Agent Keller," Atticus says, reaching out his hand for an eager shake. "It's an honor."

Keller nods and looks around the office again, taken back to her summers as an intern in the same miserable space. The investigative unit must have vastly expanded to stick this poor kid in the interns' closet.

"This used to be my office," Keller says. "I interned for the county in college."

"How funny," Atticus says. "It's small, but it could be worse. My friend Brian literally is in what used to be a storage closet in the basement." He smiles.

Keller eyes the bulletin board that takes up nearly the entire wall. It's a crime board, the Blockbuster case, by the looks of it. Photos of the employees of the video store, the victims. A man in his twenties, skinny with acne, and four pretty teenage girls, all frozen in time in what appear to be high school yearbook photos. Under them, an unnerving black-and-white picture of the Blockbuster parking lot, empty but for a cluster of cars in the employee section. At the top of the board, a mug shot. She recognizes the photo. It's of then-eighteen-year-old Vincent Whitaker. He has a swollen eye and cut lip—courtesy of the cops who busted down his door and picked him up the night of the massacre. He's handsome in that bad-boy James Dean way, the dated photo adding to the mystique.

"Impressive work. I understand you're the resident expert on the Blockbuster case," she says.

Atticus nods earnestly. He clearly takes pride in his work, and Keller likes that.

"You can brief me on the way to the scene."

"We're going to the Dairy Creamery? I thought we're limited to Blockbuster and Vince Whitaker."

"We can't do our job on Whitaker without seeing if there's any connection to the latest murders, can we?" Keller gives him a knowing look.

Atticus looks at her with those enthusiastic doe eyes: "Sweet!"

Atticus says he can drive them. Keller agrees until he stops at a faded red two-seater convertible—an old MG

Midget. She rests a hand on her belly and glances at him wearily.

"I think maybe we should take my car," she says.

It takes Atticus a moment, then the light bulb clicks on. "Sure sure sure. How stupid of me."

On the drive, Keller asks him to brief her on the Blockbuster file.

"You're familiar with the case?" Atticus asks, as if deciding where to start.

"I remember it. I went to high school in Tenafly. I was a senior when it happened. Next to Columbine, it was one of those remember-where-you-were moments for me when I was a kid." At the time, brutal murders at the edge of the millennium felt like the country losing its innocence. Back then, Keller'd had no idea that less than two years later, on September 11, 2001, it truly would become a new world.

While an intern at UCPO, Keller had heard about the Blockbuster case. By then, the search for Vince Whitaker had already gone cold. She'd never worked the investigation, and mostly did grunt work, making copies, getting coffee, filing paperwork.

She listens as Atticus gives her the basics. Vince Whitaker was arrested the night of the crime after he'd been seen at the Blockbuster earlier that night, his car later spotted in the lot at closing. Authorities also matched a print on the break room door to his index finger. It was thin, but under immense pressure, Hal's predecessor ordered the arrest. A public defender got Whitaker sprung for insufficient probable cause, and

Whitaker disappeared. A day later, in Whitaker's locker at the high school, they found the murder weapon, an ordinary chef's knife taken from the Blockbuster break room.

"That's when all hell broke loose," Atticus says. "The county prosecutor was forced to resign, and the public defender who represented Whitaker received death threats and basically was run out of town. And you all got involved with the manhunt."

Manhunt is an overstatement, but Keller doesn't say so. The FBI's file includes reports of random sightings of Whitaker over the years, many abroad. But the Bureau hasn't dedicated significant resources to finding him. The few leads, most the result of an old segment on *Unsolved Mysteries,* led nowhere.

"You've gone through all the reports and files?" Keller asks.

Atticus nods.

"Have you done any interviews?"

Atticus shakes his head. "The Whitaker file's more of a hobby. My bosses say the question isn't *who* committed the crime, just the location of the perp. They said I could go active only if I uncovered something significant to help track him down."

"Well, let's go uncover something significant, I guess," she says, turning into the parking lot of the ice cream store.

"Awesome."

Keller turns and gives him a look. "I appreciate the enthusiasm, I do. But can I give you some advice?"

Atticus nods.

"These girls had hopes and dreams, and their friends and loved ones are still coming to terms with the fact that they're gone forever. And given their horrific last moments . . ."

Atticus looks at his lap, nods.

Keller stops at the choke point that leads into the lot. A uniformed officer stationed in front of a sawhorse approaches.

"Good crime scene control," Keller says, more to herself than to Atticus.

"The CSU team's solid," Atticus replies.

The officer peers into the car. Before Keller displays her badge, the officer seems to recognize Atticus and moves aside the sawhorse.

Keller drives slowly, her eyes sweeping the area for security cameras. The Dairy Creamery is a stand-alone structure. To the west, at the far end of the large lot, is a strip of businesses. A State Farm insurance office, a pet store, a sandwich place.

"I gotta warn you," Atticus says, "the lead detective, Joe Arpeggio, can be a bit, ah, difficult."

Keller makes no reply. She's been dealing with *difficult* men—a nice way of saying condescending jackasses—her whole life, starting with her father.

The pair make their way past the police tape. Before entering, they sign a log and slip on surgical booties, latex gloves, and hair covers. Inside they're met by a tall man with a mustache in a polo tucked into his jeans. He has dark crescents under his eyes.

Keller approaches, sticks out her hand. "I'm Sarah Keller." She deliberately uses her first name, not her title, and smiles. Always best to start out friendly.

"We're glad to have you on board," Arpeggio says, as he squeezes her hand too tight. Why did they always feel the need to squeeze so tight? Arpeggio nods at Atticus.

"Walk you through the scene?"

Keller prefers to take things in without commentary, but again, better to play nice.

"That would be great."

Arpeggio steps carefully in his foot coverings along the checkered floor past the small circular tables and behind the glass case containing tubs of ice cream.

"The three employees, two high school girls and their eighteen-year-old manager, were marched into the back room. There's a panic button, a silent alarm, in case of a robbery or emergency." He gestures to a small button mounted under the register. "None of them set off the alarm."

"They knew the perp," Keller says, a statement, not a question.

Arpeggio gives a one-shouldered shrug. "Or it all happened too fast."

He turns to the back room. The door has a sign that reads, ICE CREAM MAKERS ONLY. Inside is a small space with commercial freezers and shelves packed with supplies. Stacks of napkins, cartons of plastic spoons, boxes of straws.

"All three employees were lined up facedown on the floor."

Keller studies the area. No items seem out of place.

No signs of a struggle. But three pools of blood stain the carpet. Atticus stares at the ugly red blots for a long time.

Arpeggio pushes through a side door that leads to a narrow hall with a single bathroom at the end. "Our survivor was in the bathroom. She didn't see or hear anything and was knocked in the head the moment she came out. No clue why she was spared."

"Were any knives missing from the shop?"

"We don't think so," Arpeggio says, his tone loaded with *This has nothing to do with Blockbuster.* Unlike the video store, the killer came prepared.

"Cell phones?"

Arpeggio shakes his head. "The unsub took them. Money was left in the register. Nothing else of value taken, as far as we can tell."

Taking the phones suggests that there was something on them the killer didn't want the authorities to see.

Arpeggio continues, "Cell company says all the phones went dark a few minutes after ten, just after closing. They're pulling together detailed reports for all the phones, and should get them to us today, tomorrow at the latest."

Keller nods approvingly.

Arpeggio looks at his watch. "I've gotta get over to the high school. Talk to the girls' friends."

"Mind if we tag along?" Keller asks. "It's on my list. Vince Whitaker went to school there . . ."

Arpeggio eyes her suspiciously, then shrugs his reluctant assent.

CHAPTER 9
ELLA

Ella is surprised when she opens the apartment door and Brad is there. He's supposed to be on a business trip.

"Oh, thank God, I was worried about you." He's standing, like he's been pacing circles around their small living room. His suitcase sits by the door. He gives her a long, bewildered look. Clearly, her outfit isn't helping things. "Where have you—"

"Work." Ella tries to appear nonchalant as she throws her keys on the table. "You're back early?" she says. "I thought you weren't coming home until—"

"The conference was a drag. I got in last night. Thought I'd surprise you. Apparently, I did."

She notices a bouquet of wilted grocery-store flowers and some Chinese food still in the delivery bag on the table. He's had a long night, it appears.

"Didn't you get my texts?"

She'd seen a series of messages, but hadn't read them, assuming he was just checking in.

"Sorry," she says.

Brad looks at her wearily. They've been through this before. Brad works in cyber security. He sells software to companies to help them prevent data breaches and the attendant blackmail and ruined lives that often accompany criminals roaming through high-powered executives' emails and browser histories. He could drone on about it forever—how he's the front line of defense in a new war. He was supposed to be out with fellow IT sales nerds for several days of PowerPoint presentations and watered-down drinks at an Embassy Suites in Atlantic City.

"I thought we were past this," he says, staring at her.

"Past what?"

He rolls his eyes. He's wound up, probably been stewing all night.

"I said it was for work."

He shakes his head.

She can try to explain. Tell him about what happened at the ice cream store, being called to the hospital to help a survivor. But it won't explain her outfit, where she's been all night. And, honestly, she doesn't feel like trying. She never really wanted to move in with him, much less get engaged. It just happened.

Now, for the first time in their relationship, Brad does something unexpected. Something bold. Something not boring and predictable. He looks at Ella, his eyes blazing, and says, "I'm done." He marches to the front door and yanks it open. "I'm going to the office. Have your shit out of here by the time I get back."

Good for him.

CHAPTER 10
KELLER

The conference room in the high school is more of a teacher break room than designated meeting space. It smells of burnt Folgers wafting from the ancient industrial coffee maker next to the fridge with a sign taped to its door, undoubtedly warning of the weekly food purge. Frayed workplace-discrimination signs are tacked unevenly to the walls. Keller and Atticus sit at the long cafeteria-style table, waiting for school officials to join the meeting while Arpeggio huddles out of earshot with a senior detective named Sheila Mintz. Detective Mintz has tight curly brown hair and deep frown lines, an inescapable side effect of working murders for a career.

Soon, they're joined by the superintendent of schools and the principal of Union High.

Arpeggio says, "I want to thank you for meeting with us so quickly. I know this is a devastating time, but it's these hours immediately after that we have the best chance of uncovering evidence."

"Of course," the superintendent says. She has painfully erect posture and a sharp, bobbed cut.

Arpeggio explains that they need to interview Madison and Hannah Sawyer's friends. Their mother is a mess, he explains, which is not surprising, having lost both daughters in one ghastly night. They also want to talk with friends of the survivor, Jesse Duvall.

"This may be a random robbery gone bad," Arpeggio says, "but we need to cover all angles."

The principal speaks now. "Detective Mintz asked that we make a list of the girls' friends." He slides a sheet of paper across the table. "It's probably incomplete but a good place to start."

Arpeggio nods.

The principal continues, "You can use the music room to meet with the students. It's out of the way, more or less soundproof, and won't draw attention."

Arpeggio nods his thanks again. "This is a difficult question to ask, but is there anyone—including anyone on the staff—who might have reason to hurt the girls?"

The superintendent and principal tap eyes.

Noticing this, Arpeggio says, "Anything, no matter how small could help."

The principal starts to speak but the superintendent touches his arm.

"There are confidentiality issues with employee matters," the superintendent says.

Arpeggio gives a tight-lipped smile that doesn't reach his eyes. His jaw clenches and he appears to be taking a moment to quell whatever is burning inside him. "I can appreciate that. But I think the community will forgive any confidentiality lapses if it helps save lives."

The superintendent swallows. She looks to the principal, nods for him to continue.

Principal Steadman is a serious-looking white man in perhaps his early forties. "We had a new custodian, Randy Butler. His initial background check came back fine, and he started work. But the county runs a separate check, through older databases, and it came back with a prior conviction."

"For?"

"Lewd conduct with a minor. We let him go immediately."

"Did he give you any trouble or—"

"No, we had no incidents. And he was gracious when I let him go, said he understood," the principal says, anticipating the question. "He has a son with disabilities, seemed like a decent person."

"I need his file right away."

The superintendent nods.

"The victims . . . can you think of any reason someone would want to hurt them?"

"No," the principal says. "Maddie and Hannah were popular girls. Maddie was a senior, outgoing, kind of a queen bee, but overall a good kid. Her sister Hannah was a junior, she seemed younger than the other girls, innocent, more of an introvert. Jesse Duvall is new to our school but we've had no problems. I'm told she wasn't in the same social circles as the other girls."

Arpeggio spends another twenty minutes grilling them for background. He's methodical, comprehensive, if not overly compassionate. When he's through, he turns to Keller. "Special Agent Keller, any questions?"

"I need a list of everyone who's worked in the school for the past year and everyone who worked here in 1999."

The superintendent shifts in her chair. "You don't think this is connected to Blockbuster, do you?"

"As Detective Arpeggio said, we have to check every angle."

"I can get you a list," the principal says. "It'll take a little time. But if it helps, we have a collection of old yearbooks in the office."

Keller nods. Yearbooks were on her checklist. "Nineteen ninety-eight through two thousand would be terrific. And last year's."

She has nothing else, for now. Arpeggio covered the bases, and she's never been one to ask questions for the sake of asking questions.

"Okay," Arpeggio says. "If someone can show us to the music room, we'll get started."

"Um," the principal speaks up again, "do all four of you intend to interview the students at the same time? They're already overwhelmed and upset . . ."

Arpeggio tilts his head slightly. "That's a good point. Detective Mintz and I will conduct the interviews."

Keller hides her annoyance at being shut out. "You want us to go talk to the custodian while you speak with the kids?" She knows the answer.

"I'd like my team involved in that," Arpeggio says. "We'll pull his jacket. But I suspect your shop can get the digital forensics faster, his cell records. See if he pinged near the ice cream store last night."

"I'll see what I can do."

The superintendent shows Arpeggio and Mintz to the interview room, and the principal walks Keller and Atticus down the hallway lined with gray lockers to the main office. There, he guides them to his connected office in the back.

"Thank you for your help, Principal Steadman," Keller says.

"Call me Dale," the principal replies. "On the yearbooks, you're welcome to review them here, but it may be easier for you to take them with you."

"That would be great, if it's not too much trouble."

"None at all." He picks up the phone and asks someone to collect the yearbooks.

Keller looks around the office. A bulletin board is covered with senior pictures and notes from students.

I wouldn't have made it without you.

I owe my admission to Princeton to you.

Team Steadman!

Off the phone now, the principal notices her eyeing the board. "The pay isn't great but seeing these kids succeed—particularly with the obstacles many face— it's the reason I stay."

Keller offers a fleeting smile.

"Did you work here in 1999?" Keller asks.

"Yes," he says without hesitation. "I was a teacher, not an administrator, back then. But yes, if you're looking for possible connections with people who worked here in 1999, I'm one of them. And Mr. Greer, but he's pushing eighty and I doubt he'd make much of a suspect."

Keller smiles again.

"Anyway, I'll check our files and make you a list of all current staff who worked here back then."

"Did you know the girls from Blockbuster?" Keller asks.

"I've stayed in touch with Ella Monroe, the survivor. If you're focusing on the case, you'll definitely want to speak with her."

"She's on my list," Keller says.

"Good. Actually, Ella's already met with Jessica Duvall at the hospital. Ella's a therapist."

Keller thinks about this. It makes sense. A trauma survivor wanting to help other trauma survivors.

Principal Steadman continues, "I didn't know the victims from Blockbuster well. I didn't have Candy, Mandy, or Ella in my class. And Katie McKenzie didn't attend Union; she went to a local Catholic school."

Keller nods. Picking up on a thread from earlier, she says, "You said Jessica Duvall's new to the school. It's unusual to change schools during senior year, isn't it?"

"She's in foster care. She's been to three different high schools already. Though I understand there was an incident at her last school."

"An incident?"

"They didn't tell us what it was. Confidentiality rules."

Keller nods. Arpeggio undoubtedly will look into that, but Keller makes a mental note.

"How about Vince Whitaker? Did you have him in class?"

Steadman shakes his head. "But I knew him by reputation. Which wasn't good."

"Can you think of any other connection between Blockbuster and what happened last night?"

"I'll admit, after seeing Ella this morning at the hospital, those years have been flooding back to me. I've been thinking about it. But, no."

"If you think of anything, anything at all, please let us know." She gives Steadman her card.

On the way out, Atticus retrieves the banker's box with the yearbooks.

In the hallway, Keller says, "Did the prior investigation look into him?"

"Dale Steadman?" Atticus says with skepticism. "I'll double-check the file. But if I recall, he was at a New Year's Eve party, lots of witnesses, when he got called to the hospital."

"Yeah, double-check. He's the only connection we have right now to victims from both crimes. And when you've got nothing, you turn over every stone."

"Got it."

Keller's bladder is going to give if she doesn't take care of it. She gazes down the long hallway and spies a sign for restrooms.

"I've got to go to the restroom," she says. "Get used to it."

Atticus nods, his face reddening.

Inside the bathroom, the cliché that everything is smaller when you go back to high school is true. Though maybe everything hasn't gotten smaller, and instead, Keller's grown much, much bigger. A glimpse of her profile in the mirror confirms that is most certainly the case.

"Big is good," Bob always tells her. "Two hearty souls in there."

She assesses the stall and decides she'll have to squeeze in. When she maneuvers her maternity slacks down and makes it to the toilet seat, the school bell blares.

Of course it does.

Soon there's a crowd in the lavatory. Keller's bladder isn't agreeable. This happens sometimes these days. The imminent need to pee, then nothing. Finally, the twins release their hold. By then, the masses have mostly cleared out.

Atticus must be wondering what the hell happened to her. She's about to flush when a voice grabs her attention.

"The cops want to talk to you?"

This is followed by whispers. Then: "You'd better not tell them anything."

Keller stands quietly, pulls up her slacks, and puts her eye to the crack in the door, but the students are out of her line of sight. All she can make out is a bright purple backpack. The bell rings again and by the time Keller squeezes out of the stall, the girls are gone.

In the hallway, she finds Atticus shuffling his feet.

"Did you see the group of girls who just left the restroom?"

Atticus shakes his head.

"Text Arpeggio and tell him one of the girls they're interviewing, she has a purple backpack, knows something."

Atticus sets down the box, then thumbs a message on his phone.

Back in the car, Keller ponders their next steps. She's being relegated to the Vince Whitaker file, so she might as well accept it. First things, first. She'll request the Behavioral Analysis Unit to profile the killers for both crimes, a comparison that could help determine if it's the same perp. She'll also have them do victimology, and run the crimes through ViCAP to see if there've been any similar offenses in other jurisdictions. It's all about connections.

The locals are already running crime scene forensics, pulling the digital data available on the Dairy Creamery victims, and canvassing for any video footage and witnesses. The ice cream shop had no video. All of this takes time. For now, they need to use good old-fashioned shoe leather. Systematically go back over the prior investigation. Talk to Vince Whitaker's family, as well as the families of the Blockbuster victims. Cross-check all names and evidence from the Blockbuster case with all evidence from the latest murders.

"You got an address for Vince Whitaker's parents?" Keller asks.

"Yeah, for his father, anyway. The mom took off a few years before Blockbuster."

"Let's go talk to him."

"Yes, ma'am."

"Another piece of advice?" Keller says.

"Sure sure sure."

"Don't ever call a woman in her thirties *ma'am*."

CHAPTER 11
CHRIS

On the first day of orientation at the Union County Public Defender's Office, all the new lawyers are subjected to the same ritual, a speech by the head PD, Henry ("Don't ever call me Hank") Robinson. A Black man in his late fifties, Henry has a seen-it-all demeanor, and is regarded as one of the best criminal defense lawyers in the country. Every year at orientation, he stands at the podium, in his tweed jacket, goatee flecked with silver, looking like a college professor, and tells the story of Bartholomew H. Badcock.

Chris's own orientation had been no exception. Henry had stared at the assembled faces, making eye contact with Chris and each of the new assistant PDs, and told them about the best lawyer he ever knew:

"It was New Year's Eve 1999. You all are too young but it was a momentous occasion. The new millennium. It was before social media. Before everyone had those phones you can't stop thinking about checking even while I'm talking here. I know you're thinking about them—the dopamine urging you to see how many likes you got for that amazing photo of your lunch." The room tittered, and Henry gave an exasperated shake of the head. "Anyhow, Bart was a simple lawyer. Now, make no mistake, I don't mean he was a simple man. No, he was a simple *lawyer* because he believed that no matter who you are—rich or poor, Black or white, good-looking or butt ugly—you have a constitutional right to the best defense. When three daughters of Linden were taken from this world in the most brutal way on that New Year's Eve, and our office was called to defend the accused, Bart didn't hesitate. And he did what each and every one of you will be called on to do in service of your clients: to hold the government to its burden of proof." He paused for dramatic effect. "And you know what happened then? Bart got his client released, and the man was never seen again. In the wind. *Pfft.*" Henry made a jet-airplane motion with his hand.

"And ol' Bart Badcock? You know what happened to him?" Henry turned somber. "His wife ran a small flower shop that was boycotted. His country club— the club where his father and grandfather had been members—revoked his membership. His kids were bullied at school. And this was before Twitter made it easy for cowards to join a mob."

Henry shook his head in disgust. "It was too much for his family. His wife left him. Took the kids. He couldn't go into town without someone saying something. And he eventually left, stopped practicing law altogether. He lost everything, simply for living up to everything this office stands for. He was, and still is, the best lawyer I ever knew." Henry ended the speech with three words that they all soon learned he uttered at the end of every staff meeting: "Serve justice today."

Two years ago, the speech had given Chris goose bumps. Not because the great Bartholomew H. Badcock had represented none other than Chris's brother, Vince Whitaker. But because of the sentiment—that Chris and his colleagues were part of something honorable, something bigger than themselves. That they quite literally were the guardians at the gate.

Now, Chris is less enchanted by the tale. He's since learned that the office lifers don't revere Bartholomew H. Badcock. To the contrary, they fear ever representing a client so despicable that they might lose everything. The name "B-file" is shorthand at the office for dogshit cases no one wants. And the lack of resources, pay, and respect make it hard to keep up with Henry's idealism.

Chris wonders sometimes if he should've gone for the money, gone to Big Law like his girlfriend, paid off those student loans. He's three months behind on the payments and, lawyer or not, there isn't much he can do to stop the harassment from the collection agencies. He's like many of his clients: in too deep, with no end in sight. It's not drugs that pulled him in, though. It's higher education. Soon, he might have to go back to bartending. That was how he got through college, in addition to racking up debt on his credit cards that are still compounding double-digit interest.

He's had satisfying moments on the job—like the time he helped a prostitute, trying to escape a husband who forced her to turn tricks. Chris was surprised to learn that many pimps aren't fur-jacket-wearing clichés, but domineering spouses in abusive relationships. And he once managed to get a confession thrown out after the cops pressured his intellectually disabled client. But most of his days are spent pushing paper, entering pleas for silly drug-possession charges, representing people who hate him.

Worse, to his shame, he hasn't exactly blazed a trail at the office. His friend Julia is the rising star. She already has a reputation as a passionate and superb advocate. A someday-successor to Henry. Chris is simply another one of the sheepdogs herding the flock. His adoptive father, Clint, would be so disappointed . . . if he knew.

But no matter how hard he tries, no matter how many Mondays arrive and he swears things will be different, he mostly phones it in. On his lunch break today, eating another microwaved burrito, he sits at his cubicle, puts in his earbuds, and watches more videos of the man. The anonymous travel vlogger whose life seems so exciting, so free.

Chris imagines himself on similar adventures: riding a motorbike across a rickety bridge in Belarus, staying in an ice hotel in Sweden, meeting a girl on Tinder in Reykjavík, eating reindeer burgers in the arctic, going to a water park in North Korea. Chris isn't the only one with such fantasies—the anonymous vlogger has become wildly popular in the past few months. He's been playing a catch-me-if-you-can game, a ploy to increase his followers.

Chris's eyes go to his phone, and he sees something

surprising. It's a live feed. Usually, the traveler posts videos after the fact. As always, he's off-screen, the scene an unidentified airport terminal:

"I wanted to thank everyone for your support. Today, I hope you enjoy this clip from my trip to Romania. I've just landed in the U.S., and I'll be posting all week. Who knows, maybe you'll find me . . ."

This is the chance Chris has been waiting for—an opportunity to find and meet the vlogger.

He'll find him.

He has to.

Because he hasn't seen his brother in fifteen years.

YOUTUBE EXCERPT

Mr. Nirvana, the Anonymous Travel Vlogger

(1.2M views)

"Visiting a Romanian Fortune-Teller"

EXT. ROMANIA—BUCOVINA—SUNSET

The scooter stops at a fork in the dirt road.
As always, only MR. NIRVANA's hands are in the
frame.

> MR. NIRVANA (O.S.)
> People warned me against visiting a
> village on the outskirts of town,
> known for the best fortune-tellers
> in Romania. But when has that ever
> stopped me, right? I found this guy
> online, Pavel, who agreed to take me
> there. He gave me pretty good direc-
> tions here, so I hope he shows up.

The video cuts off, then back on. A figure
emerges from the woods. It shows only the
guide, PAVEL, who shakes Nirvana's hand. Pavel
then counts bills he's given and grabs the
handles of Nirvana's rented scooter.

> MR. NIRVANA (O.S.)
> We're taking the bike?

Pavel shakes his head, and rolls the scooter
to some bramble and conceals it. He then ges-

tures for Nirvana to follow him into the woods. The camera jostles, following Pavel as the night gets darker.

> MR. NIRVANA (O.S.)
> Our guide is a man of few words. Let's
> hope I'm not being led to my death.

Pavel turns and smiles, showing missing teeth.

> MR. NIRVANA (O.S.)
> You can see the village up ahead.

Ramshackle houses are in the distance. The video turns black. When it returns, Nirvana and Pavel are inside a room illuminated only by candlelight. An OLD WOMAN looks into the camera. She shuffles a deck of cards, says something in Romanian.

> PAVEL
> (ACCENTED ENGLISH)
> She says put the money on the cards,
> and make the sign of the cross on top
> of the bills.

Nirvana puts bills on top of the deck, and makes a cross with his hand over them. The woman scoops up the money, then displays the first card on the table. The woman's face crumples. She speaks again.

PAVEL

She says you have a dark past. She's
not sure she wants to—

The old woman stands abruptly. She flings the
bills at them, starts yelling.

MR. NIRVANA (O.S.)

What's going— What is she saying?

PAVEL

She says we need to go. *Now*. Or she's
calling her sons. We're not welcome
here.

MR. NIRVANA (O.S.)

I don't understand. I thought she was
going to do a reading.

PAVEL

No. We must go. She says you're
damned.

FADE TO BLACK

CHAPTER 12
ELLA

Ella had two sessions that morning: a college kid who was flunking out and hiding it from her parents, and a seemingly perfect mother of two who purged every piece of food that entered her body. The meme is true: *Be kind, for everyone you meet is fighting a battle you know nothing about.*

She'd considered canceling all sessions for the day, but she's still wired from the hospital. From meeting this strong girl who survived the most brutal of attacks. From finally letting Brad take the parachute before the plane crashed into a ball of fire against the mountainside. So, she'd taken a scalding shower, blasted away the smeared eye makeup, put on professional attire, downed four Advil, and made her way in. Brad had told her to be out by the end of the day, but what was he going to do? Throw her stuff on the curb? It would serve her right. But that isn't Brad. She'll go stay with her mother—its own form of punishment—and get her things later this week while Brad's at work.

At lunchtime, she heads to the hospital. The nurse tells her that Jesse's been discharged.

"So soon?"

The nurse frowns. "Insurance issues."

How compassionate.

Ella calls Principal Steadman on the walk back to the car.

"They *what*?" Steadman says in disbelief.

"Discharged her this morning."

"For goodness's sake."

That was about as harsh as you could expect from Dale Steadman.

"Can you give me her address?" Ella asks. "I'd like to check on her."

She hears typing, then he reads her the address of the foster home, which is on a rougher side of town. Linden in many ways is a small town nestled in a county of a half million residents, surrounded by an area unflatteringly called the "Chemical Coast." The wealth gap is significant.

Ella arrives there ten minutes later. She raps on the screen door, which is torn and rickety.

A heavyset woman answers. Looks her up and down. A TV blares inside.

"Hi. Is Jesse available?"

"You the lawyer?"

"No. I'm a—" What is she exactly to Jesse? "I'm a friend."

"The lawyer said she shouldn't talk with anyone until—"

"It's fine, Dori," Jesse says, appearing from behind.

The woman—the foster mother, Ella presumes—shrugs. Totters back to the couch.

Jesse looks Ella up and down, examining the business attire. "I guess you aren't a stripper."

Ella smiles at that. "Wanna get a Starbucks?"

Jesse calls over her shoulder, "I'll be back soon," and pushes out the beat-up screen door.

At the coffee shop, they find a table in the back, away from the other customers.

They both cradle their cups—Ella a black coffee, Jesse some complicated sugar-filled monstrosity—and say nothing for a long time.

"Thanks for coming," Ella begins.

"It was you or the lawyers. Dori said we had like ten calls. They're saying we can sue the ice cream store."

Ella nods. "How are you?"

"Peachy."

Ella gives her a supportive smile.

"Can we just, you know, *not . . .*"

"I get it," Ella says. "After what happened to me, I didn't want to talk about it either. But I learned if you hold it all in, your mind will find other ways to deal with it. Usually, self-destructive ways."

"Like cheating on your fiancé?"

Ella is taken aback. "What are you—"

"Brad needs to learn about the privacy settings on Facebook," Jesse tells her. "And he spends *way* too much time on social media. His business conference in Atlantic City looks like torture, by the way."

Jesse's done some serious online sleuthing.

"I *loved* the sappy engagement posts. You're his *soul*

mate." She says it with mockery. "But with Brad at the conference, I wondered where you'd been in that dress."

Ella feels a tightness in her chest. Jesse grows more complicated—more interesting—by the second. She seems to be trying to antagonize Ella, push her away, but maybe she's simply testing her.

"Wow, stalker much?" Ella says with forced nonchalance. "And for the record, Brad kicked me out this morning."

Jesse eyes her skeptically, as if she doesn't believe her, then seems to change her mind. "You're better off. He's boring as shit. He also spends too much time liking bikini-pic posts from his friends—*cree-py*."

Ella's mother doesn't like Brad either. But that's because he isn't wealthy, doesn't have the pedigree suitable for a Monroe. But Jesse's right, Brad is boring as shit. "He's a good man," Ella says in tepid defense.

"Oh yes, *so* good. He makes sure everybody knows it. Very woke—a real fighter against racism, sexism, and every other -ism."

Jesse's right about Brad again. This girl's wise for her age. This no longer feels like getting coffee with a damaged teen. More like hanging with a snarky girlfriend. But she's not a friend, Ella reminds herself.

Ella says, "There are actually studies on virtue-signaling, did you know that?"

Jesse caresses the Starbucks cup and takes a sip, her eyes inviting Ella to continue. She's intrigued.

"People who virtue-signal are much more likely to have what they call the 'dark triad' of personality traits—Machiavellianism, narcissism, and psychopathy."

"I knew it!" Jesse's eyes are alight.

They fall silent again amid the whine of blenders and chatter.

Eventually, Ella says, "It's your senior year. Are you excited to graduate?"

"You have no idea."

Ella has every idea, but she doesn't say so. She remembers graduation day, skipping out on the diploma-walk, getting high under the bleachers. Her mother was livid.

"Do you have plans for—"

"For college?" Jesse interrupts. "No Wellesley in my future. Not even community college."

Ella nods, doesn't ask how Jesse knows that she attended Wellesley. "Not everybody has to go to college right away."

"I want to be a writer," Jesse says.

This surprises Ella for some reason. "Oh yeah? What kind of writer?"

"I'm thinking long-form journalism. At my old school, I was the editor of the school paper."

There's pride in her voice. Ella wonders why Jesse transferred schools. Cruel to move a kid senior year. She decides not to ask. One step at a time.

"I'd love to read some of your pieces."

Jesse doesn't respond but Ella swears she blushes, her porcelain skin briefly turning a shade of pink.

Ella raises her cup. "Here's to the next Woodward or Bernstein."

"I prefer Joan Didion."

Ella has no idea who that is. She'll look it up later. "You working on any stories now?"

Jesse sips her drink. "Yeah, a pretty fascinating one."

"Yeah?"

"A true-crime mystery."

Ella leans in to hear more.

"About an unsolved crime in Linden."

Ella feels a tingle crawl up her spine.

Jesse continues, "A fifteen-year-old mass murder at the local Blockbuster." She continues staring at Ella, waiting for a reaction.

Ella sips her coffee but makes no reply.

"So?" Jesse prompts her.

"So what?"

"Will you let me interview you? The prior reporting's weak. It's a joke, really."

The girl has clearly done much more research than Facebook-spying on Brad.

Ella's never wanted to talk about that day. Ever. In the past twenty-four hours, she's already talked about it more than she has in the past fifteen years. But she knows that Jesse's request for an interview isn't about Ella or Candy or Katie or Mandy.

It's about Jesse.

"Let me think about it."

Jesse's stare continues, strangely unsettling.

Yet, for some reason, Ella can't seem to look away.

CHAPTER 13
KELLER

Keller crinkles her nose at the smell.

"Place is downwind from the Sewage Authority," Atticus explains without her asking. They trudge up the steps to Union Self-Storage, its office housed in a cinder-block building. A chain-link fence topped with razor wire protects the rows of aluminum huts containing the remnants of people's lives. She wonders who'd want to store their belongings in a place permeated by such a stench. Spying a semitruck parked in front of one of the larger units, she realizes it might be industrial storage, a place to keep excess loads of nonperishables.

Inside they're met by a lazy-eyed clerk. Keller flashes her badge. That wakes him up.

"We're here to see Rusty Whitaker," Keller says.

"Rusty's, ah, at lunch." The man is jittery. But the badge tends to have that effect. Still, he seems to be sweating an unusual amount.

Keller follows his glance out the window to the semi. "He's at lunch?"

"He goes to the buffet at Kitten's," the guy explains, wiping his brow with his sleeve.

"Kitten's?"

Before the clerk responds, Atticus tells her, "I know the place."

Ten minutes later, they're at the front door to Kitten's Gentleman's Club, though Keller doubts there are any gentlemen inside. The flash of the badge does its thing again. The two make a sight: an eight-month-pregnant FBI agent and an Indian-American detective in a skinny tie. The burly guy with a long beard working the door taps out an anxious text and they're met inside by the greasy smile of the owner.

"Mr. Kitten?" Keller says, for her own amusement.

He starts to respond, but realizes she's kidding and displays the greasy smile again. "We don't get the privilege of having the FBI here often. How can we help you, Agent . . ."

"Keller, Special Agent Keller. This is Detective Singh from Union County." Keller glances about the dreary club. A woman wearing a bikini dances in the background to "Pour Some Sugar on Me."

"We're just customers." Keller gives him a hard stare.

The owner sucks his teeth. Calculating. The smile returns. "Welcome! For our friends in law enforcement we waive the two-drink minimum and give twenty percent off lunch. Buffet for two?"

Not on your life.

Atticus points to a man at a table near the stage who's watching the dancer while he eats chicken wings. "We're just here to meet a friend."

The owner hesitates. "You need anything, you tell them to come get me."

Keller couldn't care less about whatever the guy is nervous about. Probably more than dancing is going on in the back rooms. She has no interest being the morality police for sex workers on the afternoon shift at a strip club near the sewage plant.

She feels less sympathetic toward the patrons seated at small tables throughout the club. She and Atticus approach Rusty Whitaker's table. They sit directly across from him.

Rusty is unfazed at the presence of strangers, and continues gnawing on a chicken bone. "Who the hell are you?"

Keller doesn't answer, but displays her badge.

Rusty rolls his eyes. Begins sucking another wing.

Keller feels a wave of nausea watching him eat.

"I have no idea where Vince is," Rusty says, before they ask. "Haven't seen or talked to that worthless piece of shit in fifteen years."

"You've had no contact with him?" Keller asks.

"Nope. And I hope I never do. He's dead to me."

"Father of the year," Keller says with a hard smile.

"Kids," he says in disgust. "You'll see." He aims his chin at Keller's belly.

She restrains the urge to punch him in his teeth.

Atticus must sense her strange wave of rage, and jumps in. "Look, we don't want to create any problems for you. Just answer our questions and you can get back to your lunch."

A friendly threat that if Rusty doesn't talk they'll

create problems for him. Both the message and delivery are well-done.

Rusty shrugs for Atticus to continue.

"When's the last time you saw Vince?"

Rusty gives him a tired stare. "I just told you. The night he got sprung. I was surprised he was home."

"Did you talk with him?"

"I've been through this a hundred times, and—"

"Did you speak with him?" Atticus asks, more sternly this time.

"We had words, yeah. I told him I wanted him out. Said I was goin' to the bar and he'd better be gone when I got home."

"What time was that?"

Rusty shrugs.

"And when you got home, he was gone?"

"Yep. And I haven't seen him since, and hope I never do."

"The night Vince was arrested," Atticus says, "you told the police that you got home from work around ten, is that right?"

Rusty Whitaker frowns. "If you say so. Been fifteen years."

"Did you drive to work that day?"

Rusty throws down a chicken wing on his plate. Puts his hands in the air like he has no idea.

Atticus continues, "Because your Monte Carlo was seen in the Blockbuster that night. If you drove to work, how could Vince have—"

"No idea. Ask Vince."

"Do you have any idea where he would've gone?

Could his mother have put him up? Do you know how we can reach her?"

The club announcer's voice blares from the sound system, introducing the next dancer. Rusty moves his head to see over Atticus's shoulder. "Look, I got a half hour left for my lunch. Unless you're gonna arrest me, we're done."

Atticus looks to Keller. She considers pushing more, but that won't get them anywhere. And she *really* wants to get out of there. The smell of the wings, the sauce on Rusty's cheek, the stale air, are making her stomach churn.

The next girl totters onto the stage and the music turns louder.

Keller and Atticus head for the door.

Atticus stops, turns back. Keller follows his gaze to the stage. Rusty's on his feet, sticking a dollar bill in the dancer's G-string. The young woman—she looks no older than twenty—twirls around the pole.

Atticus says, "In the movies, the detectives always end up interviewing witnesses at a strip club, and it seemed like it would be pretty cool. But this is awful."

"You've never been to a strip club for like a bachelor party or something?" Keller says.

"No way, my mom would kill me."

Keller suppresses a smile.

Still staring at Rusty, Atticus adds, "I hate this guy so much."

"He's hiding something," Keller says, then shrugs. "Maybe we'll get lucky and find out what it is."

CHAPTER 14

"So, 'Atticus' is an unusual name," Keller says as she drives back to the office, her sidekick for the day scrolling through the Blockbuster file on his iPad. He's scanned and uploaded all the interview notes, tips, news clippings, and other documents from the old files. She admires his enthusiasm, his optimism, that they might dig up something new. She's not so optimistic.

"My father was a fan of *To Kill a Mockingbird*."

Keller nods.

"They didn't consider that the name might not go over well for the only brown kid at North Caldwell Elementary." He smiles. "And I never had the heart to mention that after Harper Lee died, they released her original manuscript and Atticus turns out to be a racist." The smile again.

It's settled. Keller likes this young detective.

"What's next?" he asks.

"Good question," Keller says, watching the road closely. Bob hates it when she talks on the phone or is otherwise distracted while driving. But Bob hates multitasking generally. He's an in-the-moment person. That works beautifully for their relationship but not so much for a fast-moving investigation.

"We rework the case file. Talk to witnesses, the families," she says. "Try to find any connections between the Blockbuster victims and the ice cream store victims."

Atticus swipes at his tablet. "I haven't been able to find Vince Whitaker's mother, or his little brother, who I think may have been adopted and changed his name. I have info on the victims' families, though. I can try to set up some interviews."

Keller nods.

"That leaves the Blockbuster survivor, Ella Monroe," Atticus says.

"I'm meeting with her tonight," Keller says. "Hal set it up for me," she adds.

"Want me to come along?"

"I think, given what happened to her, one-on-one would be best."

"Makes sense," he says, trying not to sound disappointed.

"What about all the sightings of Vince Whitaker over the years?" Keller asks. "Anything to all of that?"

Atticus lets out a sigh. "I've been trying to track those in my spare time. But most happened outside the country. If you think eyewitness testimony is unreliable, that's nothing compared to sightings by vacationers who've spent the day drinking cocktails."

Atticus's phone chimes. "Whoa," he says.

"What is it?" Keller asks.

"They went to interview the janitor from the school, the one who was fired. Apparently, the guy's barricaded himself in his home and they're gonna extract him."

"How far from us?"

"Just a few minutes." Atticus looks excited again. "Want me to reach out to the team to get approval for us to come?"

Keller grips the wheel. "Sometimes it's better to ask for forgiveness than permission."

The street is cordoned off. An officer meets them at the perimeter and lets them pass when Atticus lies and says that Detective Arpeggio is expecting them.

Keller gives him an admiring glance. Atticus is a quick study. He didn't ask for permission and would definitely be asking for forgiveness later.

They pull up to a bevy of vehicles. Keller hoists herself out of the car and surveys the scene. There are six cars, both marked and unmarked, and an armored van that probably houses a SWAT team. Keller is always surprised by the arsenals of local forces, often bought with money the federal government shares from drug forfeitures.

Arpeggio is stationed at a command center outside the van, talking to a group of men in black tactical gear.

She looks at Atticus, who's holding his iPad at his side. "You have access to the file on the janitor on that thing?"

"If they've uploaded it to the evidence portal."

"Can you check?" Keller doesn't have all the intel,

but from what she's seeing, Arpeggio's team is getting ready to kill a mosquito with a sledgehammer.

As Atticus taps on the device, Arpeggio's gaze snags on Keller. He squints, then breaks away from the group and marches over.

"I thought we agreed that you were sticking to the Blockbuster and Whitaker side of things," he says, his tone firm. "We've got this covered."

"I can see that," Keller says, her tenor hinting at the overkill. "What happened?"

Arpeggio shakes his head, like he doesn't have time for this. "Mintz and a uniform came to interview the janitor. When they climbed the porch, he surprised them, shoved them both down the stairs, and ran inside. Now he's not responding."

Keller watches the men in tactical gear, who appear too eager. "The Bureau has some top-flight negotiators," she says. "I can get one over here who can—"

"No need," Arpeggio says. "But I do need you to stay over there, where it's safe." His eyes drop to her pregnant belly. "I've got enough problems today."

Keller doesn't fight it. She and Atticus head to an area adjacent to the command center.

"I got the guy's jacket and probation file," Atticus says, handing Keller the iPad. It's short, and she reads quickly. The custodian, Randy Butler, is no serial child molester. His conviction for lewd conduct with a minor was nearly twenty years ago when he was eighteen: he got his sixteen-year-old girlfriend pregnant.

"It says he shares custody of a son with disabilities . . .

autism, apparently. The kid would be about seventeen," Keller says.

She watches as Arpeggio, followed by men in black, climbs the steps quietly. They're in stacked formation, headed to the front door.

Keller turns to Atticus. "Do you have Detective Mintz's number? I need to talk to her."

"Yeah, but she's right over there." Atticus directs his attention to a small group watching the breach team. As the armored officers reach the top of the porch steps, Arpeggio raises a hand, then closes it to a fist, and the team stops. He pounds on the door.

"Police! Open up!"

Keller hurries over to Mintz. The detective's eyes move from the breach team to Keller. She wears a sling on her arm.

"Detective Mintz, I'm glad you're all right. Did you get a good look at who shoved you down the steps? Arpeggio said it was a surprise attack. Are you sure it was Randy Butler?"

Mintz's eyes flash. "It was him. I mean, I think . . . We were coming up the porch and he just charged. We both lost our footing and he ran inside."

Keller hears a commotion from behind them. Yelling. A confrontation with the officers maintaining the perimeter. Keller recognizes the civilian from the photo she's just viewed on the iPad. He looks older than in the mug shot, but it's him. The custodian. The man who's *supposed* to be inside the house.

There's a loud *Boom*. The battering ram cracks through the door and the men disappear inside.

Keller runs over toward the custodian. By then, Randy Butler is on the ground being cuffed, two officers restraining him. Keller shouts for the officers to stand down.

"My son," Randy Butler cries, craning his neck up from the blacktop. His tone is breathless and frantic. "He's a gentle boy. But he gets scared. I don't want them to think . . ."

"Shit." Keller races to the command center and tries to speak with a man wearing a headset mic, the communications lead with the breach team. He's focused intently on the house and waves her away.

The team is likely at peak adrenaline, clearing each room in the zone. If the kid inside makes any sudden moves . . .

Keller takes a deep breath, then speed-walks across the street, holding her badge high in the air, making clear she's a friendly. The tactical lead calls out to her, but she makes her way up the steps and through the broken front door.

Inside, she moves slowly. She can hear heavy footsteps upstairs. Voices shouting the word *clear* every few seconds. Her pulse is banging in her chest, in her neck.

"I'm with the FBI," she bellows. "You should stand down!"

The footsteps continue.

She yells again, louder. *"FBI! Stand down!"*

The movement stops.

"The perp's detained outside," she yells.

The dwelling plunges into silence.

"The person in the house is his *son*! He has a disability! He may not understand what's happening."

At last, Arpeggio appears at the top of the stairs and glowers down at her. Behind him, two officers in tactical gear guide a handcuffed man, a teenager, down the staircase.

At the foot of the stairs, Arpeggio opens his mouth to speak, then closes it, then storms out the door.

Keller approaches the officers restraining the boy, who—far from struggling—appears to be shutting down.

"Jimmy?" she says softly.

The boy looks up at her.

"I'm Sarah." Keller smiles at him. "Your dad's outside. Would you like to see him?"

The boy's blank expression turns hopeful. He nods.

Keller looks at the two officers, who are conflicted now. In an overly pleasant voice, solely for Jimmy's benefit, she says, "I think these men made a *big* mistake, and since they want to keep their jobs, they're gonna take off those cuffs, if that's okay with you?"

Jimmy nods again, avoiding eye contact.

Keller gives the officers a piercing gaze. They don't question it. The burly one glares at Keller while his younger comrade unlocks the handcuffs.

Keller walks out of the house with Jimmy Butler.

She'll be hearing about this from Hal. From Stan, even. But right now, she doesn't care. This boy needs his father.

CHAPTER 15
CHRIS

Chris arrives at Clare's apartment at the Ellington, a glitzy building in Midtown Manhattan close to her office. The place has a doorman, a marble lobby, and an expensive-looking vase of fresh flowers on an elegant table near the elevators. It's a stark contrast to his shoebox in Elizabeth, New Jersey. He'd been bracing himself all week for the work party she'd coaxed him to attend. "All the junior associates are bringing plus-ones," she'd pleaded.

Chris has no interest in an evening with the masters of the universe who ruled the halls of Cramer Moorhouse, one of New York's most prestigious law firms. He imagines them gossiping about the mismatch of Clare (old money, Upper West Side, Mergers & Acquisitions shark-in-training) and Chris (no money, wrong side of the tracks in Linden, New Jersey, defender of street thugs).

"There he is," Clare says, greeting Chris at the door. She's wearing a stylish blouse—somehow corporate yet sexy at the same time—and that familiar sparkle in her eyes. She throws her arms around his neck and kisses him.

He knows he should appreciate this. She's a beautiful, successful young woman who by all accounts adores him. But on days like today, which remind Chris of who he really is, her blind affection is somehow off-putting.

"I have a surprise for you," Clare says. She gives a tiny clap of her hands, nearly vibrating with excitement.

"What's the occasion?" he asks. "I've told you that you don't have to—" But before he finishes the sentence, she's skipped down the hall.

Chris tells himself to shake off the mood. She doesn't deserve to have her night ruined by his gloom. He steps into the impressive living room. The apartment has an open floor plan. High ceilings. And the view. It sure beats the neon sign of the Chinese takeout place across from his place. Clare has already hinted that he should move in. That her dad, who owns the place, would be cool with it. Ever the optimist.

Clare's back in the living room with a garment bag.

"What's this?"

"Remember how I said my tailor could refurbish your suit?"

"Ye-es," Chris says, cautiously.

"It turns out he couldn't. But he was able to use it for your measurements," she says in a singsong voice. She unzips the bag and displays a sharp navy suit. Chris examines the label inside the jacket. Brioni, which he's never heard of but knows is expensive.

"You said you'd feel more confident for your trials if you had a nice suit." She beams.

He doesn't recall saying that—and he certainly can't wear this suit to meet his clients at the dirty Union County jail. But those sparkling eyes . . . What kind of upbringing did you need to get that sparkle? Maybe if Ms. May and Clint had gotten to him sooner, he'd have that same glint.

He kisses her and tries to sound sufficiently enthusiastic. "This is too much. Thank you, Clare."

"Maybe you can wear it tonight," she says.

So he does. The last thing he wants is to embarrass her with her friends. She's conveniently bought him expensive shirts, a belt, shoes, and even cuff links to go with the ensemble.

The soiree is at a partner's apartment that makes Clare's seem modest. At these functions, he always finds himself talking to the bartenders or women who carry around the trays of over-complicated hors d'oeuvres.

But tonight, he's been cornered by M&A guys from Clare's department. These types always are fascinated by public defenders like Chris. Occasionally it feels patronizing. But tonight, they seem genuinely curious.

It starts casually enough. Alpha small talk. Them gossiping about the party host's bad Botox, which gives his face that look of perpetual surprise. Then there's the colleague they call "Dunning Kruger," a reference to an affliction that causes the least capable people to think they're the smartest in the room. A few comments about the pretty bartender with the long legs. Then, inevitably, they turn to Chris's job.

"Do you, like, go to court?" a guy named Thad says.

His name tells you nearly everything you need to know about him. At Cramer Moorhouse, even the litigators won't see the inside of a courtroom for the first ten years. Granted, they're trying cases worth billions, not defending a purse-snatching drug fiend. But still.

"Yeah, I've had two dozen trials—mostly drugs and guns, which is what we do the first couple of years for training. I should get my first violent-crimes case soon."

Thad says, "I don't think I could sleep at night. I mean, aren't most of them guilty?"

Chris decides to spare him the usual spiel about believing in the system. And he also doesn't make the observation that Cramer Moorhouse's corporate clients—environmental polluters, predatory lenders, etc.—hurt or kill far more people.

Clare must sense trouble; she swoops in to save him. "What are you guys talking about?" She rings her arm around Chris's.

"We were just marveling that Chris actually has seen the inside of a courtroom."

This time it *does* sound patronizing.

"He is pretty amazing," Clare says.

Thad gives a razor smile. "Speaking of criminals . . . Did you all see that awful story about the ice cream shop in New Jersey? As if Jersey wasn't already bad enough."

They all laugh. If you're from New Jersey, you're used to this from New Yorkers, even the transplants.

"No," Clare says. "What happened?"

Before anyone answers, Chris says, "I'm going to get a drink. Get you all anything?"

He weaves his way through the crowd to the bar. The pretty bartender gives him a fake smile, which turns genuine when she watches him down the vodka in a single gulp.

Chris orders another as he scans his phone, looking for any new posts from the traveler.

"Is that Mr. Nirvana?" the bartender asks, obviously spying on him.

Chris is surprised, but he shouldn't be, he supposes. The vlogger has a big following. He nods.

"Any new posts? He's been hinting that he's going to reveal his identity soon," she says.

"He posted something earlier today, but nothing new tonight."

The waitress gives a fleeting smile. "What I wouldn't give . . ." She doesn't have to finish the sentence. Freedom. Adventure. No M&A assholes.

Chris glances over to Clare and her friends. "You and me both," he says.

CHAPTER 16
ELLA

Ella sits in a booth at Corky's Tavern, studying her gin and tonic and making a conscious effort at resting bitch face. She's wearing the only casual clothes she had at the office, jeans and a sweatshirt that is hardly form-fitting. Even so, she's already had to fend off the parade of men asking to buy her a drink. It's a strange blend of suitors. The regulars include men with callused hands and their names embroidered on their work shirts, overgroomed hipsters, and (more) Scotch-drinking businessmen.

There's a loud moan from the bar. The patrons reacting to something on the TV. Sports. Ella never understood the fascination. A professor explained that it's the human need to belong to something. A tribe. Ella's never felt that need.

She nurses her drink, waiting for the FBI woman, Agent Keller. Ella and Keller—it sounds like a 90s hip-hop group. Or bad cop drama. It reminds her of Candy and Mandy.

Glancing about the bar again, she feels a surge of melancholy as she recalls Candy telling her that Stevie had been a pathetic regular here. That girls led him on to get free drinks and he never scored. She remembers Candy's gravelly laugh.

"The poor dweeb. Hey, Mandy, maybe you should take pity and give him a hand-job in the break room."

"Gross!"

"Ella?"

The voice jolts her back to the bar. At her booth stands a woman. A very pregnant woman. Before Ella replies, the woman wedges herself into the booth.

"Agent Keller? Oh my god. If I knew you were . . . I wouldn't have suggested getting a drink. We can go somewhere else if you'd—"

"No worries," the FBI agent says. "This will be the wildest night out I've had in eight months."

The agent smiles. She has a kind smile. Though Keller's belly is enormous, the agent still has an athletic demeanor. Healthy. Someone comfortable in her own skin. What that must feel like.

"Thanks for meeting with me," Keller says. "After hours, I mean."

"No problem."

"I understand you were the only one able to get through to the survivor."

Ella takes a drink. "I'm uniquely qualified." The agent obviously knows her background, so Ella sees no harm in referencing the elephant in the room.

"It must be difficult for you as well."

They lock eyes. Ella tries to appear casual. She clears

her throat. Changing the subject, Ella says, "I under-stand you have some questions for me?"

The agent explains that she's tasked with seeing if there's a connection between Blockbuster and the ice cream store killings. She says it's doubtful, but they need to cover all the bases.

"You actually think that it might be *Him*?" Ella re-fuses to say his name. Always has, always will.

"Vince Whitaker?" Keller shrugs. "Like I said, we've got to cover everything."

"I guess you have to look into it, especially given what the killer said to Jesse Duvall."

"What do you mean? What *who* said to Jessica Duvall?"

Ella watches the agent for a long beat. "They didn't tell you?"

"Tell me what?" Keller looks bewildered. The agent shifts in the booth to prevent the ledge of the table from pressing against her belly.

Ella tells her. What *He* whispered in her ear: *Good night, pretty girl.* The same words murmured in Jesse's ear. She tries not to picture the bloody bodies that sur-rounded both of them.

The agent has perked up. "You told the detectives about this today?"

"Yeah, this morning. I told the lead guy. The one with the mustache."

Keller's jaw clenches. She's angry, but Ella sees that she's trying to hide it.

"The file . . . I don't think it mentions the perp say-ing anything to you. Did you tell anyone back then?"

Ella shakes her head. "I don't think so. I only started remembering after. To be honest, I wasn't sure if it was real." She doesn't mention the night terrors, the panic attacks, the blue pills.

Keller thinks for a moment. "I'm so glad you mentioned this. Before today, did you ever tell *anyone* what he said? The police? A therapist? A family member? Anyone?"

The implication is obvious. There are only three possible explanations for the killer whispering those words in Jesse's ear.

One, it's a coincidence, however implausible.

Two, a copycat, someone re-creating the crime.

Three, and this option sends a chill up Ella's back, it's *Him*.

"I never told anyone. Not until today, anyway, when I told the detective."

Keller reaches across the table and grasps Ella's hand. If this is meant to build rapport in order to get a better interview, the agent's a master at it. Ella herself uses the technique with trauma victims to elicit the same thing. But Agent Keller seems entirely sincere.

"Any idea what it means?" Keller asks. "What he said to you?"

"Not a clue," Ella says. "Not a damn clue."

CHAPTER 17

The jukebox in Corky's Tavern blares loudly, and Ella remains in the booth. She needs to shake off talking about *Him* with the FBI agent. Agent Keller left an hour ago. Ella should've headed out too, but instead she downs another gin and tonic.

One more? She shouldn't.

A man in a concert T-shirt approaches. He's rugged, handsome, in that works-with-his-hands way. The type who will take her to the restroom, turn her around in the stall, push himself into her as she palms the grimy tiles. Or take her out to the parking lot, lay her on the front seat of his truck while he stands outside, her legs in the air, her—

"Haven't seen you around lately," the guy says.

She gives him a long stare. "You've been looking?"

He reddens a trace. These types don't prattle on about Scotch, but they also aren't skilled at banter.

"I'm Mike."

"I'm Amanda, but my friends call me Mandy." The lie feels worse than usual.

"Get you a drink, Mandy?"

She shouldn't. She peruses the bar for any familiar faces. She's no longer an engaged woman, so why not? She edges over in the booth, signaling he can sit.

He turns and gestures to the waitress and slips in next to her.

One drink, then she'll go. But where? To Mom's house, she supposes, though she hasn't had the energy to tell Phyllis about the breakup. Maybe she'll get a hotel room. Or maybe Mike will be more persuasive than she anticipates.

The drinks arrive. *Just one* becomes two more. He's sitting closer now. She keeps touching him as they talk about nothing, encouraging him. His hand is on her thigh now.

"Hey, want to get out of here? Get a drink at my place?" he says.

She feels the trickle of desire. She's about to suggest the bathroom instead, but her phone snaps her out of it.

She doesn't recognize the number but her clients sometimes call from unfamiliar lines. "Hello," she answers, trying to sound sober.

Mike's leering now, his eyes wolfish.

"Ella? It's Jesse."

Right. She remembers giving Jesse her business card.

"Hey." It's late to be calling. Ella inches away from the guy.

"I'm in some trouble, and I need someone to come."

Ella pushes Mike to slide out of the booth. He does so quickly, as if assuming they'll be leaving together. But Ella shoves past him and marches out of the tavern, speaking into her phone:

"I'm on my way."

Ella fast-walks into the Target in a shopping plaza off Edgar Road. Why in the hell there's a twenty-four-hour Target in Union County, she can't understand. She scoops up a tin of Altoids from a stand near a register, opens the can, and pops a mint. She sobered up considerably on the Uber ride over, but she probably still reeks of Corky's. She'll have to leave her car in the Corky's lot tonight, but that's all right. It won't be the first time.

Finding the door at the back of the bed-and-bath section, Ella breathes in a whiff of the soap-scented air and knocks timidly.

"Come on in," a voice calls out.

Ella turns the knob and goes inside. She'd expected some type of sophisticated command center—walls of monitors and surveillance equipment—but finds a small room with a bald man wearing a short-sleeved button-up shirt behind a desk. He looks more like a high school guidance counselor than head of security at a major corporation's store. Across from him, Jesse sits, arms crossed tightly.

"Mr. Bowling?" Ella says.

The man stands, walks around the desk, and shakes her hand. He's all-business, but has kind eyes.

"You're Ms. Duvall's guardian?" he asks, skepticism in his voice.

Ella hesitates. "Jesse's in foster care. I'm a therapist. I work with her."

Mr. Bowling bunches his lips like he's debating whether to be a stickler and say he can speak only to a legal guardian. Ella turns to Jesse, gives her a look, then turns back to Bowling. "What's going on?"

"It seems Jessica decided to redeem what we call the 'five finger discount.'" He gestures to a pile of items on his desk. Two bags of Skittles, some Bubblicious gum, a Red Bull, and a bag of Flamin' Hot Cheetos.

"I didn't fucking steal anything," Jesse protests. "I just didn't have a shopping cart so I put them in my bag."

Mr. Bowling blows out a breath. He pecks on a battered laptop on his desk, then twirls it around so the screen faces Ella and Jesse.

It shows Jesse looking around nervously in the aisle. She snatches a shirt from a rack and proceeds to the snack section, then tucks the items inside the shirt so you can't see them. The screen jumps to what looks like a dressing room. Jesse peers out the door and then takes the items from the shirt and shoves them in her backpack.

"You were spying on me in the dressing room?" Jesse says, indignant. "That's against the law. You're ogling teenage girls in the fucking dressing room. I have a lawyer. I'm gonna sue!" She's building steam now. Teenage Diversion 101.

Mr. Bowling ignores her and looks at Ella. "Our policy is normally to deal with first offenses informally, but I told her if she keeps cursing at me, we're gonna have to call the police."

Ella nods at Bowling. He's had a long day, probably doesn't want the paperwork. But if Jesse doesn't cool it, she'll find herself arrested.

"Mr. Bowling, can you and I have a word?" Ella asks. "In private?"

Bowling makes another audible sigh. "Sure. Ms. Duvall, if you could wait outside for a moment."

Jesse opens her mouth but is cut short by a hard look from Ella. She stalks out of the room, closing the door too hard behind her.

Bowling waits for Ella to speak.

"I'm sorry about that."

He waits.

"She's been through a lot. Have you seen the news about the ice cream store murders?"

Bowling perks up now. "Yeah, those kids. Devastating."

"There was one survivor . . ." Ella says pointedly.

Bowling blinks a few times. "You mean . . ." He doesn't finish the sentence. "Sweet Jesus." He slumps back in his chair. He thinks for a moment, then does two things. First, he lifts a sheet of paper, the incident report, and tears it in half. Second, he gathers the items Jesse had stolen, puts them in a plastic Target bag, and hands the bag to Ella.

"Talk to her about this," Mr. Bowling says. "She can't be—you know. Just talk to her."

"I will," Ella says. She holds up the bag. "I'm happy to pay."

Bowling shakes his head. "It's on me."

CHAPTER 18
KELLER

Keller lies in bed, mind churning. Even before she was pregnant, she had trouble leaving work at the office. Tonight, her thoughts swirl with the photos of four teenage girls pinned to Atticus Singh's crime wall; Rusty Whitaker sucking on chicken wings at a dreary strip club; and the three pools of dried blood staining the carpet of the Dairy Creamery.

Bob rolls onto his side, facing her.

"Go back to sleep, sweetie," Keller says.

He stares at her in that way he does. He knows her so well. "I'll go back to sleep if you do."

She frowns.

"If you're gonna work through something, it will be faster if you have help."

He often stays up with her during her bouts of insomnia from the pregnancy, usually watching old movies or bingeing on Netflix.

"Where are you going?" Keller asks as Bob lumbers out of bed and shuffles to the hallway.

"We need every G-man's secret weapon for investigations."

"What's that?"

"Ben and Jerry's."

Twenty minutes later, in the twilight glow of the muted television, Keller and her husband sit on their bed, empty bowls with smears of Cherry Garcia gracing the nightstand.

Keller starts by explaining the eerily similar crimes. Night shift employees attacked with a knife, in each case, a lone survivor. "And then the weirdest thing happened . . ."

Bob looks at her, eager. The goon loves *weird*.

"The killer whispered the same thing to both surviving girls."

"Wait, *what*?"

"Yeah, he said, 'Good night, pretty girl.'"

"Then it's gotta be the same guy, right?"

"Yes, unless that's what the killer *wants* us to think. Vince Whitaker has dropped off the face of the earth for fifteen years. We're checking but it's hard to imagine he had anything to do with the ice cream store killings."

"So, a copycat?"

"Well, that's the problem. The survivor from Blockbuster, she swears she never told anyone what the killer said. She said it came back to her later and she wasn't clear whether it was real or a false memory. She says she never told anyone . . . until the new survivor told her what the killer said."

Bob scratches his chin. "It had to be crazy traumatic, is she sure?"

"She's a therapist now. I believe her."

"So it's either the same killer, or she told someone she doesn't remember telling, or it's a weird coincidence."

Before Keller responds, Bob asks, "There's no DNA or video or cell phone pings or—?"

"For Blockbuster, no. It was 1999. People were starting to carry cell phones then—remember those Nokias?— but it's not like today. The file is pretty thin. They got a customer who reported seeing someone arguing with a Blockbuster employee in the parking lot earlier that night, but they didn't get a good look at the guy. An anonymous caller reported seeing Vince Whitaker's car in the lot at closing around the time of the murders. And police found his print on the break room door. After he fled, they found the murder weapon in his locker at the school."

"Sounds like enough."

Keller nods. "For the ice cream store, we're checking cell records. The perp took all the phones. They're trying to find any businesses or ATMs nearby that might have footage, but they've got nothing so far. Maybe the crime scene unit will find something, but it's not like TV."

Bob thinks for a moment. "Let's say the first survivor—"

"Ella," Keller says.

"Let's say Ella told someone what the killer said to

her but she doesn't remember. Who would she have likely told?"

The same question has floated around in Keller's head all night, but she's avoided facing it. Now, it dawns on her.

"The investigators," Keller tells her husband. "She would've told a cop."

CHAPTER 19
ELLA

In the Target parking lot, a concrete field speckled with lamplight, Ella faces Jesse Duvall.

The teenager's scowl has turned to a gaze of admiration. As if Jesse's thinking that Ella not only got her out of the jam, but also got her the merch.

"Want to talk about it?" Ella says.

"No."

Ella wants to tell the girl that she's lucky, that she could get in real trouble. That she's being reckless. That she needs to get help. But a lecture won't help. And, really, who is she to give advice about sensible, safe behavior? And the truth: she likes the admiration in those eyes.

"Need a ride home?"

Jesse takes an exaggerated look around the empty lot, like she's looking for Ella's car.

Ella holds up her phone. "Uber."

"No, thanks. I'm gonna walk."

Ella feels her eyebrows creasing. "Won't your foster mom be—" She stops. She's not this girl's mother. But she's also not keen on letting a teenager walk home by herself from an isolated Target surrounded by woodland.

"Walk?" Ella gestures around the same empty lot.

"What time is it?" Jesse asks.

Ella looks at her phone. "Eleven-fifteen."

"Good, there's still time. If we're fast, we'll make it. Follow me."

Soon, Ella is traipsing through the forest on the outskirts of the parking lot. She's breathing heavily, trying to keep up with Jesse, who negotiates the trail like a skilled hiker. The kid's obviously done this before. The woods hum with insects and the wind rustles the treetops.

Lights wink ahead. Ella stops at the edge of the forest, finally catching up with Jesse. They're at a gravel road. A tall, chain-link fence spans the distance on either side of them. On the other side of the fence, railroad tracks. A platform, a gray concrete slab, borders the tracks. It's not for passengers, a storage or work area for rail employees. Ella hears a train in the distance.

She watches as Jesse steps to the fence and grasps a section at the bottom near a support pole, and yanks upward. Someone has cut this piece of fence so it opens like a hatch. Jesse lifts the fence and crawls under.

"I don't think this is a good—"

Before Ella finishes the sentence, Jesse is running toward the platform. "Hurry! It's coming."

The rumble is louder. Fuck. A train. Ella's concern about breaking into a rail yard turns to terror as she watches Jesse standing on the ledge of the platform, facing the tracks. The ground is trembling now. Ella yanks at the fence and climbs through the opening, then sprints toward Jesse, who is lit by the approaching train's head-lamp, her shadow stretching across the platform.

"Jesse!" Ella screams as she pumps her legs over the grass and weeds. Her heart is pounding.

Jesse stands precariously close to the platform ledge. The roar of the train buries Ella's pleas.

The train is speeding toward the platform. The scene is surreal, Ella struggling to process it. She has to reach Jesse before . . .

The teen stands at the platform's lip, her arms raised and spread, head raised to the sky like she's on the prow of the *Titanic*.

Ella makes it to the platform with little time to spare and finds Jesse still in the same position. Jesse turns as the train approaches and gives Ella a look. A faraway smile.

It's the first time Ella has seen Jesse smile.

"No!" Ella screams.

CHAPTER 20
CHRIS

Chris lies in the dark, the city lights twinkling through the thin sheers covering the window in Clare's bedroom.

Her voice breaks the quiet. "Is something wrong?"

Chris waits for the briefest of moments. "No, why do you ask?"

"You've just seemed quiet since the party," she says. "My friends weren't giving you a hard time about your job, were they?"

"No. Not that I'd care if they did."

That is met with a long silence. Then: "They're good guys, if you get to know them."

"If you say so."

"I do, actually," Clare says. It isn't biting, it's earnest. That's the thing with Clare, you can't get her ire up. How can she be so *good*? The better question is how can someone so good be with *him*? And why is he sporting for a fight?

"Maybe I should get going," he says.

She faces him on the bed now. "Get going? It's late.

What's going on, Chris? Are you mad at me? Did I do something—what's going on?"

He examines this lovely woman in the faint light. Her strong jaw and perfectly sculpted eyebrows. Beauty inside and out. What's next isn't an epiphany, since he's experienced it before, but more of a piercing revelation: Clare doesn't deserve his shit. And he should quit pushing her away out of fear that she'll leave when she understands who he really is.

"There's something I have to tell you."

The look in her eyes nearly causes him to chicken out.

"What is it?" She swallows audibly.

Chris takes in a deep breath. And he tells her. About grisly murders on New Year's Eve 1999. About his brother's arrest. About Vince's release for insufficient evidence. About his disappearance. About the adoption, his name change.

While Clare absorbs it all, he reaches for his phone and pulls up an app. It displays a map with small blue dots with dates next to them. When enlarged, the map reveals dots spanning from Ukraine to Paris to India.

"These are all the sightings of Vince over the years."

Early on, Chris speculated that his brother had somehow managed to change his appearance. Cut the long hair, got plastic surgery, perhaps. Taken a job as a trucker or drug mule, something that kept him on the road abroad. Given Mr. Nirvana's arrival in the U.S. today, Chris believes that his chance to find Vince has finally arrived, but he doesn't tell Clare that.

Her first question surprises him. "You *want* to find him?"

"He's my brother," he says. "He couldn't have done it. I was with him that night. And you don't understand what he did for me. Who he *is*."

"Then why did he run?"

Chris makes no reply. He knows she'll find the answer; it's only a quick Google search away: someone seen arguing with one of the victims outside the video store; his car in the lot after closing; the fingerprint; the knife in his locker at school. Vince disappearing the same day that the public defender somehow got him sprung.

Clare opens her mouth to speak but stops. She doesn't ask the questions he'd always anticipated and had rehearsed answers for: *Why didn't you tell me? Chris Ford isn't your real last name? Don't you trust me? Did I ever really know you?*

Instead, she releases a cynical laugh and says, more to herself than to Chris, "I thought you were going to say there's another woman."

"Would that have been worse?"

Clare's answer is a gut punch, revealing that sweet, perfect Clare might not be so sweet and so perfect after all.

"I'm not sure."

YOUTUBE EXCERPT
Mr. Nirvana, the Anonymous Travel Vlogger
(2M views)
"The Radioactive Wolf"

EXT. CHERNOBYL—WOODS

MR. NIRVANA's hand points to a sign posted to a tree in a desolate woodland. The metal sign is faded, rusted, and written in Russian.

> MR. NIRVANA (O.S.)
> The sign says "Radioactive Danger, Entry Forbidden." But when's a sign ever stopped us, right?

The video cuts off, then turns back on. He's in an abandoned house. The paint is peeling from the walls. Pictures still hang on them. A doll sits on the rotted timber floor.

> MR. NIRVANA (O.S.)
> It looks like they quickly packed up their belongings and never looked back. I hope there's no dead bodies in here.

Nirvana hears a noise and freezes. He pulls a hunting knife from a sheath, walking slowly with it held in front of him, on-camera.

                    MR. NIRVANA (O.S.)
                    (WHISPERING)
The most dangerous places in the zone
are the houses. Why? Because although
the land is contaminated, berries and
nuts and roots still grow, attract-
ing animals. Bears and other creatures
take shelter in the abandoned—Oh shit!

The camera jostles and the sound of the wind
rasps the microphone as Nirvana runs. There's
growling, a vicious animal giving chase. The
camera turns off briefly. When it comes back
on, Nirvana is inside a small room. The camera
focuses on the door. Something is scratching
on the other side, nails digging into the wood.

                    MR. NIRVANA (O.S.)
You hear that? It's a big, mangy,
Chernobyl wolf, right outside. He
didn't much care for me intruding on
his home. I do *not* want that radioac-
tive fellow to have me for dinner, so
it appears I'll be here for a while
until he gives up. If you don't see me
post again, you know what happened.
Until then, campers, when you view
this, I'll be back home in America. If
I survive.

                    FADE TO BLACK

CHAPTER 21
ELLA

Jesse doesn't jump.

When Ella reaches her, she's standing with her toes over the ledge, the freight train barreling by less than two feet away, the air roaring like a tornado. Jesse extends an arm to make sure Ella doesn't get too close to the edge. And they both stand there, the train blurring past, the two of them lost in a world where nothing matters but being in the moment—a dreamlike quality born of noise, danger, and the allure of death.

Jesse yells into the night, a joyous howl barely discernible amid the thunder of the train. And to her own shock, Ella joins in.

When the train is gone, they both fall on their asses, sapped by the adrenaline rush, laughing hysterically.

They sit on the dirty concrete slab for a long time, saying nothing.

Jesse dumps the contents of her backpack, snatches up a pack of Skittles, and tosses it to Ella.

In that moment, Ella realizes that shoplifting the snacks is part of the ritual.

"First time you ever catch a train?" Jesse asks, chewing on the candy. She grasps her phone, like she's battling with herself about whether to check it. It has a large plastic case in the shape of Hello Kitty. She's clearly not one of those teens who is glued to her phone, which is a good thing, Ella has learned from her practice. Jesse shoves the phone back into her bag.

"Yes, I'm a catching-a-train virgin," Ella says. She's never heard of the reckless activity before. But one thing she's learned in her practice is that in small towns with no organized teen activities, kids improvise.

"I love it here," Jesse says, still smacking on the candy, her lips bright red from the dye.

Ella assesses the area. The grungy platform. The train tracks strewn with trash. Even the woods look ratty and bleak.

"What do you love about it?"

Jesse looks up at the starless sky. She doesn't answer. Ella isn't sure if it's because she doesn't want to share or just has no idea why she loves it here.

They sit awhile longer.

Ella's coming down. From the adrenaline crash. Or maybe it's a sugar crash from the candy. She stands, dusts off her jeans, signaling it's time to go.

Jesse glances up at her. She's cultivated a tough persona. But right now, she looks like a vulnerable little girl.

Ella is surprised when she sees a tear roll down Jesse's cheek.

"Are you okay?"

Jesse brushes the tear away. "Last night . . ." She shudders.

Ella doesn't say anything. She wants her to finish.

"Last night," she says again. "About what happened." She swallows hard. "I lied."

DAY 2

CHAPTER 22
ELLA

"You lied about what?" Ella asks.

It's just after midnight and Ella hears another train in the distance, the only other sound insects in the dense forestland surrounding the rail yard.

They're interrupted by the rotating cherries of a police car on the dirt road at the far side of the tracks. Jesse jumps to her feet. There's a crackle of a police radio, flashlight beams.

Before Ella has time to protest, she's chasing after Jesse, who's running through the weeds, down an embankment, and onto the tracks. Soon, they're both sprinting—breathing heavily, their pace panicked—into the gloom.

This is crazy. She should stop; she's the adult. She can't run from law enforcement. But her legs keep pumping, trailing after Jesse, who jackrabbits ahead, the only sound their shoes pounding gravel between the long beams of iron.

They're trespassing. Ella has placed herself in a difficult position. So she runs.

It goes on like this, making their way along the grim trail—past graffitied walls, piles of garbage, overgrown shrubs—until the police lights disappear behind them.

Jesse takes a sharp left off the tracks through a path stomped into the weeds. A chain-link fence stops them, but this one's low, and Jesse vaults over it. Ella isn't so graceful.

They're in an industrial area now. In the distance, a dilapidated warehouse and figures huddle in front of a fire dancing from a metal drum. This isn't right. It isn't safe.

"They're harmless," Jesse says, as if reading Ella's thoughts, or more likely, her stiff body language.

"We need to get out of here, Jesse. I'm not comfortable with—"

"Suit yourself."

"Wait," Ella calls after Jesse, who's marching toward the fire.

Ella checks her phone. It's already on low-battery mode and will shut down at any moment. She taps on the Uber app. The nearest car is thirty minutes away. She wonders if an Uber driver would be foolhardy enough to venture here at this hour. She orders the car, then follows after Jesse, who's approaching the group, masked by smoke wafting from the barrel.

When Ella catches up, she realizes they're kids. A boy and a girl. They can't be more than fifteen years old.

It's unclear if they know Jesse. But she's surely been here before.

The boy, looking worn for his age, speaks first. "We told you not to come back." It's said with exasperation rather than menace.

"You're not still mad?" Jesse says. "He had it coming."

"You broke his nose."

Jesse shakes her head. "Then he shouldn't have been acting like that. You have a sister, Kevin." Jesse looks at the girl. "You should be thanking me."

The girl next to Kevin studies the ground, not wanting to get involved.

Ella says, "We should go. I have a ride coming."

Jesse doesn't budge. In the firelight, she looks older. Harder.

"I'm not gonna say it again," Kevin says. "Listen to your friend." A shadow crosses his face.

"We don't want any trouble," Ella tells him. "We'll stay over there . . ." She looks over to the old warehouse. It has a single bulb illuminating its front. The boxy structure has shattered windows and peeling paint.

The boy sniffs. "Just keep her away from us."

"Fuck you, Kevin." Jesse makes a threatening gesture, like she's going to lunge at him, and the boy flinches. She wears a wicked smile now but lets Ella drag her away.

Ella catches her breath in front of the warehouse. They wait in leaden silence until the headlamps of the Uber miraculously appear on the desolate road ahead.

Ella is learning a lot about this girl. That she's tough. Brave.

And has a violent side.

The Uber driver eyes them skeptically in the rearview. Ella wants to ask Jesse what she meant about lying to the police. Wants to probe. But Jesse closes her eyes and falls asleep—or pretends to sleep—the entire ride. Eventually, the car pulls to a stop at the wrought-iron fence of a grand estate on Beekman Terrace in Summit, New Jersey.

Jesse's eyes pop open. "Where the hell are we?"

"My mom's house."

"You didn't say you were, like, rich." Jesse stares at the mansion in the distance.

"I'm not. I said it's my *mom's* house."

Ella instructs the driver to push the call button on the security system outside the gate. She asks him to pull the car up so the camera can focus on the rear window, which Ella has lowered. She sticks her head slightly out the window so that her face is visible in the yellow glow.

A man's face appears on the video monitor.

In a pronounced English accent, he says, "This is private property. What do you—" He stops. "Eloise?"

Ella smiles. The family's longtime butler—or "estate manager," as Charles prefers—has aged. More lines on his face, more gray hair. But still distinguished and decidedly British.

"Hi, Charles."

The gate creaks open, and the Uber pulls down the

long lane lined with old-growth trees. The tennis courts on the left are lit up. So are the stables on the right. The car maneuvers along the cobblestone circular driveway and comes to a stop in front of the porticoed entrance of the colonial revival that's been in their family since the late 1800s.

Ella and Jesse are met at the front door by Charles. Even at this late hour, he's buttoned up and looking 8 a.m. sharp.

"It's been too long," he greets Ella. "Shall I wake your mother?"

Ella cocks a brow like it's an insane question.

"Yes, the morning's better." He looks at Jesse. "Shall I make up the guest room?"

"That would be lovely. Thank you, Charles."

Charles disappears.

Jesse's mouth is agape as she looks about the foyer. The high ceilings, chandelier sparkling even in the dim light. She wanders into the library with its expansive bookshelves and ladder attached to a rail that spans the length of the wall.

They sit in the two leather chairs. Ella's dad would spend hours in this room, reading, thinking, seeking refuge from her mother.

Ella notices that Jesse hasn't checked her phone for worried messages from her foster mother. Her heart aches at that. The girl survived an attack out of a horror movie, and she seems alone in this world.

They remain silent for a long while. Ella finally breaks the ice: "When I went back to school after what happened, I felt like a different person. Like I was in one of those alien movies—my body was the same but something had taken over inside."

Jesse stands, walks to the bookshelf, pulls a leather-bound volume, and flips through it absently.

"But I'll tell you," Ella continues, "it gets better."

Jesse whirls around. Her elegant features are shadowed, giving her the appearance of a 1950s movie starlet. She'll be a beautiful woman one day. She already is.

"Does it really?" she asks. "Get better?" It's a challenge, calling Ella on her bullshit.

"Yes."

"Does your fiancé agree?"

Touché.

Ella feels a sting of guilt. She's been a serial cheater. She pictures Brad's face from earlier. It wasn't angry. Just run-down, exhausted because, no matter how hard he tried to make things work, she wouldn't stop. She's a horrible person, she knows. What the hell is she doing? She's the worst person in the world to give advice.

Ella says, "Earlier, at the rail yard, you said you'd lied about what happened."

Jesse's glance returns to the book, flipping the pages. "I'm really tired. Can we talk about it tomorrow?"

Ella doesn't want to talk about it tomorrow. She wants to talk about it now. But she doesn't push. She waits.

At last, Jesse says, "I hated Madison Sawyer."

Ella doesn't understand. *Who's Madison Sawyer?* Then it hits her: one of the ice cream store victims.

"I went to the store to confront her."

This was the lie: Jesse told the police she went to

the store to use the bathroom. That she didn't know the victims well.

"Confront her about what?" Ella asks.

"She was talking shit about me. Her and her friends. And I wanted them to stop."

Before Ella has a chance to respond, Charles appears and says their rooms are ready.

Jesse leaps at the chance to escape. They follow Charles up the spiral staircase.

Jesse says, "We'll talk more in the morning."

Ella wants to protest. Wants to know more. But Jesse disappears into the guest room and shuts the heavy wooden door.

Back in the familiar comfort of her childhood bedroom, Ella falls into the bed. She's exhausted, but not sure she can sleep. She has a knot in her gut. Anxiety prickling under her skin at the unanswered questions: What happened at that ice cream store? What else might Jesse be hiding? And, critically, what is Ella supposed to do with this new information? As the hours pass and darkness gives way to a purple hue, she wonders what further chaos the day will bring.

CHAPTER 23
KELLER

The phone pings at the breakfast table. Keller fights the urge to check the text as she downs the porridge and fruit Bob has made her. He has a thing about using phones at the table and she tries to respect that.

"Do you have your thermos?" he asks, retrieving a blender pitcher filled with green sludge from the refrigerator.

She grimaces. "I'm sorry, I left it at the office." More likely it's still rolling around on the floor of her car, where she left it yesterday.

"Nice try," he says, pulling another thermos from the cupboard. "I bought two."

Keller's phone pings for the fourth time.

"Go ahead, check it," he tells her.

She scans the device. A series of texts from Stan:

Turn on TV
Today show

Or any morning show
Call me

Keller goes to the living room and turns on the set. She assumes it's another segment on the ice cream store murders or even the Blockbuster case. But the *Today* show anchor is smiling, upbeat. On the screen: "We've been showing you this all morning, but the internet has been ablaze with a video they're calling 'Agent Bad-ass.' Yesterday in New Jersey, local police were storming a house to detain a suspect when a federal agent learned that the suspect wasn't there. Instead, his autistic son was inside, and the police didn't know it. Fearing for the boy's safety, the agent . . . well, watch this."

The screen skips to cell-phone footage of Keller— looking extremely pregnant—holding her badge in the air, crossing the street, and barging through the shattered front door.

Bob has joined her in the living room. "Is that *you*?" He looks at her. "You said you went inside for the kid, but you didn't mention it was mid-siege. What were you—"

"I didn't want you to worry."

"Worry? You mean worry about you intervening on a bunch of amped-up cops with assault weapons?" He's angry, a rarity for Bob.

"It wasn't like that."

On the screen, Keller emerges from the dwelling, guiding a young man who looks terrified and confused, then leads him to his father. It turned out that Randy

Butler had an airtight alibi and was cleared of any involvement in the Dairy Creamery slayings.

Keller's phone starts pinging again. News is spreading.

"Shit. This is bad," she says. The Bureau isn't an organization that appreciates attention—unless it's cultivated through the Public Affairs office.

The anger drains from Bob's face. "It'll be fine," he says, knowing what she's thinking.

As he hugs her, she experiences a wave of emotions: fear for her job, embarrassment at being a national spectacle, shame that Bob thinks she acted recklessly with their unborn twins.

"Look at me," he says.

She does.

"It's gonna be okay." Bob gives a half smile. "And, I mean, let's face it, you are a badass."

On the drive to the Union County Prosecutor's Office, she calls Stan. It goes straight to voice mail. She worries that's because her boss is on the phone dealing with his bosses at HQ in D.C. about the viral video.

Her phone chimes and she answers immediately.

It isn't Stan.

"This is James Nicoletti with the Secret Service," the man says in a deep baritone. "I got a message that you're looking for intel on Russell Whitaker."

Keller had asked the field office to run a search on Vince Whitaker's father in federal databases. But *Secret Service*? How could they be involved with a low-life like Rusty Whitaker?

"Yes, thanks for reaching out, Agent Nicoletti."

"Call me Nico," the agent says. "What can I do you for?"

Keller hates expressions like that. They permeate the lingo of law-enforcement agents of a certain age.

"The Bureau's helping the locals with a mass killing at the Dairy Creamery in Linden," she begins.

"I heard about that. Tragic."

"We're running down whether the murders may be connected to a fugitive on our Top Ten: Vincent Whitaker, the key suspect in similar murders fifteen years ago. Russell Whitaker is his father."

"Quite the family," Nico says.

"We interviewed the father and he's uncooperative, so if you have something we could use as leverage to get him to talk, the Bureau would appreciate it. I'll admit, though, I didn't expect to hear from the Secret Service. Did he threaten the president or something?" Keller imagines Rusty tapping out a venomous political post on social media, or, more likely, making a drunken call to the White House switchboard.

"Hardly." Nico chuckles. "It's about cigarettes."

"I'm sorry?"

"We've been investigating a ring of cigarette counterfeiters."

"You all cover that?"

"We do, indeed. And before you say it's a waste of time, these cigarette smugglers make more than drug dealers. In case you haven't noticed, cigs are taxed at more than three bucks per pack in New Jersey. Illegal factories outside the U.S. actually manufacture and sell counterfeit brand-name cigarettes. You take a truck full of fake cartons and charge half price, you're still making more per kilo than selling heroin. And that money sometimes funds terrorist groups."

Keller didn't know that. The ingenuity of criminals never ceases to amaze. It also dumbfounds her—why don't the smart ones take their talents and go legit?

"What's Rusty Whitaker's connection?"

"You get a giant shipping container at the Port of Newark filled with a load of counterfeit product, you need somewhere to store it."

It hits her. "He's renting out space at the storage business."

"Bingo."

Keller recalls the semitruck at the facility yesterday. The nervous desk clerk.

"I don't want to step on anything you're doing," she says, "but I'd love some leverage on this guy. He may know how to find his son." Keller doubts that Rusty knows the whereabouts of Vince Whitaker, but her instincts tell her he's hiding something about the case.

"You're in luck."

Keller waits.

"A new shipment just landed at the port this morning. We're taking it down soon."

"How soon?"

"You got plans tonight?"

She smiles. "Sounds like I do now."

CHAPTER 24
CHRIS

Chris knows he has an unhealthy obsession. Sitting in the interview room of the Union County jail, he pulls up the anonymous travel vlogger's site on his phone. During these long morning breaks between clients, he often falls down the rabbit hole and watches video after video of Mr. Nirvana's adventures.

He imagines what it would feel like to be so free. Free of his student loan debt. Of a job he's come to hate. Of a relationship that's destined for failure. Though, maybe it's already failed. Clare normally springs out of bed, but not this morning. He'd sensed she was waiting for him to leave so she wouldn't have to talk to him. He'd taken a shower, put on his fancy new suit, and is now the sharpest-dressed man in the morning cattle call of indigent defendants.

Chris has spent many hours trying to get a glimpse of Mr. Nirvana's face. And he's far from the only internet sleuth on this case. But the vlogger has evaded being outed thus far. Comments and forums speculate that he scrubs the videos before posting, editing out reflective surfaces or anything else that might identify him. Some theorize that Mr. Nirvana stays anonymous because he's on the run from something. Others say he's doing it simply to add to his mystique.

In the past, Chris considered traveling abroad to track him down. Put an end to this wild fantasy, once and for all. Prove that Mr. Nirvana is—or is not—his brother. But he couldn't afford it. Not even close. Now, though, the vlogger's in the U.S. And he's been taking more chances of late, posting live feeds, challenging his fans to find him. Why would Vince hazard that? Maybe the excitement from the risk. Or more likely it's just a tactic to get more subscribers, more ad revenue from the posts.

Chris waits, refreshing his phone. New videos usually pop up in the morning or late at night. Sure enough, a new vlog appears. Chris feels a wave of excitement as he reads the title: "Five-Star Hotel in NYC."

The anonymous traveler is in New York City, a short drive from here.

Mr. Nirvana has finagled a free room at a five-star hotel in the city for a single night. In the new video, the camera tours the room: five stars but still tiny. That's New York for you. The traveler takes the elevator and continues filming until hotel security shuts him down. The camera turns black for a beat, then filming resumes, now surreptitiously. He's on the platinum-member floor of the hotel, eating a buffet breakfast. In the background, a large-screen television plays the news. Chris freezes the frame and zooms in. Nothing on the TV gives a clue to the date. The traveler could be toying with viewers. There's no real way to know when and how long he's been in the U.S. Chris resumes the clip. The camera focuses on an average-looking plate of bacon and eggs that the traveler treats like something extraordinary. The camera scans the room again . . . *There.* Chris pauses the video. A man is reading the paper. It's spread wide, perhaps the guest's effort to stay off-camera. Chris zooms in. He can't make out the date but the headline is visible: DIVIDED JUSTICES SPAR OVER RIGHT TO GAY MARRIAGE. He jumps to the *New York Times* website and there it is—the same-sex marriage headline. The front page, above the fold, in this morning's paper. The traveler is really here.

This might be Chris's chance to find Mr. Nirvana. But to what end? He's the clichéd dog chasing the car, not clear what he'll do if he catches it. On the screen, the traveler wheels his bag out of the dining area and outside to a Manhattan sidewalk heavy with foot traffic. The traveler had the room for only one night. Hopefully, he'll post more on his quest for free accommodations. He usually does that.

And when he does, Chris will find him.

A calendar reminder pops up on his phone. His next client will be brought down in five minutes. Another day of drug cases. He takes the file from the top of the stack on the table and opens it. His client, Brenda is her name, has a thick jacket, though she's only twenty years old. The booking photos from her prior arrests take his breath away. The early shots show a pretty teenager. But with each photo, the toll of the methamphetamines becomes more apparent. If he stacked the mug shots together and flipped them at the corners like you did with little stick-figure cartoons you made in middle school, it would show the evolution of a monster. The eyes sinking. The hair receding. The skin scabbing. The teeth disappearing.

He's so tired of the drug war, which is really just a war on broken people, many who've suffered childhood trauma. Locking them up does nothing. Plenty of people in the system want to help. But his clients are like an army from a zombie movie. Help one, and a hundred more appear.

An officer escorts Brenda into the room and pulls out the chair. She plops into it. She's thin, and looks even worse than in the photos. She smiles at Chris. A row of blackened nubs.

He goes through his script. He has it memorized by now: he's her lawyer, he can never reveal what she tells him, she can trust him. He explains the charges and likely sentence if she pleads out versus if she loses at trial. He asks her questions about her background that might inspire the softer prosecutors to cut her a break.

Despite her scary appearance, Brenda is sweet. When she speaks, if you don't look at her, you can almost imagine life before the streets. High school football games. Prom. College.

"Ow, that looks like it hurt," Brenda says in her high-pitched voice, her eyes fixed on Chris's palm as he pages through her file.

Chris places his hand flat on the table, concealing the half circle of three parallel grooves seared into his skin.

"Yeah, when I was a kid, I was screwing around and tripped and grabbed the stovetop trying to break the fall."

He's explained the scar so many times over the years, he almost doesn't think of Rusty clutching his wrist, his face wrinkled with fury, spittle flying from his mouth, pressing Chris's hand to the burner. But, really, Chris should've known better than to drink the last Coke in the fridge.

Brenda gives Chris a skeptical look. You don't live on the streets selling yourself for drugs without knowing bullshit when you hear it. Without learning that scars like that don't happen by accident. Without understanding the dark side of people—people who take pleasure in inflicting pain. But maybe Brenda isn't skeptical, maybe the expression is one of pity.

Chris rubs his shoulder involuntarily. Whenever his thoughts drift to Rusty, no matter how hard he tries to fend them off, his hand always goes to the indentation on the ball of his shoulder. He can still feel the cigar like a cattle brand and smell the burning flesh. That time it hadn't been for some trivial offense, like drinking the last soda. He'd been nine years old and was defending Mom, who lay bloody on the kitchen floor. Chris had been terrified. Vince normally was the brave one. But his big brother was out. Chris stepped between Rusty and Mom. And he paid for it. In his view, it had been one of his finest moments. Still the most courageous thing he's ever done.

Where has that brave kid gone? Has Rusty stolen that from him too? He needs to find that bold side of himself: quit playing it safe. Leave this job. Start over. Do something to help kids like him, who've grown up victims by sheer chance. He supposes that, in a way, he's doing that for Brenda. But for her, it isn't a parent tearing her apart bit by bit. It's a bag of white crystals.

He examines Brenda. She's so damn thin.

"You hungry?"

"A Cherry Coke and chips would be nice." She smiles, and he fights the urge to look away.

Chris has a rule never to buy vending-machine snacks for his clients. He'd made that mistake early in his career at the PD's office and word had gotten around inside the jail. The characters in lockup started requesting him as their public defender simply for the food.

But Brenda is getting to him. He thinks of that first photo in her file. If only someone could've gotten through to that girl. It's just so goddamned sad.

He stands, knocks on the door. The officer lets him out. He ventures to the vending machines and buys the drink and some Doritos.

Back in the room, they talk more about her options. He recommends a plea. They have her dead to rights on possession. He doesn't tell her, but he's going to call in a favor a prosecutor owes him to get her a good deal.

Brenda listens intently as she eats the Doritos, her fingers smeared in orange. She sips the Cherry Coke like it's vintage cognac.

Ultimately, she agrees to let Chris broker a plea. Something with no jail time. Treatment.

He feels good about that. It's worth calling in the favor. Maybe this time it will be different for her. Maybe she'll escape. Get back with her family. Fix her teeth, get some meat on those bones. Live a nice life. Have kids. A family of her own.

"I think we can make this work, Brenda." He smiles. "But before I approach the prosecutor, I want to make sure this is your decision, that you understand all the options. I'll be by your side no matter what you decide. My job is to tell you the risks of each option, my views on the best choice, but it's your decision."

"I understand."

"Great." Chris scoops up the paperwork and puts it back in the folder. "Any other questions?"

"Just one," Brenda says.

Chris nods for her to continue.

"If I suck your dick, will you get me another Cherry Coke?"

CHAPTER 25
KELLER

Keller pulls her Volvo into the lot of Workers Insurance Company headquarters next to Atticus's tiny car. Atticus lifts his small frame out of the vintage MG. *Vintage* is being kind, since the vehicle's a wreck. Blistering paint, a soft-top repaired with duct tape, a dented fender.

He gives her his trademark beaming smile. Despite his doe-eyed, aw-shucks demeanor, Atticus is sharp. Analytical. He's a data person like her. And he has something you can't teach most young law-enforcement professionals—he doesn't need to hear himself talk. He listens, observes. He doesn't have anything to prove. And he's not one to tell you how things *really* are. He soaks things in. When he speaks, it tends to matter. Hal's right, he'll be a good detective once he gets some seasoning. Maybe that's why Hal assigned him to Keller. No, Hal probably thinks she needs a little seasoning herself.

"They know we're coming?" Keller asks.

"Yep. Got us an appointment with the department head."

"You tell them who we're here to see?"

He shakes his head. Not confidently, like he's unsure it was the right call. "The notes in the file said this guy acted unusually during the investigation, was uncooperative, but it didn't give a reason why, so I thought he might refuse to see us. Better to ask forgiveness than permission and all that." He smiles again.

Keller nods.

Before they head in, Atticus gives Keller a look.

"Something the matter?" she asks.

"Um, I don't know if you're on social media, but there's this video from yester—"

"I've seen it," Keller cuts him off, signaling she doesn't want to talk about it. Stan still hasn't gotten back to her, so it's giving her anxiety. For his part, Bob has texted her several GIFs: a clip of Will Ferrell in *Anchorman* regalia saying, "That's the most badass thing I've ever seen." Another of Chuck Norris giving the camera a simmering gaze: "You're a badass."

Inside, they're met by a guy in a suit that's seen better days. He escorts them to his office. The company's in-house lawyer is there as well.

"What can we do for you, Agent Keller?" the lawyer says. He wears a tie that has a stain on it. Workers is a low-cost insurance provider, and company culture is obviously no-frills. You don't want to show up in a nicer suit or car than the CEO.

Keller explains that they're working the ice cream

store murder case, which the lawyer and department head have of course seen on the news. Keller tells them the visit has nothing to do with the company. Instead, they need to speak with Walter Young, an employee.

The men don't need any explanation. They know Walter's daughter, Mandy Young, was one of the Blockbuster victims.

"He works in the actuary department," the department head says, walking them through a winding series of hallways. Six-foot-tall cardboard cutouts of a worker bee, the company's mascot from its cheesy commercials, are displayed in the elevator banks.

"We think the architect of our building was a fan of mazes. I still get lost," he chuckles.

They take the elevator down several floors. The structure has a deep underbelly.

"We have a football field's worth of computers. They gotta stay cool," he explains.

The basement has a long hallway painted turd brown.

"I'll warn you," the department head says. "Walter is, um, eccentric. Not a people person. He asked to have his office down here. He's a brilliant actuary. But . . . you'll see."

Keller and Atticus tap eyes.

They reach the closed door at the end of the hall. No nameplate. The department head knocks, waits a beat, then opens the door. A man sits behind a cluttered desk. He wears thick glasses and keeps blinking, giving his eyes an insect quality.

They hang back as the department head speaks with Walter, explaining why they're here.

Under his breath Atticus asks Keller, "You ever see the movie *Office Space*?"

"No, why?"

"Never mind."

The department head speaks louder now. "Agent Keller and Detective Singh, I'd like you to meet Walter Young, our best actuary." His tone is sincere. Cautious and over-the-top, but sincere. "Walter designed our computer risk model. If you tell him three things about yourself, he can predict with near certainty whether you'll get in a car accident." He smiles. "Text me when you're done and I'll come see you out. We don't want them to get lost in the maze, right, Walter?" The manager lets out a forced laugh.

Walter cricks his neck. Like a tic.

"That won't be necessa—" He cricks his neck again. "That won't be necessary. I've got nothing to say to you."

Keller says, "Mr. Young, I understand this may be a difficult subject. But you may be able to help us catch—"

"I've got nothing to say!" he shouts.

The department head's eyes widen. "Walter, I think these agents just need to—"

"Get out!"

"Walter, I'm—"

"Out!" Walter lurches from behind his desk. Keller, Atticus, and the department head bump into each other walking backward out of the small office. Walter slams the door.

The department head escorts them out of the facility, apologizing for Walter's behavior. It's a difficult topic, his daughter's murder, he explains. And Walter obviously has some social issues.

Outside, Atticus says, "What the hell was that?"

"No idea." It was weird, but they need to push forward, go systematically through the prior investigation.

"Who's next on our schedule?" Keller asks.

"Candy O'Shaughnessy's mother. But not until two o'clock. Still no word from the other parents," he says, checking his phone.

"More parents . . ." Keller lets loose a breath. They have time to kill. She thinks about her discussion with Bob last night—that perhaps Ella Monroe told a detective what the killer said to her. "I'd like to talk to the original leads on the investigation."

"There were two leads," Atticus says. "One died a few years back; the other, his name is Tony Grosso, retired shortly after the killings."

"You got an address for him?"

"No, but I can ask the HR department. He probably gets a pension, so they'd have it."

"If he still lives nearby, we've got some time, so let's see if he'll talk."

"Why? You think the file's missing something?" Atticus asks.

"It always is," Keller says. "It always is."

CHAPTER 26
ELLA

"You grew up *here*?" Jesse looks about the ornate dining room.

Ella doesn't answer. She's sipping coffee from one of the Shelley teacups her mother spent a small fortune on. Charles has checked in on her more than once, offering breakfast. But she has no appetite. Maybe it's because of last night, the weight of the secret Jesse told her. Or maybe it's being back in this house, dreading the visit with her mother.

Jesse drops down on the chair across from her. "But you, like, went to public school in Union County. You worked at a video store. I don't understand—"

"Neither did my mother. It's a long story."

"I want to hear it," Jesse says, not letting it go. She's already got a journalist's taste for the red meat of a story.

"My father insisted. After my older brother—Shane—overdosed. Dad blamed the money. That they'd spoiled him . . . the lifestyle."

Jesse scrunches her face. "And he thought sending you to public school would—"

"Do me a favor," Ella says, interrupting her. "Don't bring this up when you meet my mom."

Ella's mother never forgave her dad for his little experiment—removing Ella from boarding school, sending her to Union High—and even letting her have a part-time job, the thing that ultimately ruined Ella. It was the last straw that broke their marriage. Or, as Phyllis would say in her wannabe English manner, it was the drop that made the cup run over.

"Why?" Jesse asks. "Does she blame your dad for what happened to you?"

Ella doesn't answer.

"How'd they get so rich?"

"You'll have to ask my great-great-grandfather."

Jesse thinks about this. "Is that why the stories about Blockbuster have hardly any information about you? I mean, like, because you're Bruce Wayne's daughter or something?"

"More like Martha Wayne," Ella corrects. "I imagine my mom's army of lawyers and political connections didn't hurt."

"Where's your dad?"

"Where's yours?" Ella shoots back.

Jesse cocks her head to the side, seeming surprised—or maybe amused—at the edge in Ella's response.

Ella immediately regrets it. "My father died," she says in a softer tone.

It happened when Ella was in college. But her father really died on New Year's Eve 1999, if Ella's honest about it. Correction: he died the night police arrived at the house about Shane.

Jesse doesn't react, only says, "This is gonna add a nice twist to my story."

Ella frowns. She needs to talk with Jesse about this story she's working on. She's humored Jesse so far, but now it's getting uncomfortable.

Charles appears in the dining room. He nods. It's time.

"You ready to meet *Mother*?" Ella says in a posh accent.

Jesse's face lights up. "Am I ever."

She's excited about this. No fear whatsoever. Who knows? Phyllis may like this girl after all.

Outside on the veranda, Ella's mother is dressed in an expensive-looking blouse, her hair up in a chignon.

"Eloise," she says with a nod.

"Phyllis," Ella replies. She ignores the frown. Her mother hates being called by her first name. But she hated being called *Mommy* too, so you couldn't win.

"And who do I have the pleasure?" Phyllis says, studying Jesse.

"I'm Jesse." She reaches out her hand.

Phyllis doesn't take it. She stands, says, "That's a man's greeting. Don't lower yourself to their rituals." She walks over to Jesse and gives her cheek kisses, while Jesse stands ramrod straight. Then she gestures for them to take a seat at the table, which is covered in white linens.

Charles appears with a teakettle.

"Tea?" Phyllis asks.

Ella tries not to roll her eyes. Her mother is such an Anglophile.

"No, thank you," Ella says.

Jesse shrugs. Like, *What the hell, why not?* "Sure, I'll have some."

"Did you eat?" Phyllis asks.

"Not yet," Jesse says.

"Eloise Monroe, where are your manners?" Phyllis turns back to Jesse. "What would you like?" She directs her gaze to Charles, who is standing by.

"Um," Jesse says, thinking.

"Anything at all," Phyllis says. "French toast. Eggs. Whatever you'd like."

"A cheeseburger, I guess."

Phyllis's lips are a seam, but she nods to Charles, who scurries off. Then she leans back in her chair, quietly scrutinizing them both. Waiting. A trick designed to unnerve, as Ella knows too well.

"Are those your horses?" Jesse says, looking toward the stables. It's another break in that hard facade, and she suddenly seems like a young girl again.

"They are." Phyllis turns to Charles, who somehow is already back from giving Jesse's order to the kitchen. "Can you give the young lady a tour while we wait for her meal to arrive?" It's not a question and it doesn't matter because Jesse's already on her feet.

Charles says something into his sleeve and a moment later a young groundskeeper arrives in a golf cart. Charles and Jesse climb into the cart and it zips away, the whine of the engine fading in the wind.

Phyllis looks at Ella again. Waits.

Nope, Ella thinks.

Finally, Phyllis relents. "So . . ."

It's so like her mother to pack so much into a single word. With that word she asks, *Why the hell did you show up at my door after midnight? Who's the girl? What's going on with Brad? And what on earth are you wearing?*

"So," Ella says. *Mirroring,* the communications experts call it. It's one of those things she remembers from her time at boarding school, where half the curriculum was aimed at teaching you how to be charming at a dinner party or charity gala. It was one of the reasons Ella's dad let her transfer to public school.

Phyllis smirks. "That's the same thing you said when I discovered that stray dog you hid in your room." She shakes her head. "You and your father always had a thing for strays." Her glance turns to the stables, where Jesse stands on the first rung of the horse fence, feeding an apple to a Thoroughbred.

Ella releases a loud breath. "Have you seen the news? About the ice cream store?"

Phyllis tenses. Her back is straighter now. Jaw tight. She doesn't respond but it's clear, she's seen the reports.

"Jesse's the sole survivor. They asked me to meet with her."

Phyllis's brow creases.

"What?" Ella says. "They think I can help her. I'm obviously well qualified."

Phyllis lets out a breath of her own. "That's good, dear, I'm sure you can."

Her mother can push Ella's buttons like no other.

"Then what's with the frown?"

Phyllis makes no reply. She's never wanted to talk about *it*. Ella can't remember ever talking about *it* with her mother. Her father tried, but Ella stopped when she realized how much it hurt him too. He would go out to his private garden, the one he tilled and minded himself, and spend hours in solitude. Once, Ella came out and found him weeping. She'd heard the same sound of his despair through the doors of the estate's library. That's why Mr. Steadman became her lifeline.

"What is it? Say it, Phyllis." Her tone is severe.

Phyllis's mouth remains a slit. "Now isn't the time."

"The *time*? The time for what? What are you—"

"The time to discuss that you need to quit defining yourself by that day."

That's a punch to the gut. Ella feels her blood turning hot. *How dare she?* Phyllis never had the fortitude to hear about that night; about Ella waking up to Katie's lifeless body on hers; the terror of the figure leaning over her; nearly dying herself, surviving only because the blade missed her pulmonary artery by two millimeters. Yet she has the gall to tell her to *get over it*?

"Maybe it's *time* for you," Ella says, venom in her tone.

"For what? I face my demons, dear. And until you do, you'll continue to be a mess."

Ella feels tears welling.

Jesse returns before their visit can get any worse. She's smiling until she sees Ella.

Ella stands. She's leaving.

Phyllis shakes her head. "Don't be so melodramatic, Eloise." She turns to Jesse. "Sit down. Eat."

The food's on the table. Ella didn't even see the kitchen staff deliver it.

Jesse stares at the cheeseburger with longing. Grade-A beef smothered in melted cheddar with a side of fresh-cut fries.

But, as if sensing Ella needs backup—needs someone on her side—Jesse says, "I've actually lost my appetite."

Phyllis makes a sound of amusement from her throat. Like Ella and Jesse are kindred spirits. Two damaged souls.

And what's worse: she's right.

"Wait," Phyllis says as Ella walks to the door, Jesse at her side.

Ella stops, twists around. Something in her needs Phyllis to apologize. Not just about today, but about the last fifteen years. About every single fucking night that Ella woke up in a cold sweat and wanted her mom there to rub her back and tell her everything would be okay.

She looks at Phyllis, waiting. *Just this once, for fuck's sake, say it. Say you're sorry.*

Finally, Phyllis speaks: "Charles can drive you."

CHAPTER 27
ELLA

Oddly enough, she likes the smell. Popcorn combined with plastic from the VHS cases displayed on rows and rows of shelves. She doesn't even mind the unsightly Blockbuster uniforms, blue polos with gaudy yellow collars. She feels older, more mature, getting to hang out with seniors. And they seem to be warming to her. It's about time.

At nine on Sunday night, it's pretty quiet. Mostly customers rushing in, stuffing cases into the return slot to avoid late fees. That part of the job is unpleasant. Dealing with all the gripes about surcharges. It's not like Ella invented late fees.

Candy smacks her gum and seems to be eyeing Ella. Sizing her up. She's the queen bee of the store. She has mostly ignored Ella. Until now.

"You party?" Candy says.

"Pardon?"

"I said, 'Do you party?'" She says it loudly, exaggerated, like Ella's deaf.

"Leave her alone, Cans." Mandy calls her "Cans" because of Candy's large breasts, which the boys are obsessed with.

"Yeah, I party." It's weak, unconvincing. But there. She said it.

Candy continues smacking the gum. Her look is skeptical. "We're gonna hang out after shift. You can come if you want." She looks over at Katie. "You too."

It's the first time Candy and Mandy have invited Ella out after shift. Ella's mother is already furious about her taking the job. Hanging with the "townies," as she calls them, might send Phyllis off the deep end. That settles it: "Sure. I'll come."

Candy nods. "I'll drive. So you can give Jeeves the night off," she adds.

On Friday, Ella closed the store for the first time. Her father worried about her driving in Linden late at night, so he sent Charles to pick her up. It did not go unnoticed. The kids at school seem to know that Ella's from money. Candy had already been making rich-girl cracks. Having a chauffeur pick Ella up didn't help.

"I drove myself," Ella says.

Their manager appears from the back office and marches over. "Candy, can I speak with you, please?" Stevie stabs a finger in the direction of the office, then heads back there.

"O-o-oh, you're in trouble," Mandy says, drawing out the words, like Candy's being called to the principal's office.

Stevie tries so hard, but it's tough to take him seriously.

He's not that much older than they are and has a sweetness he can't hide.

Candy smacks the gum with more vigor now. She shuts the register hard and struts after Stevie. He's no match for her.

Katie makes eye contact with Ella. A slight smile. Ella and Katie are the counterweights to Candy and Mandy. The older girls are graduating, heading off to college soon, and they know that Stevie doesn't have it in him to fire them. So they disappear during shifts, take nights off without notice, flirt with the boys who come in just for a gander at Candy's work shirt, which she altered to accentuate her cleavage.

Katie and Ella are more reserved. Both juniors. Both unlikely candidates for part-time jobs. Ella lives in a mansion in Summit; Katie is from a deeply religious family. No dating allowed. No drinking. No swearing. She seems to live vicariously through Candy and Mandy. The store is a place where she can be herself. Out from under God's smothering reign.

From the back of the store, Candy bursts out of the office. She has a twinkle in her eyes.

"This is your last warning," Stevie bellows after her.

"Yeah, yeah, yeah."

"Are you coming tonight?" Ella quietly asks Katie as they empty the overflowing return bin.

Katie looks torn. "I don't think so. My dad freaked that I was even scheduled to work on a Sunday. Said he was going to call Stevie. And I still don't have my license, so my mom's supposed to pick me up."

"You could tell your parents we're doing night stocking or something," Ella says. "I can drive you home after."

Katie thinks about this. "Let me call my mom."

At ten-thirty, the four of them are parked in the lot of ShopFresh. It's empty and Ella's slightly disappointed. She's imagined where Candy and Mandy go after work. In her mind, it was way more exciting than parking in a vacant grocery store lot drinking warm bottles of Zima.

A muscle car, engine rattling, veers into the lot too fast. It takes a sharp turn and Ella swears it's going to crash into them. Her stomach flips as it screeches around and pulls up parallel to Candy's car.

A blond guy, Sean Morris from the football team, leans out the window and stares at Candy, who responds with a lazy, couldn't-care-less glance.

"Hello, ladies."

"Hi, Sean," Candy says flatly.

"And who do we have here?" Sean cranes his neck to see who's in the backseat.

"Friends from work," Candy says.

Ella has to admit that it stings a little being called a work friend.

Sean gives them a sly smile. "We're going to Brody's for some beers. Wanna come?"

Candy looks around the empty lot. Sighs. Then nods.

Sean nods back, then tears out of the lot in his loud car.

Ella has butterflies now. It's exciting, going to a get-together—a party—with the seniors. But it's scary at the same time. Katie looks like the blood has drained from her face.

Ten minutes later, they're in a basement that smells like the inside of a bong. Lounging on an old sofa and two beanbag chairs are six boys and two girls.

Candy introduces Ella and Katie. The introduction has a maternal quality to it. A warning underneath: *they're too young for you, so back off.*

One of the girls, her name is Scarlet, is cold, unfriendly. As if she doesn't like the way the boys are looking at them, particularly Candy. Scarlet rises from the sofa and joins one of the boys on the beanbag, sitting on his lap, marking her territory.

Mandy hands Ella a beer. Ella tries to act nonchalant. She subtly poured out the Zima earlier, but there's no way to avoid drinking here. It's the first time she's tried alcohol. Katie accepts the bottle but doesn't sip from it.

Soon, the boys are goofing around. They're not the brightest bunch, but they're funny. One of the guys mentions that a dealer's coming over to sell them pot. And Sean Morris has just lowered an empty bottle to the floor and placed it on its side.

Spin the Bottle.

She's spared the indignity of refusing to play when a new guest arrives.

He makes an entrance, this boy. He's handsome. Everyone yells "Vinnie" in unison when they see him.

This mysterious boy captivates the room.

But no one seems more mesmerized by him than Katie.

CHAPTER 28
KELLER

Keller and Atticus stop by the Union County Prosecutor's Office before continuing their interviews. While Atticus tracks down the address for the former Blockbuster lead detective, Tony Grosso, Keller decides to take her medicine and speak with Hal about the Agent Badass fiasco. Keller hasn't spoken with Stan yet, but maybe Hal has.

Hal responds to the knock on his door with a bellowing, "Enter."

Keller stands tall and walks confidently into the room. She learned this much from her father: if you slink into a room, you'll be treated as such. Walk in like you own the place, same principle.

"Well, well, well, if it isn't Agent Badass." It's playful, but Hal isn't smiling.

"I'm sorry. I didn't know anyone was filming. I just didn't want—"

Hal holds up a hand. "You don't have to explain

anything to me, but Arpeggio . . ." Hal grunts. "He didn't care much for his team looking like a bunch of idiots."

Keller nods.

Hal gives her a mischievous grin. "But like I always say, if you don't want to look like an idiot, don't act like one."

Keller says, "I hope Stan sees it that way."

Hal shrugs. "He won't. He hates attention. Not sure what kind of number his folks did on him, but geez." Hal sits back in his chair, like he's reflecting on his old friend. "One thing you don't need to worry about: if you're on Stan's team, he's got your back."

Keller knows that much. With Keller's fifteen minutes of fame out of the way, she broaches a topic that's been bothering her since last night: that Arpeggio hadn't told her about what the killer said to Jesse Duvall, the same words spoken to Ella Monroe fifteen years before.

"I've actually got my own beef with Arpeggio," Keller says. "He withheld some key intel from me, something important that—"

Hal holds up a hand again. "You'll have to take it up with him. I don't interfere with how my lead detectives handle their cases."

"Stan would be proud," Keller deadpans. "Okay, I'll go talk to him."

"You just missed him. Arpeggio and his team darted out of here. Apparently, they caught a big break in the case."

"What is it?"

Hal shakes his head.

"Got it," Keller says. "I'll have to ask him myself."

"A badass *and* a quick study," Hal says.

Twenty minutes later she and Atticus are on I-95 South, headed to the Carteret Fishing Pier. Atticus not only tracked down Tony Grosso's address, but also called Grosso's house and charmed his wife into telling Atticus where to find her husband.

"Hal said that Arpeggio caught a big break. You hear anything?"

"Nope. I knew something was up, though. They were all buzzing around. When I asked, one of the A-holes on Arpeggio's team said that me and the Feds need to 'stay in our lane.'"

"Sorry about that," Keller says. She doesn't want the rookie detective to take heat because of her. She'll be gone soon enough, and he's just beginning his career. She wonders if Arpeggio's break came from the kid in the purple backpack Keller had overheard talking in the school's bathroom.

Atticus smiles. "I'm not worried about it."

"So, what's Tony Grosso's story?" Keller asks.

"I don't know much about him. Retired years ago; looks like Blockbuster was his last big case. I asked around and was told he was solid. Not an out-of-the-box thinker or a workhorse, but honest, solid. Frankly, from the file, it seems like he was all too eager to accept that Vince Whitaker was guilty and wrap things up."

"Why do you say that?"

"It's like, once Whitaker took off and they found

that knife in his locker, the investigation screeched to a halt. No more interviews, no trying to deal with discrepancies."

"Like what?" Keller asks.

"Like how the hell would Vince Whitaker have made it to the Blockbuster if his dad had the car and didn't get home until ten when the store closed? Like why would Whitaker kill them all? A customer saw someone fighting with Katie McKenzie in the parking lot, but Whitaker's little brother said Vince was going on and on about a girl that night. Like he was in love."

"Still no luck tracking down the little brother?"

"I'm having a heck of a time. He was taken away from Rusty when the investigation team saw signs of abuse. And if he was adopted and changed his name, it's gonna take a while to track him down."

"After meeting Rusty, I hope he was adopted." Keller pulls off the interstate and merges onto a narrow road. She can see the green water from the Arthur Kill in the distance. Along the road, there's a chain-link fence topped with barbed wire. Behind the fence is some type of truck yard with about two dozen delivery trucks with their backs to the fence.

"Speaking of Rusty, I'm going on an operation with the Secret Service tonight," Keller says. "Want to come?"

Atticus's face lights up. "Heck yeah."

Keller briefs him on her call with the Secret Service agent, and Rusty Whitaker's suspected participation in a cigarette counterfeiting ring.

They park in the pier's spacious lot. The air smells

not of the sea, but of industry—they call it the "Chemical Coast" for a reason.

A man walks ahead of them, carrying a pole and tackle box.

"I never took to fishing," says Atticus. "My father and I went one time, and that was all I needed."

Keller regards him in his skinny-tailored suit. He certainly doesn't scream outdoorsman.

"I went fishing, hunting, camping, we did it all," Keller says. "My father wanted a boy."

Truth be told, her dad, a high-powered lawyer, isn't much of an outdoorsman either. But in his worldview, men need to do such things. He and his law partners and clients get dressed up in hunting getups and go on retreats. When she was younger, Keller enjoyed experiencing the great outdoors with her dad, the only meaningful time she'd ever spent with him. Then came the affair with his secretary, the divorce, and the move from the city to Tenafly with her mom. When she graduated from college, her dad wanted her to go to law school, follow in his Big Law footsteps. And he didn't hide his disappointment when she chose the Bureau; he viewed agents as *the help*. But the final straw, the thing that broke their relationship, was his reaction to Bob. It shouldn't have come as a surprise that her narcissistic father would not take to a man so unlike himself.

Atticus points to a fisherman at the far end of the pier. "Grosso's wife said he'd have on a ridiculous fishing hat with lures all over it, so that's probably him."

The man wears the hat, but also has the unmistakable

gait of a cop. Keller can't describe it—it's one of those know-it-when-you-see-it things.

Her phone chimes. At long last, it's the dreaded call from Stan.

"Can you give me a minute?" she asks Atticus.

"Sure. I'll get things started with Grosso if that's okay?"

Keller nods as she walks out of earshot.

"I'm told you have more than a million views on YouTube," Stan says without pleasantries.

Keller braces for what is going to be an unpleasant call.

CHAPTER 29

Tony Grosso smokes a cigarette, not bothering to put it out when pregnant Keller joins the conversation.

She regards the retired cop. As Grosso's wife warned, he wears a lure-covered fisherman's hat. He has a lined face covered in stubble.

Keller considers reminding him that tobacco smoke isn't good for unborn children, but she doesn't want to break any rapport Atticus has built, so she positions herself upwind instead.

Atticus gestures his chin to the cigarette tucked in Gross's fingers, then to Keller's belly. "You mind?"

"Oh, god, sorry." Grosso crushes the cigarette on a plank of the pier.

Keller gives a nod of thanks, then introduces herself. Apologizes for taking a call before joining them. Stan's call didn't take long. It was as direct and efficient as Stan himself. In his dry way, he implored Keller to try not to rile up the locals; to focus on Whitaker, not the new murder case; and for the love of God, try to not go viral for the rest of the week.

"Catch anything?" she asks Grosso, eyeing the rod jutting from a stand built into the pier, the slack line blowing in the breeze.

"Nothing yet. I rarely catch much. But it gets me out of the house. It's been nearly fifteen years since I retired, but my wife's still adjusting to me being home all the time."

Keller offers a transient smile. "I don't want to repeat any ground you guys already covered about Blockbuster . . ."

"We just got started," Atticus says. "I was just catching up Detective Grosso on doings at the office."

"Hard to believe the division has gotten so big. I retired pretty young—got my twenty-five years when I was only fifty—but all my friends have retired or moved on. I see in the papers that Hal's still hanging on."

"That, he is," Atticus says.

"He got the big job after I left. It was one of the few times the powers that be got something right."

Keller presses forward. "We'll try not to take too much of your time."

"I got all the time in the world. But I'm not sure how much help I'll be. We closed that file a long time ago. It was my last major case, but my memory isn't what it used to be. But I'll try. Fire away."

"We get it," Keller says. "We're kind of coming up empty, and you know how that goes."

Grosso gives a knowing nod. "I can't believe Whitaker's still out there. That was one hell of a disappearing act."

Keller nods back. "I know it's been a long time, so maybe it would help dust off the cobwebs if you walked us through what you remember about the investigation, take it from the top."

"One thing I'll never forget is that crime scene." Grosso shakes his head, like it's a memory he'd gladly discard. "So much blood. The four of them, the manager was a young guy, and the three teenage girls on that break room floor." He exhales loudly. "My family used to go to that video store every weekend, but we never went again, not after that."

Grosso explains how he was called away from a New Year's Eve party. How a traumatized teenager had been found outside the store covered in blood on the brink of death. The grim discovery inside. The tips that led them to Vince Whitaker.

"Do you know who called in the tips about Whitaker being at the scene?" Atticus asks.

Grosso shakes his head. "I vaguely recall a customer had seen one of the girls, Katie McKenzie, having an argument with someone in the lot, though they couldn't identify who she was fighting with. But someone else had seen Whitaker at the store around the same time."

"How about who gave the tip about seeing Whitaker's car in the lot later at closing," Atticus asks. "It's not in the file."

"I think it was an anonymous tip, but I honestly don't remember."

"So, you get these tips," Keller says, "and you all immediately think Whitaker's the perp?"

"We also got a print on the back door to the break room, compared it to Whitaker's, and it matched. You gotta understand, we had nothing to go on, so we brought him in. If I could go back in time, you know, twenty-twenty hindsight, I would've waited to make the arrest. Particularly since that dirtbag lawyer got him out for insufficient evidence. I mean, we found the knife right after he was released. But by then, Whitaker was long gone."

Keller looks out at the water, which is murky and choppy. "After you found the knife, the investigation seemed to slow down. The file kind of winds up."

Grosso nods. "The county prosecutor at the time was getting a lot of heat because we'd made the arrest too soon, that Whitaker got out, so he was eager to close the investigation. Declare some type of win, that we'd identified the perp. He assumed they'd scoop up Whitaker soon enough and all would be forgiven. Didn't quite work out that way for him—or for any of us."

Keller realizes that Grosso's decision to retire young wasn't completely voluntary. The county cleaned house after the Whitaker debacle.

"But it was for the best. I was burned out on the job, got a good government pension. I can fish whenever I want, so it all worked out." He says this like he almost believes it.

"Were you okay with the investigation being shut down so abruptly?" Keller asks. Most detectives want a case solved, not merely administrative closure.

"Didn't matter what I was okay with. But, yeah, I mean it seemed pretty open-and-shut. The kid takes off, we find the blade in his school locker, he had motive . . ."

"What was the motive?" Keller asks.

"You know, he'd been seeing one of the girls, Katie. We figured he visited her at work, they had a fight. He came back at closing to pick her up, maybe they went at it some more and he stabbed her in the heat of it, used a knife that was in the break room. Then maybe the others stumbled on the scene before he was out of there, or maybe they'd seen him there earlier, so he took out all the witnesses."

"Except for Ella Monroe."

Grosso releases another loud breath. "I haven't heard that name in a long time. Yeah, she got lucky, that one."

Keller looks at Grosso closely now. "Did you interview Ella?"

Grosso nods, staring out at nothing, like it isn't a pleasant memory.

"Did she ever tell you about the killer saying something to her?"

"No, she'd been knocked out cold during the attack. Ella and Katie came into the break room together, so he needed to incapacitate them both. He clocked Ella, then stabbed Katie repeatedly. Before he left the store, the guy stuck Ella in the chest, and must've thought she was dead too."

"You're sure no one ever mentioned anything about the killer saying something to Ella?"

Grosso gives a decisive nod. "I'd remember that."

He didn't hesitate, didn't waffle or seem defensive.

"Did anyone else on the investigative team interview Ella Monroe?"

"I don't remember. But I imagine so. You'll have to check the file."

Atticus speaks up. "You mentioned the motive. Did you all ever learn what Vince Whitaker and Katie McKenzie were supposed to be fighting about?" He's been hung up about discrepancies in the file.

Grosso looks conflicted now. He sighs, like he's deciding there's no harm in saying it. "There was one thing, which we left out of the official reports. The press was in a frenzy and we didn't want it to leak."

Keller and Atticus stare at Grosso, eager for him to explain.

"The girl—"

"Katie McKenzie," Atticus says.

"Yeah," Grosso says. "We thought the perp had gotten her pregnant, so we thought it might be about that."

"The autopsy report didn't—" Atticus begins.

"No, I mean she'd already gotten it taken care of. So maybe the fight had something to do with that. The family had been through enough, and they were super-religious types. And her mother was old friends with someone from our office . . ."

"Who was that?" Keller asks.

Grosso shakes his head. "He wasn't on the task force. I don't remember his name. But he was tight with the mother. Said it would devastate the family if it came out. So we kept it quiet. I figured it might need to come out if Whitaker was ever caught and went to trial." Grosso looks up, like he's trying to conjure the memory. "For the life of me, I can't remember the fella's name. He was lucky that he wasn't officially on the team; probably saved his job. If it's not in the file, you can ask the victim's mom."

Keller nods. Someone from the Union County Prosecutor's Office had a connection with Katie McKenzie's family. Maybe this someone knew what the killer had said to Ella Monroe. Or maybe there's more to it.

CHAPTER 30
ELLA

In the back of the limousine, Jesse's fascinated by the luxurious interior. She plays with the mood lights. Ella shakes her head to stop. Jesse plugs her phone in its Hello Kitty case into the aux cord and her playlist, loud and angry, comes through the speakers. Ella gestures for her to turn it down. Jesse opens the mini bar and peers inside. Ella gives her a *Don't even think about it* look.

When the novelty wears off, they sit quietly, the only sound the hum of tires on asphalt.

Ella tries to contain her emotions. She's angry. At Phyllis, for being Phyllis. At herself, for letting her mother get under her skin. At Mr. Steadman, for pulling her into this mess. At Jesse, for making Ella lose all sound judgment. She chides herself for getting angry at a victim, a traumatized child, at that.

Jesse turns to her. "You're giving me great color for my story."

Traumatized kid or not, Ella is tiring of this game. But she bites: "Like what?"

"Like, you've got to have a trust fund, right? So what the hell were you doing working at a video store? What were you trying to prove to your mom? To yourself? And why the hell do you live in a low-end apartment complex in Linden?"

How does this girl know where she lives—actually, where she used to live, since Brad has thrown her out?

Jesse continues: "And what's with the beat-up Nissan?" She looks out the window at Ella's car as the limo pulls to the curb in front of Corky's Tavern.

The privacy window hisses down. Charles twists around. "I'm sorry, Eloise. But I need to drop you here. The car won't be able to maneuver out of the lot—it's too narrow."

Ella's car is the only vehicle parked at Corky's. Right where she left it last night, before her intoxicated Uber ride to the Target. There's some type of construction work at the far end of the lot. Orange cones surround a hole in the asphalt covered with a slab of steel.

It takes her back to the Blockbuster parking lot. Stevie standing in the empty space on a Sunday before the store opened. He'd put out cones and was shaking his head as Katie ran them over, trying to parallel park. Stevie may have acted exasperated but he had a soft spot for all the girls. Katie finally had gotten her permit and her driver's test was coming up.

Stepping out of the limo, Ella suppresses a sob. Katie passed the test the day before she was killed.

As she drives to Jesse's house, Ella rehearses in her head what she'll say to the foster mother. How to explain?

Keep it simple, she supposes. There was a misunderstanding at the Target and Jesse called her. It was late, so they went to Ella's mother's house and stayed over.

She imagines the foster mother asking the obvious question: *Why didn't you call?* There's no good answer for that. And unless the woman's as indifferent as Jesse claims, this is going to be a disaster.

"You okay?" Jesse asks.

This makes it even worse: Jesse thinking she has to manage Ella.

"I'm fine," Ella says, rounding the corner to Jesse's street. "So, when we talk to your foster mother, I think I'll tell her—"

From the passenger seat, Jesse holds up a hand, her face bloodless.

Ella follows her gaze. In front of her house are several police cars.

What the hell? That's a ridiculous amount of backup for a teen missing less than twenty-four hours.

"Pull over," Jesse tells her.

"What? No." Ella hesitates, thinks. "I'll come with you. I can explain."

"Please." Jesse's tone is desperate, the tough kid morphing into a little girl again.

Ella turns down a side street and eases to the curb. "Look, it's going to be okay. You won't be in trouble. I'll talk to the police and your foster parents."

But Jesse already has her seat belt off. She flings open the door. "It'll be better if I go alone."

"I don't think that's—"

"I don't want you to get in trouble," Jesse says.

Ella thinks about this. She may indeed face some consequences. She's a therapist and she's kept a teen girl out all night without permission. Not to mention the breaking and entering at the rail yard. Running from the police.

No, she won't leave her. She's the adult. She needs to act like it.

But in the nanoseconds that it takes to complete the thought, Jesse's out of the car.

"Thanks for everything," she says, slamming the door shut.

"Jesse, wait."

But she's already running. Down the street and through someone's backyard. Away from her house.

CHAPTER 31

Ella's knuckles are white, clenched to the steering wheel, as she drives aimlessly. What to do? She's already canceled all sessions for the day. She doesn't have a home. She's at odds with her mother (again). And she doesn't really have any friends. No one to talk to about what she's feeling. Dread is consuming her.

What's causing this sense of imminent doom? Obviously, it's what Jesse told her. That she'd lied about what happened: she'd had a dispute with one of the victims at the Dairy Creamery.

But it's more than that. It's the feeling that Ella's had ever since Y2K. The foreboding has dulled over the years. From the pills. From the denial. From the faking it with Brad. But the beast is back.

She decides to stop by the apartment—what Jesse called her "low-end" abode—to change her clothes, pack some things. Brad will be at work, so better to go now. At the front door, she slides the key into the slot, relieved when it clicks open. Brad hasn't changed the lock at least. Not yet, anyway.

After showering and getting dressed, she finds two empty suitcases in the storage closet: one is Brad's but, oh well. She begins stuffing her clothes in. On the nightstand, she sees that the photograph of them—one of Brad's favorites—is facedown.

She's feeling guilty. Not for leaving. That's the best decision she's made in a long time, one Brad will thank her for one day. She feels remorse for betraying him. For pretending for so long. He may be boring as shit, as Jesse said, but he's not a bad person.

In the bathroom, she packs her toiletries. She finds the small makeup bag behind the box of tampons, a place she knew Brad would never venture.

She unzips the bag. Inside are a cluster of orange pill bottles. She pulls one out and walks to the toilet. She's going to dump them. Flush every pill from this bottle and every other vial and never look back.

Uncapping the bottle, she catches a glimpse of herself in the mirror. She stares at her reflection. This could be one of those moments in life, a turning point, something she'll want to remember.

Who's she kidding? She rolls a pill from the bottle, pops it in her mouth, then clicks on the childproof cap. She stuffs the bottle in the makeup bag and carries it and her toothbrush and jams them in the suitcase.

She debates what else to take.

He can have the rest, she decides.

No, there is one more thing. She heads to the bookshelf

in the corner of the room. It's stuffed with those mo-
tivational business books Brad loves and some paperbacks. She pulls one of the few hardcovers from the
shelf: *A Farewell to Arms*. A book her father gave her
after Blockbuster. She riffles through the pages and
stops at the bookmark—a photo booth strip, black-and-
white photos taken shortly before her world changed.
When she was herself. She can see the difference in
her face. Next to her sits a boy. Oh, god, where is he
now? In a different life, she'd be on Facebook stalking
him. Reconnecting with a first love. She finds the pas-
sage her father highlighted in yellow: *The world breaks
everyone and afterward many are strong at the broken places*. The world certainly hadn't made her father
stronger at the broken places.

She closes the book and then shoves it in her handbag.

She then drags the heavy bags to the front door. She
refuses to turn around and do that last-look thing people
do. She doesn't need this shot on her mental camera reel.

Back in the car, she fights the urge to cry. "Hurt," the
Johnny Cash version, plays on the radio, a song both
beautiful and crushingly heartbreaking at the same time.

Now what?

She'll find a hotel, she supposes.

She thinks about Jesse, then texts Principal Steadman to see if he can meet her after school. She needs
to know more about this girl. What happened between
Jesse and the victims. What happened at her last school.
What happened to her family.

At the same time, she fears what she'll learn.

CHAPTER 32
KELLER

Keller breathes through her teeth in the tobacco-stained living room of Tawny O'Shaughnessy, mother of Blockbuster victim Candy O'Shaughnessy. The space is cluttered, filled with porcelain figurines of angels, and shag carpet that has seen better days. The woman across from Keller and Atticus has also seen better days. She's either in her fifties or sixties, it's hard to say, and she has bleached-blond hair and wears dark liner around watery eyes, like she's taking style tips from a 1980s Def Leppard video. But she has a sweet demeanor and welcomes them into her home.

"He's so handsome," she says in her gravelly voice, staring at Atticus, who's perched on a worn lounge chair across from the couch, looking uncomfortable. Between them, a coffee table holds several remote controls and an ashtray filled with butts.

Keller smiles. She's standing, explaining that it's because of her back.

"I've been there, honey," Ms. O'Shaughnessy says. "My Candy, she was a kicker. Two days of labor and, I swear . . . she grabbed onto my ribs and they had to yank her out." She gives the saddest of sentimental smiles.

"We're sorry to barge in on you, but we have some follow-up questions," Keller says.

"I assumed," Ms. O'Shaughnessy says. "When I saw what happened at the ice cream store, I thought I might get a visit."

"Why is that?"

"The case seems to perk up when something happens. Usually it's a TV show about the murders, or a mass killing somewhere, and reporters call. Not as often anymore, though. And rarely a home visit from the police, much less the FBI. I used to call over to Union County every day, but after a while you just have to accept it."

It's true, Keller knows. Vince Whitaker's trail went cold long ago. The only reason she's here is another tragedy. And if they don't find Whitaker, there probably won't be another visit to Tawny O'Shaughnessy until another mass slaying or new *Dateline* episode. But, looking at Atticus, the earnest detective who took a keen interest in the cold case on his own time, even before the ice cream store tragedy, Keller hopes she's wrong.

"I'm sorry you have to relive this every time," she offers.

Ms. O'Shaughnessy nods. "It's okay, hon, you're just doing your job. And Detective Singh can come by *any* time." She smiles at Atticus, who tries not to blush.

"We're going back through the file. Looking at it with fresh eyes. And we wanted to talk a little about Candy, if you wouldn't mind?" Keller says.

Ms. O'Shaughnessy smiles. "I love to talk about my daughter. People forget that. It makes them uncomfortable. But she was my baby, my life. And after her no-good father left, she was my best friend. We told each other everything."

Keller isn't a mother yet, but her heart hurts for this woman. She's gotten a taste of what's to come. On those days when the twins haven't kicked in a while, she waits for long, excruciating minutes until she feels movement. That sensation only gets more intense, exponentially stronger, with each second of our children's lives, Keller surmises.

"I wonder if you could tell us a little about your daughter's life at the time."

Keller doesn't need to know so much, it's a question that risks a long, irrelevant detour, but she feels like Ms. O'Shaughnessy needs it.

"Oh, where to start? She was wonderful. A spitfire, like me when I was young. But she knew who she was and made no apologies for it."

Ms. O'Shaughnessy reaches for the glass of brown liquid, which Keller assumes is *not* iced tea. Jameson, by the faint aroma and slight slur in Ms. O'Shaughnessy's voice.

She tells them about a headstrong young girl who was fiercely independent. Candy didn't want or need a boyfriend, and probably partied more than she should. She worked hard to help her mom, given that her deadbeat dad was years behind on child support. Her mom worked as a bartender at a Hilton hotel, and Candy worked at the Blockbuster. She'd been accepted to nursing school over in Irvington.

"She had the temperament for it. She liked to help people, but she also took charge of situations, didn't rattle under pressure, and most certainly would put an arrogant doctor in his place if she needed to." Ms. O'Shaughnessy has a faraway look, possibly imagining her daughter in a nursing uniform, living the life that was stolen from her.

"Did she ever talk about Vince Whitaker?"

"Ah, 'he who must not be named,'" Ms. O'Shaughnessy says. "I don't remember her talking about him directly, but she talked a lot about the gals she worked with at the store."

"What did she say?"

"She said one of the gals, I always mixed up their names, was seeing some boy her parents wouldn't approve of. You know teenage girls."

Keller has never been one for drama and in high school she surrounded herself with sensible girls, but she understands.

Ms. O'Shaughnessy continues, "Candy told me one of the girls got herself in trouble."

"Pregnant," Keller says, a statement, not a question.

Ms. O'Shaughnessy nods. "And the guy was obsessive, abusive. Candy said she was gonna give him a piece of her mind. Her and Mandy both."

"By Mandy, you mean the other victim, Amanda Young?"

"Right."

"So you think maybe they did that, and—"

Ms. O'Shaughnessy cuts in with an exaggerated nod. "It's the only thing that makes sense. I mean, why else kill them all?"

It's the same theory as Grosso's. Yet something bothers Keller. If Katie McKenzie had taken care of the pregnancy, would Vince Whitaker kill her over that? Or were they fighting about something else?

A tear spills down Ms. O'Shaughnessy's cheek. "It was just so like her, speaking up for someone. Trying to help."

Keller and Atticus remain quiet, allowing Ms. O'Shaughnessy to collect herself. She dabs her eyes with a tissue, the eyeliner smearing now.

Keller finally asks, "Did Candy ever talk about the survivor, Ella Monroe?"

Ms. O'Shaughnessy thinks about this. "I always get them mixed up. You know, back then, they were mostly her work friends. She and Mandy were tight, but the others, they ran in different circles. I think she talked about Ella, the rich kid, but nothing sticks out in my mind. I mostly remember her saying they were gonna help the religious girl with all that drama she was having with the older guy."

"How about the parents of the other victims? Do you keep in touch with them?"

Ms. O'Shaughnessy shakes her head. "At first, we got together, you know, for support. But I didn't really connect with any of them."

"Any particular reason why?"

"The fathers were all macho, you know? Like they were gonna break into the jail and beat the kid up. And I've had enough macho types in my life. And, I don't know, one girl's parents were Bible-thumpers. And the other dad had some condition, so it was hard to be around him."

Keller thinks about Walter Young at the insurance company.

"I met Ella's folks only once. And they were hoity-toity." She takes a pull of the drink. "And after a while, we all lost touch. At some point, I just decided that I needed to accept it and that Candy would've wanted me to move on."

Keller turns to Atticus to see if he has anything more. He leans in, looks Ms. O'Shaughnessy in the eyes, and speaks in a soft voice: "She was lucky to have you as her mom." It's unnecessary, serves no purpose since they're closing the interview.

Ms. O'Shaughnessy gazes at Atticus. "This one," she says, pointing her drink at Atticus, then directing her gaze to Keller. "We've gotta find him a nice girl. He's a keeper."

CHAPTER 33
ELLA

Mr. Steadman looks tired. He's probably had little sleep since Ella saw him at the hospital yesterday. Could that have been only yesterday?

Like most educators, Steadman's job doesn't end when the bell rings. *Terrible hours, but at least the pay is bad,* he always jokes. To make ends meet, he has a couple side hustles, including tutoring and running a driving school.

He agreed to meet with Ella at their usual spot, Daisy's Delights, a cupcake store in downtown Linden. They'd been meeting in this spot on and off for fifteen years, though for the first ten Daisy's had been a coffee shop. Mr. Steadman brings two cupcakes to their table, a red velvet and a vanilla.

"How are you holding up?" he asks.

"I should ask you the same thing," Ella says, watching him peel the cupcake's paper shell. This has to be his only vice.

He shrugs. Typically, these meetings resemble therapy

sessions, but with Ella as the patient. Mr. Steadman isn't one to go under the microscope, and he usually ends up filling all the time asking her loaded questions, never talking much about himself. It's an occupational hazard, a principal of a high school needs to be beyond reproach, and keeping life close to the vest helps.

She knows he isn't married. A year ago he let slip that he had gotten back on the horse and had started seeing someone. He used the pronoun "she," so that answered another one of Ella's long-standing questions. She also knows he lives in Asbury, far enough from the school district to allow some privacy. And she knows that he spends summers traveling, typically to African countries.

"How's Bradley?" Steadman says.

"Don't ask."

"How's your mother?"

"*Really* don't ask."

Steadman doesn't push. The restraint and patience of a man who's spent years dealing with demanding parents and mouthy teenagers.

Ella considers telling him about her night with Jesse. What the girl told her. But Steadman is a straight arrow. She knows what he'll say: she needs to tell the authorities everything, for her own good and Jesse's. She needs to establish boundaries with Jesse. Start acting like a therapist, or at least an adult, not the girl's friend.

Instead, she asks what he knows about Jesse's background. The incident at her old school.

"You know student information is confidential," he tells her.

Ella frowns.

"I suppose since you're working with her, it's okay to talk about it. But I don't know much." Steadman glances around the shop to confirm no one is eavesdropping. "When she transferred, I was told there had been an 'incident.'" He makes air quotes around the word with his fingers. "I saw that her test scores were off the charts, so I was curious, and I called the principal at her old school."

Ella waits, anxious to hear what he learned.

"The principal told me that her parents died in a car accident when she was in middle school. I asked about 'the incident' and he clammed up. Said there were legal issues."

"How are you supposed to help a student if they keep it from you? I mean, I think Jesse is a good kid. But what if she'd been violent or troubled?" Ella recalls the homeless kid from last night. *You broke his nose.*

"You're preaching to the choir. It's just how it is with these things." Mr. Steadman scratches his chin, creases his brow like he's debating something internally.

"What is it?"

"I can't. It's just gossip."

Ella holds his gaze, not letting him off the hook.

He wipes his mouth with a napkin, then looks around again to see if anyone's within earshot. In a quiet voice, he says, "The gossip mill says the incident involved a teacher."

Ella doesn't like where this is heading. "An improper relationship or something?"

Mr. Steadman shrugs.

Ella gives him another long look. A classic Phyllis move. Say it with silence and your eyes.

Mr. Steadman lowers his voice. "I can't talk about it, Ella, you know that." He pauses. "But schools like Middlesex East have online directories. It wouldn't be hard to compare last year's staff with this year's . . ." He holds her stare.

Ella grins. "And see who might be missing."

Steadman shrugs again. She didn't think he had it in him to break the rules.

"Ella," he says, his tone serious.

"Yes?"

"Are you okay?" He says it like he's regretting bringing her in to help Jesse. That he's thinking it's too much, too many memories.

"Okay? When have I not been okay?" She smiles.

Mr. Steadman does not.

CHAPTER 34
KELLER

Keller and Atticus stop at a greasy spoon for lunch, and Atticus eats a burger that looks absolutely delicious while Keller picks at a salad and forces down the green sludge smoothie from her thermos. Over the meal, Keller runs down their thin leads. First, the new piece of information, that one of the victims, Katie McKenzie, had been pregnant. Second, Katie was from a strict, religious family and was keeping her boyfriend, presumably the father of her unborn child, a secret. Third, the guy she was seeing was being obsessive, abusive, according to Tawny O'Shaughnessy. Fourth, at least two of her coworkers at the Blockbuster, Candy O'Shaughnessy and Mandy Young, were having none of it and planned to confront the guy. Perhaps doing so resulted in him killing Katie in a rage, then the rest of them to cover his tracks. Finally, the other new bit of intel: the Union County task force buried the fact that Katie had been pregnant. And they did so, according to Grosso, because Katie's mother was tight with a detective.

It isn't much to go on. And it certainly doesn't get them any closer to finding Vince Whitaker. But you chase the leads you have.

After lunch, they knock on the front door to the home of the McKenzies, Katie's parents. The lawn is immaculate, the cars washed, the exterior of the house meticulously maintained.

A woman answers the door timidly. She's mousy and wears a necklace with a cross pendant outside her sweater.

"Ms. McKenzie, I'm Special Agent Keller with the FBI. This is Detective Singh with the Union County Prosecutor's Office. We wondered if you have a minute to speak with us?"

Ms. McKenzie starts to speak as a man's voice calls out from behind. "Who is it?"

Before Ms. McKenzie turns around, the man has joined her in the doorway. He has a sharp part in his hair and a sharper demeanor.

Keller introduces Atticus and herself again.

The man's face turns to stone. "I'm sorry, but we have nothing to say to you."

Before Keller can get another word out, the door slams shut.

She looks at Atticus, confused. That's now two fathers who've refused to talk about the case. It doesn't make sense. She considers knocking again, but she's distracted by Atticus, who's intently studying his phone.

"What is it?" she asks.

"They caught the perp." His eyes jump up from the device. "Arpeggio's team just made an arrest."

"Who is it?"

"You're not gonna believe this."

CHAPTER 35
CHRIS

When Chris arrives at the office, he feels an electricity in the cube farm. Their work area is normally filled with the clatter of typing and the din of calls with clients, prosecutors, and witnesses, but today there's an ominous quiet.

"What's going on?" Chris asks Julia, who's stationed in the cubicle next to his.

"You haven't heard?" Julia is eating fruit from a plastic container. They both started at the Public Defender's Office two years ago, but unlike Chris, Julia still has true-believer idealism.

"Heard what?" Chris asks.

She swings her long braids over her shoulder. "They caught the ice cream shop killer."

Chris takes in a breath. "When did they—who?"

"A high school kid."

Déjà vu ripples through every part of Chris.

"I know, crazy, right?" Julia says. "The Blockbuster case all over again."

Once, Chris came close to telling Julia his secret—his real name, his connection to a notorious crime that had made this very office notorious. The inspiration for Henry's *the best lawyer I ever knew* speech. They'd been out drinking, talking shop when he started to tell her, figuring she'd be someone who would understand and not hold it against him. But they were interrupted by Roger, one of the newer lawyers in the prosecutor's office, who stumbled over, tanked up on artisan beer. He frequently hit on Julia while gloating about his office's convictions of their clients. Roger is one of those prosecutors who treat the justice system like a game. Maybe he's right.

Chris looks about the room. The tension is palpable. Then he realizes why. Everyone is worried they'll be assigned to defend the kid. A quintessential B-file.

Henry Robinson approaches the podium. The head of the office scans the room from over his reading glasses pinched on his nose.

"I imagine you've heard that there's been an arrest in the murders at the Dairy Creamery."

The room is morgue-quiet now.

"The accused is being brought before Judge Armstrong this afternoon. The judge called me personally to make sure we had someone there. No way this kid can afford a private lawyer."

Whoever the kid is, he's gotten lucky so far. Judge Armstrong is fair, not a hanging judge. She worked at the PD's office for a decade before taking the bench. She and Henry are old friends. She believes in the Bill of Rights. Won't rush to judgment. But even Armstrong,

Chris knows, will have Bartholomew H. Badcock on her mind.

"I'm going to appear myself," Henry tells the group. "But I need a couple volunteers who can get their arms around this quickly. I don't want to assign someone who doesn't want it."

The room remains quiet.

"All right," Henry says, after a long pause. "Give it some thought. If you're willing to help this seventeen-year-old"—he's laying on the guilt now—"come to my office. If there're no takers, I'm going to have to—"

"I'll do it." The words escape Chris's mouth before he has time to think it through.

Julia looks over and gives him an openmouthed nod, as if to say, *That's what I'm talking about.*

Henry stares past him. The case is out of Chris's league. He's still doing lightweight work, drugs and guns. This is a murder case. And not just any murder case. One that will be covered heavily by the media. One that could summon a mob at the courthouse steps.

Chris remembers the media footage of his brother's arraignment. The throng of angry people holding signs. The disdain and grief etched into the faces of the victims' parents.

Henry still hasn't responded to Chris's offer.

"I'll do it," Chris says again, this time with conviction.

"I heard you, Ford." Henry's lips are tightened into a thin line. He waits for others to jump in. Hoping that his *best lawyer I ever knew* speech had meant something to them all.

But the room remains still.

Henry waits an uncomfortably long time for more experienced lawyers to jump in. But they're the ones with kids and mortgages and college tuition who can't risk being the next Bart Badcock.

Henry gives a disappointed look around the room.

Then, another voice: "I'm in."

Chris turns to Julia, who's making a point of not looking at him. He could've hugged her.

Henry's shoulders sag. Then he says it. "Okay, Chris and Julia, my office. The rest of you, serve justice today."

CHAPTER 36

Chris stares out the window from the backseat of Henry's rust-blotched Subaru hatchback.

The courthouse is only a short walk from their office, but dark clouds loom, so perhaps that's why they drove. Or maybe Henry wants to avoid any journalists staking out the place. Chris sees no reporters out front. The building has a wide staircase that leads up to the porticoed entrance. It's a small, narrow structure, like an old schoolhouse struggling to look majestic with its columns too close together. Julia sits silently up front next to their boss.

Henry pulls around to the rear of the building. No portico there, just a blocky structure with windows that are too small for the concrete facade. The back contains the holding areas for defendants with windows built small to prevent ill-conceived bedsheet-tying escape calamities.

"Shoot," Henry says, looking to a news van lingering across the street outside the lot. "The prosecutors haven't even announced the arrest, but the vultures are already circling. Damn leaks."

A pack of reporters will soon swarm all sides of the building. And probably the PD's office too. The press has already established a campsite outside the prosecutors' office complex, so the lawyers there will welcome the reprieve. Share the love.

After a checkpoint at the garage entry, Henry parks. Chris feels abnormally excited. It's his first big case. But he's also anxious. He hadn't fully considered the media coverage. That the defense team will be featured in newspapers or on the six o'clock news. Chris is merely a supporting member of the cast, someone in the background. Still, if someone recognizes him, it could create problems: Vince Whitaker's brother defending another accused mass killer.

Before getting out of the car, Henry pauses, as if collecting his thoughts. He twists around so he's mostly facing Julia but can also see Chris in the backseat.

"A few ground rules," he begins.

They nod, both wanting to know the rules of engagement. This isn't one of their usual cattle-call drug prosecutions. It's a major case, albeit an infamous B-file.

"From the moment you step out of this car, you exude confidence. Your facial expressions, the way you walk, the way you talk, it all needs to project that we're not worried one spit about this case. Our client is not guilty. No laughing, no smiling. This is serious business and we don't want it misperceived by anyone."

They nod again. Henry's instructions so far are familiar.

"We'll hopefully avoid any reporters today, but you need to be on alert because they're crafty. If they shout questions at you while filming, pretend like they don't exist. Viewers can't tell if you hear the questions, so don't say 'no comment' or acknowledge them. They're invisible."

He looks to the pair for acknowledgment. They nod again.

"Last, with our client, it's all about building trust and rapport right now. A seventeen-year-old is more likely to take a shine to a younger person rather than to me, so we'll play it by ear on who takes the lead in the interview."

The trio leaves the car. Henry cracks his neck, a boxer about to enter the ring, and leads them to a grimy elevator. They get out on the seventeenth floor. At the security checkpoint, they pass through metal detectors and are allowed into the inner sanctum of the courthouse. An officer stands guard outside a door near another checkpoint at the end of the long hallway.

"Dammit." Henry points to a man outside the perimeter with a smartphone filming the defense team.

The guard turns and sees the guy and shoos him away.

Standing at the door to room 1754, Henry nods to the officer outside, who opens the door for them.

It's time to meet their client.

CHAPTER 37
ELLA

It's troubling how quickly Ella identifies the only teacher who hasn't returned to Middlesex East high school from last year—less than fifteen minutes on Google. His name is Chad Parke. Until his quiet departure from Middlesex, he taught English and—another clue—he ran the school newspaper. Where a budding young Bob Woodward worked. No, wait . . . who was the journalist Jesse claimed was her role model? Ella can't remember.

Now, how to locate him? She runs a search on his name, date-restricting it to the past year. Boom. Up pops a page for Chad Parke Landscaping in Rahway, New Jersey. A new business. An unusual career change for an English teacher. Unless teaching is no longer an option. But maybe it isn't the same guy. She navigates the page. On the "About Us," there's a photo of the owner of the business and his crew standing in matching shirts on a landscaped yard. It takes only a few more searches to find a photo of Chad Parke from his days as a teacher. He's tagged in a social media post about an after-school club—the Culture Club. He and a group of students stand in front of a Broadway marquee. It's the landscaping guy. But it isn't the photo of good-looking Mr. Parke that's so jarring. It's the young woman standing next to him amid the lights of Broadway. If you weren't looking, you wouldn't notice it—the adoring, some might say sultry, gaze at her teacher.

Jesse.

Twenty minutes later, Ella's sitting in her parked car at the curb in front of Parke Landscaping.

"What do you think you're doing, Eloise?" Ella says aloud, mimicking her mother's voice.

How many times has Phyllis asked her this? Too many to count. Along with *What are you wearing, Eloise? Why are you living like a pauper, Eloise?*

She gets out of the car, her head floating a little from taking another pill.

The office is a small structure, not much bigger than a two-car garage. She takes a breath before going in. The door swings open unexpectedly. Two men in the same company shirts from the website photo smile at Ella as they walk toward a truck that has a trailer loaded with mowers, rakes, and bags of mulch.

Ella catches the door and steps through. A man sitting at a desk doing paperwork looks up at her.

"Can I help you?" He smiles. Good teeth. Dimples. The kind of teacher Ella might have swooned over back in the day.

"Hi. I'm Ella Monroe."

"Hi," he says back, still smiling.

"This is going to sound weird," Ella says. "But I'm

a therapist. And one of my clients is the survivor of the attack at the ice cream store in Linden. You may have heard about it?"

His smile fades, but he seems curious.

"My client, she's a high school student. You used to work at Middlesex East, right?"

Now the smile is gone.

"Yeah, I used to teach—before I decided to become my own boss." He smiles, gestures around. It's rehearsed. An explanation at the ready, in case he's asked why he left the school. "But I don't understand how I can help with your—"

"Jesse Duvall," Ella interrupts. "She's the survivor."

Parke's face turns dark. "I'm going to have to ask you to leave."

"Please, I'm just trying to understand what happened, why she left your school, so I can help her."

"Go!" He's on his feet now, finger stabbing at the door.

Ella has a choice to make. There's a quote she's always loved. She can't remember who said it. *Speak the truth, even if your voice shakes.* She decides she's going to stand her ground even if her voice shakes.

"I'm going to call the police if you don't leave." Parke yanks his desk phone and puts it to his ear.

Ella takes a deep breath. Then: "Go for it." Her voice isn't shaking.

This prompts a befuddled look. "What? Look, please just go."

"Just so you know, if the police come, I might have to mention some rumors I've heard about why you *really* left Middlesex. Maybe talk to some of your crew, the other business owners nearby."

Parke looks defeated now.

"I just want some information," Ella says. "I'll keep it off the record. I'm just trying to help Jesse. Trying to understand her."

Parke puts the phone back in the cradle. "You have your work cut out for you."

CHAPTER 38

"Jesse has a high IQ. Mature for her age," the former teacher says.

Ella feels her skin crawl. The justification of the older man. Chad Parke is in his late twenties so the gap is not a gulf. But he knows better. Particularly with a vulnerable girl who's bounced around foster homes and is possibly looking for parental figures.

Parke sinks into his office chair, a distant look in his eyes. "She worked on the school paper and she's a talent. Better than most cub reporters at major newspapers."

Ella listens patiently, figuring he needs to work his way up to the damning part. Start with the rationalizations.

"I tried to help her. You know, took her under my wing. Tried to get her internships at local papers. Talked to some contacts at a couple of colleges about getting her a scholarship."

He goes on like this. After a few minutes of babbling, delaying, justifying, Ella finally decides to cut to it.

Decides to say it for him so he doesn't have to: "And then the relationship turned into something more."

"No," he says emphatically. "She's just a kid."

Ella makes a skeptical face.

"You don't have to believe me. No one else did either."

"What happened?"

Parke's jaw pulses. Finally, he says, "It started off with the school newspaper. Me editing her pieces, giving feedback on story pitches, like I did with all my students. But, like I said, she's talented, so I probably gave her more attention. She joined the Culture Club, which I supervised. I used to take the kids—I tried to focus on kids without involved parents—on field trips to the city. I mean, New York's a short drive away, yet many kids have never been there. I'd take them to the Met, to plays, try to expose them to the world." He stops, thinking. "She has this way of making you forget she's a kid. Like she's a friend, instead."

That part rings true to Ella. She lets him continue.

"I started to get concerned, you know, that she was misreading things. So I made sure to always have someone around when we were in the same space at school. Stopped doing things off-campus with the students. Made it clear I was engaged. But then she starts running into me places. At my gym. Then the coffee shop near my apartment. Then I start getting weird Facebook requests from people I didn't know."

"You think she was cyberstalking you?" Ella's mind wanders to the Starbucks, Jesse talking about Brad's social media posts. Her research on Ella.

He nods. "Then my fiancée . . ." He pauses, corrects

himself, "My *ex*-fiancée, Mara, she comes to my place one night—she used to come over on Tuesday nights after her yoga class." He stops, suppresses the emotion bubbling to the surface.

To her surprise, Ella feels for him. He's lost his job, his fiancée, and he's an English teacher, a lover of literature and culture who's now maintaining yards.

"Mara comes in my place and there's someone in my bed. At first, she thinks it's me, then she turns on the lights."

Ella's mouth drops open. "Jesse?"

"Yes, and she's not just in my bed. She's naked."

Ella feels her heart rate accelerating. He has to be lying, right? Covering up an inappropriate relationship with a teenage girl.

Parke's staring at nothing now. "The next day, our principal gets an email from Mara. It includes a photo of Jesse in my bed."

"Your fiancée turned on you? Just like that? Didn't let you explain?" Ella hears the accusation in her tone.

"That's just it. Mara swears she didn't send the email to the school. That someone must've hacked into her account."

"Do you believe her?"

"I do."

CHAPTER 39
CHRIS

Chris doesn't know what he expected, but she isn't it.

In the interview room at the Union County courthouse sits a young woman . . . a girl. She has delicate features. Flowing black hair.

You'd expect someone her age to be crying. Terrified. But she just sits there, calm and collected.

His mind skips to Vince's face on the night the cops busted in. His brother had cultivated a tough-guy persona. He *was* a tough guy. He'd taken countless beatings so that Chris and their mom wouldn't have to. But when the police dragged him out of the house, his eyes screamed terror.

But this girl?

Nothing. Maybe she's in shock.

As Henry introduces them, Chris has another thought: her demeanor will kill her in the media. The press will call her the "Stone Cold Killer" or "Ice (Cream) Queen" or other clickbait-inspired names.

Henry takes the lead, his manner with their client

parental but no-nonsense. "We can never tell anyone anything you tell us," he says. "Do you understand?"

The suspect nods but doesn't say anything.

"Here's how it's going to go. The first step is called an arraignment. That's where you plead guilty or not guilty. We'll plead not guilty. You can change that at any time but we need time to assess your case before we give you our recommendation. Then the judge is going to address bail. Whether you can go home," he explains.

The girl's eyes widen a trace. Still no other reaction.

"In a case like this, it's rare to be released before trial. But you'll be safe. You won't be held in an adult facility, for now."

Chris swallows at that, imagining this pretty young girl housed with the hard cases at the Union County Juvenile Detention Center, much less in the adult population at the jail.

"This is a lot to take in, I know. Do you have any questions?"

The girl shakes her head, then turns her gaze to Chris and Julia, as if deciding whether she's satisfied with her legal team.

There's a knock on the door.

"You ready?" Henry asks her.

Chris stands, expecting they'll be heading to the courtroom. But in walks Judge Armstrong, wearing her robe, unusual outside the courtroom. Next to her, a fit-looking white guy with a Marine haircut. Hal Kowalski, the Union County prosecutor.

Chris understands now. Henry arranged for the arraignment to happen here, not in the courtroom. Out of the ordinary, sure. But this is no ordinary case. The judge doesn't want a circus any more than Henry does.

Kowalski has aged since Chris first saw him all those years ago. He remembers Kowalski's face creasing in despair when he got a look at Chris. The bruises on his arms. The scar on his hand. He'd been the one who'd taken Chris to the foster home.

"You're not in trouble. And this has nothing to do with your brother, Christopher. It's for your safety. We have a nice couple who you can stay with for a while till this all gets worked out with your dad." Chris had been angry about it. Funny how that works: abused, neglected, but upset about being removed. His anger slowly faded under the tender care of Ms. May. Under the strength of Clint. Going to bed without worry of being woken by a fist.

Hal Kowalski has risen in the ranks over the years. Chris had wondered at times whether the prosecutor remembered him. Today, Kowalski doesn't give him a second look.

The session lasts less than five minutes. Judge Armstrong denies bail without argument. And Henry doesn't fight it. The ghost of Bartholomew H. Badcock and Vince's case hang heavily over the room. No one will be released, only to disappear. Not this time.

When the judge and Kowalski leave the room, Henry says, "We only have a little time before they're going to take you to the juvenile facility. We need to ask you some questions." Henry shifts in his chair. "Remember: we are *not* here to judge you, and lying to us will only hurt your case."

That isn't necessarily true. If a defendant confesses to the crime, it constrains the defense. A lawyer can't knowingly suborn perjury.

As if reading Chris's mind, Henry adds, "And just so you understand the rules, we can never tell anyone what you say to us. But if you confess to something, we can't claim innocence as a defense." He all but winks at her as he says this. "We've got only a couple hours, so let's make good use of our time."

For the first time, Jesse Duvall speaks. "I'll tell what happened."

Henry looks hopeful now.

"Not to you," Jesse adds.

Henry suppresses a frown. He gestures to Chris and Julia: "I'd be happy for you to talk to—"

"You're not getting it," she says, holding Henry's gaze. "I'll only talk to Ella Monroe."

Henry cocks his head; clearly, he doesn't recognize the name.

Julia shakes her head; she doesn't know either.

Before Chris opens his mouth, Jesse speaks again: "She's a survivor . . . like me."

CHAPTER 40

In the courthouse hallway, Henry convenes with Chris and Julia. They plan to track down Ella Monroe, but before leaving, they'll take another run at getting their client to talk. Henry asks Julia to go back into the room by herself. Jesse might be more comfortable talking to a female. But it takes only a few minutes before Julia sheepishly exits the interview room.

Henry checks his watch, frustration showing on his face. "Your turn," he says to Chris in an exasperated tone. "Maybe a pretty boy is what she needs to talk."

Nice.

Chris rises from the hard bench and Julia takes his seat.

"I'll give it a shot."

As he walks into the room, Jesse's mouth tugs to one side, a lazy smirk. "I've heard of Good Cop/Bad Cop," she says. "But Dad Cop/Girl Cop's a new one. What are you, Dumb Cop?"

Chris can't hold back a smile. He decides to try

something different—to not treat her like a kid. She sure as hell doesn't act like one.

"You think this is a joke?" he says.

She makes no reply.

"The prosecution's about to go on a speaking tour. The subject? A monster named Jesse Duvall. They'll tell anyone who'll listen that you belong in prison for the rest of your life, and if you don't talk to us—give your defense team a chance to help you—that's going to be the narrative."

Jesse remains quiet.

"We're the ones—and let me tell you, maybe the *only* ones—who are one thousand percent on your team. We're required by law to try to save you. So you might want to quit screwing around. And talk to us."

Jesse slouches in her chair. "Nice speech."

Chris sighs and shakes his head. "Tonight, when you hear the clank of your cell door slam at juvie, when you hear the wails of the damaged souls in there with you, remember: those are just kids. When they move you to the adult system—and rest assured, they will—juvie'll be a picnic by comparison. I'm not saying this to scare you. I'm saying it because you need to take this seriously, like your life depends on talking to us. Because it does."

For the first time Jesse's face doesn't look amused. There's a trace of concern now. He's reaching her. Jesse's about to speak.

Chris prepares to summon Henry and Julia into the room so they can get past this bullshit, and start building their defense.

"I said I'll talk with Ella Monroe."

"Really?" Chris shakes his head. "You're not stupid, Jesse. I know that much. Please, talk to us."

She stays low in her chair, holding Chris's eyes. "I know something too," she says.

"Oh? What's that?'

"You tell *me*, Chris Ford. Or should I say, Chris Whitaker?"

CHAPTER 41
ELLA

Ella checks into the Roadside Inn just off Edgar Road. It's tired in every way imaginable. Tired desk clerk. Tired fake flowers in the lobby. Tired elevator scuffed from years of tired suitcases banging around. Tired room with tired drapes.

She's starting to regret having words with her mother. She could be having Charles bring her dinner rather than contemplating a takeout order from the fast-food place across the street.

She separates the drapes and cracks the windows as far as they'll open to let in some air. She yanks the bedspread so it rests on the floor at the foot of the bed. Never sit on the bedspreads.

There's a mini fridge, and she nearly cheers when she sees the miniature bottles inside. They'll be outlandishly priced, but she downs two Tito's in two seconds. She pulls out one more and sits on the sheets.

She thinks about the last thirty-six hours. Jesse

hugging her knees on that hospital room floor. The girl howling into the night at the rail yard. The shrewd-beyond-her-years girl at the Starbucks who's done a deep dive into Ella's background. The hard girl in the firelight being told to leave by the homeless kids. The girl who stood by her when Phyllis had pushed Ella to the brink. Then she imagines the teen in her teacher's bed—naked, if Chad Parke's to be believed—*Fatal Attraction*-style.

And, of course, she recalls Jesse telling her that she'd lied to the police. Jesse wasn't at the ice cream store by happenstance. She'd been there to confront one of the employees—one of the *victims*. That's not some trivial investigative detail. Ella decides to let it all marinate. Then she'll decide what to do.

She downs another mini bottle, then scuttles over to the fridge and pulls out the last two. Street noise filters in from the open window.

She turns on the TV and channel-surfs. She catches the end of *Before Sunrise,* a movie she's always loved; a story about a young couple meeting on a train and spending a magical night together in Vienna. It reminds her of a special day she'd had with a boy at Coney Island before her life turned upside down.

She flips to Bravo and watches a reality show for a couple of minutes, two grown women are arguing, acting like teenagers. She flips to the next channel, and it's the local news.

There's a clinching in her chest at the Breaking News alert. The man she remembers from the hospital, the guy with the mustache and polo shirt and jeans, stands at a podium, a throng of microphones in front of him.

A banner at the bottom of the screen scrolls on a loop: SUSPECT IN LINDEN ICE CREAM STORE MURDERS ARRESTED. POLICE WITHHOLDING IDENTITY OF JUVENILE ACCUSED.

Ella turns up the volume and moves closer to the set. The detective at the podium answers a question from a reporter:

"The suspect was arraigned today and bail was denied. We don't have a clear motive right now."

Ella's heart hits the floor.

The detective answers another question. "We're not releasing the suspect's name right now. We can confirm the suspect was a classmate of the victims and is a seventeen-year-old female. If the court permits her to be charged as an adult, we'll release her name at that time."

A reporter says, "My sources say you identified the suspect through a tip."

"I don't want to get into any specifics. But, yes, a classmate bravely came forward with information that allowed us to obtain a warrant. We've also uncovered evidence connecting the suspect to the crime."

Ella watches in a haze, her thoughts muddled. *It can't be her. No.*

Back on the screen, the reporter presses: "Physical evidence? You mean the knife, the murder weapon?"

The detective shakes his head. "I'm not going to get into specifics at this time. We will keep you updated as the case progresses."

Ella races outside to her car. She needs to know if it's Jesse. But how? She could go to the foster home. But she remembers the police cars there. Not a good idea. She could call Mr. Steadman. The police probably told him. But if so, why hasn't he called her?

She's startled by the chime of her phone. She reaches for her handbag on the passenger seat, but in her haste, knocks it over, the contents spilling onto the floor. She misses the call.

She reaches over and scoops up her belongings—the pill bottle, lipstick, hand sanitizer, tissues, her wallet—and shoves them back in the bag. She snakes her hand under the edge of the seat to feel for anything else. She feels something and pulls it out.

It's an iPhone. It was deep beneath the seat, so it didn't simply fall under there by accident. It was hidden.

Ella clasps the phone. It has a Hello Kitty case.

Jesse's phone.

CHAPTER 42
CHRIS

They slip out of the Union County Courthouse the way they came in. Only a few reporters manage to get a shot as they race from the parking garage. Chris thinks he evaded the photos by crouching low in the backseat of Henry's car. For his part, Henry is silent on the drive back to the office, working the case in his head.

Julia has already tracked down information on Ella Monroe. "She's the survivor from the Blockbuster case, all right. And get this, when Jesse was nonresponsive at the hospital, they called Ella Monroe in. She's the only one Jesse would speak to."

"How'd you find that out?" Henry asks.

"I have my sources," Julia says coyly.

Chris knows what that means. Every young prosecutor in Union County has a thing for Julia.

Henry gives an admiring nod, clearly impressed not only that she has a contact, but that she didn't disclose the source's name, even to her boss.

"I've got Ella's number," Julia says.

"Give her a call," Henry says. "See if she'll come to the office."

"Already done. It went to voice mail. I left a message."

Chris half listens as Julia makes another call. Henry's on his phone now too, barking something about getting the file from the prosecution.

All the while, Chris's mind remains fastened on what Jesse told him. How in the hell did she know his real name? And why didn't she tell Henry or Julia when they wrapped up the meeting? Chris knows that *he* needs to tell them. But he wants to think about it first. Maybe he doesn't *need* to tell them, not yet anyway.

But that thought is shattered when Henry finishes his call.

"Damn reporters know more than we do." He whips around another car on West Jersey Street. "They're saying the cops were tipped off. There are text messages—Jesse threatening one of the victims."

Julia looks crestfallen.

Henry continues, "They also found one of the victim's cell phones hidden in the hospital room where Jesse was treated. And it gets worse. At her foster home they found a research file."

"How's that worse?" Julia asks.

Chris feels his pulse in his neck.

Henry says, "She was researching the Blockbuster case."

CHAPTER 43
KELLER

It's early evening and Keller and Bob stroll near the curb of their neighborhood, Bruno, their fourteen-year-old bulldog, trails behind them. The years are catching up with Bruno, and Keller worries how much time he has left. And how her husband will deal with the inevitable loss. Bob rescued Bruno from a shelter before the couple met, then babied and pampered the animal, a prelude to what she can expect with their twins.

"So, you're done with the county now that there's been an arrest?" Bob asks.

"I need to talk with Stan. But I won't be surprised."

Bob nods. "They think a seventeen-year-old is capable of . . ."

Keller shrugs. They walk under the gray sky, the smell of a spring rain lingering in the air. One of the neighbors calls out to Bob as the man drags trash cans to the curb. "You catch the game, big man?"

"Missed it," Bob says. "Don't tell me. I DVR'd it."

The guy smiles, waves, then goes back inside.

An SUV moves slowly toward them. Their neighborhood has no sidewalks so the culture is to take it slow. The vehicle emits two friendly beeps in greeting.

"I forgot what it's like to take a walk with the mayor of Bob Town," Keller says.

Before Bob responds, the SUV stops next to them. The window comes down. Donna, their neighbor from two doors down, smiles. The rear of the SUV is packed with kids.

"I'm glad I caught you," she says, more to Bob than to Keller. "I spoke to the director of Shining Lights, told her about you guys, and I think she may find room for the twins, if you're interested."

Among the many surprising things about preparing to have children is the cutthroat world of getting a spot in the best day care centers.

"That's awesome," Bob tells her. "When I called, they said there's a two-year waiting list."

"I guess not," Donna says. She then gives an exaggerated wink.

Keller's father often said, *"It's not always what you know, but who you know."* She's always hated that sentiment, particularly on days when it's true.

Donna's six-month-old starts crying in the back of the SUV, which ignites a cacophony of whines from her preschoolers. "I have to get these monsters home. But call Susan at the center. She's expecting you."

The SUV forges ahead, the wails from its interior audible even a block away.

"You think we're ready for this?" Bob asks.

"Is anyone?" Keller replies. It's a question that bounces around in her head on those nights when she can't sleep. *Is* she ready for this? Not one, but *two* babies?

Keller changes the subject back to their recurring debate over baby names. Keller's criterion is that the names have meaning, personal significance. Bob isn't so demanding and leans toward names with pop-culture significance, which isn't going to happen. When each of their proposed names elicits a frown from the other, they agree to try again on their walk tomorrow.

"I'm sorry I have to work tonight," Keller says.

Within hours, the Secret Service will launch its cigarette-counterfeiting op targeting Rusty Whitaker. And, thanks to Agent Nicoletti, Keller will have a front-row seat. It's not capturing Vince Whitaker or the Dairy Creamery suspect, but it will have to do.

"Don't apologize, I have to work nights all the time. But you need to take it easy. No Agent Badass stuff."

She shakes her head.

"After all, we need to keep Luke and Leia safe." Bob hoists his brows.

"Never. Gonna. Happen."

They stop, let Bruno do his business.

"Are you bringing the young guy with you tonight?" Bob asks.

Keller nods. "He was so excited when I mentioned it, how could I not?"

"Is his name really 'Atticus'? Like from *To Kill a Mockingbird*?"

Keller smiles. "Yeah, it's a sweet story. I think you'd like him."

"If he keeps my babies—Arya and Jon Snow—safe, I'm sure I will."

Keller ignores him.

They turn back toward the house, but Bruno plants his feet.

"Come on, buddy," Keller says to the dog. But she knows from experience, the pooch isn't going to budge.

"Well, this is humiliating," Bob says, bending down and scooping up Bruno in his arms. He carries the dog all the way home, smiling and waving to more neighbors along the way.

CHAPTER 44
CHRIS

"We're sorry to drag you in like this," Henry says to Ella Monroe. Henry sits at the head of the rectangular table in the large conference room at the PD's office. To his right, Chris and Julia. Ella sits on the edge of her chair across from them. Behind her, a wall of photographs. The annual staff photo. Henry is in nearly every shot. He stands out in every photo. Not only because he's one of the few Black guys in the early years at the office, but because of the intensity of his gaze.

"It's no problem," Ella replies.

"We met Jesse today, and she wouldn't talk to us," Henry says. "She said she'll only speak with you."

Ella doesn't seem surprised. She explains how she'd been called to the hospital yesterday morning after the attack. That she and Jesse had made a connection.

"We're in a bit of a bind, Ms. Monroe," Henry says.

"How's that?"

"If we let Jesse speak with you, whatever she says won't be protected by the attorney-client privilege. If the prosecution calls you as a witness, anything she says to you is fair game."

Ella considers this. "I'm a therapist, and we have privileges for communications with clients too."

Henry nods. "That's true. New Jersey has a victim-counselor and other privileges. But is she under your care? If there's any question about that, then we need to assume there's no protection. If she tells you anything incriminating . . ."

Ella seems to ponder that. "Can I ask you something?"

"Sure."

"What if I was a member of your team? An expert or consultant or whatever. Wouldn't that protect what she says to me?"

"Hypothetically," Henry says, "yes."

"How about things she said to me previously?"

"Not under the attorney-client privilege. But if you were part of the team, no one would likely ask you. They'd know we'd raise hell and that you'd probably not disclose anything helpful to them anyway."

"So . . ."

Henry pauses, then says, "Can you give us a minute to discuss?"

Ella nods.

Henry steps out of the conference room, Julia and Chris at his heels. In the hallway, he asks, "What do you think?"

Julia says, "I'm not sure what choice we have, if Jesse won't talk to us."

"I don't know," Chris says. "She seems to want to tell us something, like she knows something about Jesse." He hesitates. He doesn't have the experience, the years under his belt, but his Spidey senses are telling him this is a bad idea, so he goes out on a limb and voices his concerns. "I'm not sure we want to hear whatever it is she has to say. It could bite us down the road. Once she tells us, we can't unhear it. And if Jesse really was researching the Blockbuster case, the press could have a field day with us working with the original survivor." Chris recognizes the irony of this last part.

Henry seems to be doing a risk assessment in his head. "I think we're better off having her on the team, hearing what she knows. And maybe it helps to have a former victim on Jesse's side. I mean, if Ella believes and supports her, that could work in our favor with the public."

He says this like it's open for further discussion, but Chris can tell he's made up his mind, so he doesn't fight it.

Back in the conference room the deal is struck. Ella Monroe will be a consultant for the defense. They print a form agreement and she signs it.

Ella then fishes out a cell phone from her purse, places it on the table. It's a standard iPhone with a cracked face and large Hello Kitty case.

Henry's face turns sour. Chris doesn't understand.

"It's hers," says Ella.

Henry's head drops, an exaggerated show of vexation.

"And there's more," Ella continues. "Jesse lied to the police about why she was at the ice cream store."

Henry sighs and leans back in his chair. "The hits keep coming."

CHAPTER 45

After Ella Monroe dropped her live grenade—Jesse Duvall's cell phone—Henry tasks Chris and Julia with some research. What are their legal obligations to turn over the phone to the prosecution? If they don't hand it over, they're potentially obstructing justice. But if they do turn it over, they're potentially sealing their client's fate. The phone could contain damning information. Also, simply delivering a device that everyone assumes the killer had taken could itself be incriminatory. Especially now that another victim's phone, the Dairy Creamery manager's, had been found hidden in the hospital room where Jesse had been treated.

Henry said he'd encountered the question before—a client handing over a murder weapon to an assistant public defender—but the law had been unclear at the time. He needs them to research whether there are any new legal precedents.

Julia taps away on her laptop, searching Westlaw for the answer. Chris separately searches the PD's office intranet—a database of past research the office had performed on recurring legal issues.

"Hey," he says, "you mind if I duck out for an hour or so tonight? I promised my parents I'd come for dinner. I can come back to the office after."

Julia looks up from her screen. "Sure, and you don't need to come back. I can take care of the research."

"No, I don't want to leave you hanging. I wouldn't go, but it's a weekly thing, they make a special meal and look forward to it."

Julia smiles. "That's so sweet. How about you text me after dinner and I'll let you know if I need help? Really, it's no problem."

Chris nods his thanks.

The door opens and Bea, the busybody receptionist, appears. "Chris, you have a guest."

Behind Bea stands none other than Chris's girlfriend—or perhaps *ex*-girlfriend, he's not so sure—Clare.

Chris stands, surprised, confused. There's been radio silence between them, not a single text, since this morning.

"I'll give you the room," Julia says, offering Clare an insincere smile. Chris catches Bea giving Julia the eye as they shuffle out.

"Hey. What are you doing all the way out here? Is everything—"

"Are you insane?" Clare says.

"What do you mean? I don't under—"

Clare cuts him off with a hand in the air.

"You're part of the defense team for the ice cream store murders?"

Chris doesn't answer.

"A friend told me they saw you in one of the news stories." It sounds accusatory, like she expects he'll deny it.

"So what? It's my job."

"You wanna lose your bar ticket?" She stares at him intently. When he doesn't reply, she says, "It's a conflict of interest, Chris."

"I don't see it that way."

"Oh, you don't?"

He shakes his head.

"There's a crime alarmingly similar to the one your brother—your *fugitive* brother—is accused of committing, and you don't think your client might want to suggest that maybe *he's* the perpetrator?"

"Don't be ridiculous," Chris says. But his mind leaps to Mr. Nirvana's post. He's in New York, only a short car ride away from the crime scene. If the vlogger is Vince, any defense lawyer worth their salt would have a field day with it.

"Have you told your client? Have you told your boss?" Clare was top of their class, works at one of the best law firms in the world. And even though he hasn't wanted to admit it to himself, she's right about the conflict: his client might be better off if the defense blamed Chris's own brother for the crime.

"That's what I thought," Clare says to his silence.

"I won't let my brother's case interfere with giving Jesse Duvall the best defense possible."

"That's what everyone who has a conflict says. That's why the rules exist. You're not in a position to assess the situation objectively."

"What do you want, Clare? Are you working for the New Jersey bar now? Why are you even here?"

"I'm here because I care about you. I don't want you to throw away your—"

"I can take care of myself." He always has.

"You've put me in an awkward spot."

"What are you talking about?"

"As an officer of the court, I have a duty to report an ethics violation if I'm made aware of one."

"Really? You can't be serious."

Her arms are folded now. She starts to speak, then stops. She turns back to the door and pushes it open. Before marching out, she looks at him again. Shaking her head, she says, "Nice suit."

On the drive to his parents' house, Clare's voice runs through Chris's head: *"Nice suit."* What did she mean by that? Whatever. And who's she to tell him how to practice law?

He pulls into the driveway of their modest home. Clint still hasn't taken down the tire swing they'd hung together from the big tree in the front yard. He says it's too much work, but Clint has never shied away from hard labor. Ms. May says he leaves it up because he likes it when the neighborhood kids sneak into their yard and play; it reminds him of Chris.

"Something smells great," Chris says, stepping into the small kitchen. Ms. May is wearing an apron and removing baked ziti from the oven. On the lime-green refrigerator is a photo of Chris from his law school graduation. By outward appearances, that had been a good day. The sun shining. His parents beaming. An amazing girlfriend at his side. The world at his feet. But Chris mostly remembers the day for another reason: it's when he finally decided to let his mother go.

He'd been so angry with her. She hadn't only left without saying goodbye—she'd left Chris and Vince with Rusty. She of all people understood what that meant for them. Rusty said she'd run off with a no-good bastard who hung out at the bar; that if they ever spoke of her again it would be their last words. That she was a whore and they were better off without her. She'd abandoned them. Still, every birthday, Chris would check the mail for a card. On his high school, then college, graduation days, he'd stare out into the stands, searching. But nothing. He fantasized that Mom and Vince had reunited, that they'd appear when things were safe. But part of him always knew the truth: she'd escaped the prison known as Rusty Whitaker and never looked back. Thus, on that seemingly perfect day with his law school diploma tucked under his arm, Clint and Ms. May beaming with pride, he'd let Mary Whitaker go forever.

"I made your favorite," Ms. May says.

"It won't compete with the ramen I usually have, but it will do." The smell brings him back to the first time he'd ever had a meal without the threat of violence. Clint and May lacing fingers, saying grace, a quiet calm making it clear that he was home. Vince had promised that their new life, nirvana, would smell different. Maybe this was the smell: Ms. May's ziti.

Clint comes in from the back door. He's sweating, his shirt damp over his ropey, muscled arms.

"The counselor is here." He sticks out his hand. Clint isn't a hugger. A firm shake is what makes a man, he'd once told Chris. And you'd better look 'em in the eye when you do it. Chris makes sure to do that whenever he greets Clint.

"I hear you're building a shed," says Chris.

"More like a guesthouse for when May kicks me out."

"That's gonna be sooner than you think if you don't get upstairs and take a shower. Dinner's in ten."

Clint widens his eyes for Chris's benefit, but he rushes out obediently. They all know who's the boss.

Ten minutes later, on the dot, they sit at the small dining room table, joining hands.

Clint says, "Bless this family and thanks for this food and our health. Bless those less fortunate." And that's it. No scripture. No drawn-out version of grace. Straightforward, like Clint.

Ms. May scoops a giant portion of ziti onto Chris's plate. And for the next few minutes, the only sound is silverware on china. Ms. May always brings out the good dishes for their weekly dinners.

"How's work?" Clint asks. Standard Clint small-talk.

"I got assigned to a big case, actually," Chris says. He decides it's better if they hear it from him. Clint has never said so, but Chris surmises he's not thrilled about Chris working on behalf of criminals.

"Good for you, dear," Ms. May says. She doesn't ask for elaboration, and normally that would be the end of the discussion. Dinnertime was for family talk, not work talk. But Chris needs to do this.

"I wanted to mention it, since you may see it on the news." Chris forks at his plate.

Ms. May and Clint stop eating. Chris can feel their eyes on him. He keeps his eyes on his plate.

"You gonna keep us in suspense, son?" Clint says. It's lighthearted, as if he senses trouble and wants to convey that it's safe to continue. They've spent years helping rebuild Chris and have an uncanny ability to read him.

Ms. May reaches across the table and puts a hand on his.

"You saw they made an arrest in the ice cream shop case?" Chris asks.

Silence.

"I'm on the team assigned to represent the defendant. She's a teenager, a kid."

Clint makes a grunt. "I saw that. News said you may have your work cut out for you."

Chris doesn't reply.

"There's usually more to it than what they say on TV," Ms. May says.

Chris says, "People may say some unkind things about me and my colleagues. But I think it's the right thing to do." He's not sure why he feels the need for the hard sell. "I just wanted you to hear about it from me."

Chris expects them to ask questions: *What will happen if they find out about your brother? Is there a chance your client will try to blame Vince for the crime? Are you sure this is good for your mental health, son?*

Instead, Clint says, "I've only got one thing to say about it." He holds Chris's gaze, waiting an eternity to spit it out. "She's damn lucky to have a skilled lawyer like you."

Chris feels a fist in his throat.

"Amen to that," Ms. May says. "Eat some more, dear, you're looking too thin."

CHAPTER 46
KELLER

They huddle near a stand of shrubs under the starless sky. Keller scrutinizes the entrance to Union Self-Storage through her binoculars. Atticus and Secret Service Agent James Nicoletti stand next to her. Nearby, parked on a dirt road off the highway, there's a van with two more agents. A skeleton crew, but enough for tonight.

She hasn't found Vince Whitaker, and the locals have made an arrest for the Dairy Creamery murders, but this could at least be a consolation prize: busting Rusty Whitaker on a federal rap. If they take down Rusty, who knows? Maybe the old bastard knows where his son is hiding and will give him up for a deal. If not, it will still be gratifying to throw the disgusting man in prison.

Keller looks over at Atticus and tries not to smile. He's wearing all black and has his badge hanging around his neck by a chain. Attire inspired by TV cop shows.

Nico puts a hand on Atticus's shoulder. "You okay, partner?"

Atticus nods, like, *No big deal. I do this all the time.*

Nico says, "Our intel is that he usually gets shipments at closing time. They finished unloading the containers at the port an hour ago, so hopefully we'll be in business."

The plan is simple. The team will stop the semi driving on the desolate patch of highway. They'll threaten the driver with all kinds of trouble, then promise leniency if he lets them stow away in the truck and ride into the facility. Nico calls it a Trojan horse operation. Keller wants to be in the truck. But Nico shot that down. He joked that it was because she wouldn't fit. But he clearly didn't want to be liable if the pregnant lady got hurt.

Nico's a good man, but like many men, he treats pregnant women like fragile flowers. They overlook the fact that, over the course of history, through famines, epidemics, and other extreme conditions, women survived longer and better than men. Having babies? A walk in the park next to what most men could endure. But whatever.

Nico presses a finger to his earpiece. "Son of a—"

"What?" Keller asks.

"It's a bigger load than we anticipated. There're three trucks." They'd planned on having to deal with only one semi, not three.

"Pull them all over," Keller says.

"No chance we can time it without one of them calling ahead, warning Whitaker."

Pulling over one truck in a routine traffic stop is plausible and could avoid suspicion. But three trucks? That's an obvious raid.

"How far out are they?" Keller asks.

"About two miles."

She looks at Atticus's MG parked on the dirt road. Then Nico's unit car.

"I have an idea. Follow me," she tells Atticus, pointing at his car.

Before Nico can protest, Keller is in the driver's seat of the unit car. Nico follows her and hops in as dust kicks out from the tires. Keller smiles at Nico gripping the handle above the window as she tears through the dark streets. Keller drives fast, Atticus close on her tail, finally stopping at the intersection on the only road leading to the storage company. She parks in the middle of the intersection and then directs Atticus to pull his car facing hers. Like they've been in an accident. She gives Nico instructions, and he calls his team in the van, then hides in the trees along the roadside.

Headlights appear ahead. Keller takes a bottle of water from Nico's car and splashes her face.

As the trucks approach, Keller stands in the street and waves her arms frantically at the lead truck heading toward them.

On the ground near the MG, lies Atticus. A red flare burns next to him. A nice touch that Atticus added to ensure the drivers didn't miss him in his dark clothes. Smoke from the flare floats in the air, adding to the sense that a serious accident has occurred.

The lights are blinding now. But the truck stops. The two rigs behind it pull over as well.

The door to the first truck swings open. Keller runs over.

"We had an accident," she says, gulping for air. "We weren't going fast, but I think he may be having a seizure or something." She turns back to Atticus, who remains on the asphalt.

The trucker, a heavyset guy with a scraggly beard, appears torn. He has his CB in hand. He mutters something into the radio, then lumbers out of the truck.

"I called 911," Keller says. "Do you know CPR?"

The guy hesitates. A 911 call means cops will soon be on the scene.

Keller glances over the trucker's shoulder and sees figures approaching the cabins to the other two rigs. The trucker follows her gaze and looks behind him. In the headlamps' glare, the two drivers are pressed against the sides of the trucks, hands behind their backs. Nico gives her a thumbs-up.

The trucker turns back to Keller. "What in the hell?" That's when his expression turns to dread at the sight of Keller's badge.

CHAPTER 47

It takes less than fifteen minutes for the rigs to pull into the storage facility and the team to make arrests. They've separated Rusty Whitaker from the desk clerk. Rusty's in the back of Nico's car, wearing a dirty white T-shirt and a scowl. Nico is in the front office grilling the clerk, who's likely spilling his guts.

Standing in the half-light near a cluster of storage units, Keller glances inside the car, sizing up Rusty. He doesn't seem overly concerned. He knows counterfeit cigarettes aren't the highest priority of the justice system. He probably assumes he'll get a slap on the wrist.

He has an ugly disposition, Rusty Whitaker. Not his physical features. His aura. Under the unkempt facade there's a once-not-so-bad-looking man. His son Vince is a looker. She wonders what became of the youngest child in the woebegone Whitaker family. Keller hopes the kid got out from under Rusty's rule before his disposition turned ugly too.

Nico's agents continue to process the evidence. The

three trucks have been seized, but the storage units already contained another two loads of product that will need to be inventoried and transported to federal evidence storage.

Rusty sits bored in Nico's backseat, not a care in the world.

Until . . .

Keller notices him sit up straight, his attention locked on Atticus, who's examining a storage unit protected by a rolling metal door. It's far from the cigarette units, but for some reason it's caught Atticus's attention.

Rusty seems even more agitated when Keller heads over to Atticus.

"What's up?" Keller asks.

Atticus holds his iPhone's flashlight over a printout. "The owner gave me a list of all the units and owners." He swings the beam of his light to the unit in front of them. "But this one doesn't appear on the log."

Atticus moves the beam back to the printout. Keller's eyes follow Atticus's index finger down a column. It lists units 1400, 1401, 1402, and so on until Atticus stops at 1452. The next number is 1454. There is no unit 1453.

"It could be just a misprint, but it's weird, like someone is trying to hide the unit." He shines his light on the storage unit's number: 1453.

It's probably nothing, Keller thinks. But what the hell, they're here.

She calls over to a member of Nico's team. "Can you bring over the cutters?"

The woman nods, disappears a moment, and returns

with bolt cutters. Keller moves aside so the woman can do her work. She snaps the padlock on the first try.

Keller looks back at the car. Rusty is all stares now.

Inside, the unit is dark. Musty. There's an old mail sack with U.S. POSTAL SERVICE printed on it. Envelopes are scattered across the floor.

Keller picks up one of the pieces of opened mail. A Christmas card in a partially torn envelope. The postmark is from 1996.

"Hmm," Atticus says. "Someone stole a bag of mail for the Christmas money and gift cards, I guess."

Keller shrugs. A federal offense, but it pales in comparison to the counterfeit cigarette charges. And it's decades old, so there's likely a statute-of-limitations problem.

Then why does Rusty look so worried?

In the corner sits a large drum. The kind that holds fuel or toxic waste. Maybe that's it—Rusty's illegally storing waste from one of the nearby chemical companies.

The drum is old, covered in rust and dirt.

Keller gestures at the agent with the bolt cutters. "Got a crowbar?"

Five minutes later, Keller's prying off the barrel's lid.

"You sure about this?" Atticus says. "I mean what if it's like poisonous or toxic waste or something?"

"You can wait outside."

Atticus's lips press together.

The lid makes a hissing sound when the seal is broken. The smell is pungent but not like chemicals. Keller turns and realizes that she has an audience. Nico's team watches as she continues.

Atticus is covering his mouth with a handkerchief. He must be the only twentysomething man in the country who carries a cloth hankie.

Keller covers her mouth and nose with her hand. The lid makes a loud clank when it hits the concrete floor.

Keller beams the light inside the drum and adrenaline rips through her.

A decomposed body. Mostly skeleton.

Is it Vince Whitaker? Is that what's happened to him? His father killed him?

No, Keller realizes. The skull still has hair, long hair.

And the victim is wearing a sundress.

CHAPTER 48
CHRIS

Chris arrives at the office as Julia is powering down her computer. The office is empty save for the cleaning woman, who wears earbuds and occasionally belts out a tune while emptying the trash bins.

Julia briefs him on her research. "I think we have to turn over the phone to the prosecution."

Chris nods. "Even if it has something incriminatory on it?"

"The case law is surprisingly spotty. But yeah, that's the safest course."

It makes sense. Otherwise, criminals could simply give their lawyers murder weapons and other inculpatory evidence to conceal from authorities. And here, it wasn't even their client who'd given them the cell phone, it was a third party.

"Anything you need me to run to ground in the research?"

"If you wouldn't mind." Julia loads up her briefcase.

Chris waits for her to explain.

"Some of the cases say we can keep the evidence for a reasonable amount of time. A law review article says in some instances we're allowed to run tests on the evidence before turning it over. I didn't see any New Jersey case law or ethics decisions on that. If you could run that down, maybe we'll be able to analyze the data on her phone before turning it over."

"Makes sense. I mean, we don't even know that there's anything incriminating on the device. It seems reasonable we can analyze the texts and digital forensics before handing it over. I'll research that piece and report back tonight."

"Cool, thanks," Julia says.

"You heading home?" Chris asks.

She shakes her head. "I'm gonna hit the bar. I imagine Roger and those clowns will be there celebrating their new big case."

Chris smiles at that. Julia will let the junior prosecutors buy her drinks while listening to their banter. Between the booze and bravado, she'll probably learn more about the case than anything the prosecution will give them in discovery.

"Have fun," Chris says.

Julia pauses. "Sure you don't want to come? We don't meet with Jesse until late-morning tomorrow, so if we got in early and split it up, we could probably finish the research in time."

He considers joining her. But Henry will want to know the best course of action with the phone before the interview. The digital forensics guy also is awaiting permission to analyze the device. And, honestly, he's not in the mood.

"Have a drink for me," he says.

Julia disappears and Chris does a deep dive into the Westlaw database. He reads every decision, every treatise, every law review article, every ethics opinion, and writes up the results. They'll need to use extreme caution, document the chain of custody at each step, but they can analyze the phone before turning it over.

At just past eleven, his phone pings. A text from Julia.

This is their theory.

She includes a link to a news story. Chris clicks on it.

It's a newspaper article about a workplace attack a few years ago in the Washington, D.C., area. An employee at a high-end athletic-wear store bludgeoned her coworker with a hammer, then staged the scene, claiming she and the employee had been the victims of masked intruders.

So this was the prosecution's working theory: that Jesse killed the employees at the Dairy Creamery, then pretended to be one of the victims, like in the Washington, D.C., attack. She'd taken all the victims' phones with her to cover up her previous dispute with one of the girls, hidden them in the hospital room, but inadvertently left one behind when she checked out.

Is Jesse Duvall capable of such a ghastly crime? Could any teenager concoct such an elaborate scheme? He recalls their meeting with the seventeen-year-old.

She's a cool customer. An old soul for sure. But a murderer?

Chris's phone chimes again. He expects another text from Julia, but it's a notification that a new travel vlog has posted.

Chris takes a deep breath, then lets it out slowly, excitement chasing away his fatigue.

Nirvana awaits . . .

YOUTUBE EXCERPT
Mr. Nirvana, the Anonymous Travel Vlogger
(18K views)
"The Ship Graveyard"

EXT. DAYTIME—ARTHUR KILL SHIP GRAVEYARD

MR. NIRVANA stands on the hull of a steel
freighter that has turned scarlet from rust
and is consumed by decay. It's partially sub-
merged in murky, brown water.

> MR. NIRVANA (O.S.)
> When I was a kid, I'd come to this
> ship graveyard, which is on this
> tidal strait that divides New Jer-
> sey and Staten Island. We'd maneuver
> rowboats around these corroded hulks
> at night and party in battered old
> ships. I used to camp at a spot not
> far from here, and I might stay there
> tonight.

The camera spans the area, where the ghostly
remnants of vessels litter the waterway.

> MR. NIRVANA (O.S.)
> But you couldn't appreciate it at
> night, so I'd come out here by my-
> self in the daylight, like now. It's
> so peaceful and it has this ethereal

beauty. Back then, it helped me escape some stuff I was dealing with. But I can't show you this properly on my own, so today I'm going to do something new.

The video switches to another camera, one affixed to a drone. Aerial shots of the dead fleet appear on-screen.

> MR. NIRVANA (O.S.)
> Look there, on top of the mast, a bird's nest.

The camera floats over a ruined old ferry. Seagulls squawk in the distance.

> MR. NIRVANA (O.S.)
> It used to be a junkyard for ships, and it had about four hundred vessels, some predating World War One, but most have been used for scrap now or sunk to the bottom. It's an accidental marine museum.

The drone captures small boats closer to the shore that are splattered with graffiti, then drifts farther out, hovering over old tugboats, a warship. Piles of tires and splintered wood and debris cover the vessels.

MR. NIRVANA (O.S.)

This is where ships go to die. There are worse places for your final resting place, trust me on that.

FADE TO BLACK

CHAPTER 49
ELLA

Ella is parked outside the boarded-up building again. She needs to stop this. Lurking outside the old Blockbuster store is weird; it's unhealthy. It's past eleven. She considers heading into the city, meeting someone, taking him back to her tired hotel, having tired sex. But she *needs* to stop this.

She eyes the book on the passenger seat, *A Farewell to Arms.* The photo booth strip she used as a bookmark sticks out from the top. Why hasn't she thrown it away? Torn it up?

Her mind wanders to the movie from earlier, *Before Sunrise.* And her thoughts trip to a cold afternoon from before.

"Where's Katie?" the boy asks Ella. He's standing in front of the Cyclone, the old wooden roller-coaster, their designated meeting place. His hair pushes in the cool breeze, his cheeks rosy from the cold. Ella's never been to Coney Island. It's not somewhere her mother would ever dream of taking her, much less in December.

"Katie's parents found out and she can't make it. She asked me to come and tell you so you didn't think she stood you up."

He thinks on this.

The boardwalk is empty. The beach vacant. The rides all shuttered for the season. It's oddly beautiful.

"Want me to show you around?" he asks.

Ella rams her hands in her pockets. "I should probably get going."

He nods.

She studies him another beat. He has high cheekbones and tender eyes. She's taken the long train ride all the way there, she might as well.

"Actually, I have a little time," Ella says.

He smiles, gestures for her to follow. He walks for a while, his breath pluming in the cold.

"My mom grew up in Little Odessa." He points a finger down the long boardwalk. "When I was little, we'd come here most summer days while she was at work. My grandmother lived in Brighton."

"I've actually never been to Coney Island," Ella says.

He stops. Looks at her. "You and Katie are the only people I've ever met who haven't been to Coney."

She shrugs.

"You haven't lived until you've been on top of the Wonder Wheel on a hot summer night." He glances to the Ferris wheel, which is locked down.

Ella imagines the scene—not the ghost town it is now, but on a muggy night, crowded with teens, the smell of fried food and cotton candy in the air.

"You hungry?"

They go to Nathan's to get hot dogs. She'd seen Nathan's at the crappy food court in the mall so she wasn't enthusiastic about the choice. But this wasn't the same. This was the site of the *original* Nathan's, he tells her with pride. The best hot dogs in the universe. And he's right. Granted, it's one of the few hot dogs she's had in her life—she's been to a Yankees game and had one there—but it's delicious.

Soon they're playing video games in the arcade, one of the only businesses open. They crowd into a photo booth. Afterward, he hands her the black-and-white strip of pictures.

They walk on the beach—the only souls braving the bite of the wind. The sky has turned pink.

He asks Ella about herself. Her plans for the future. He's heard she used to go to boarding school, which seems to fascinate him.

She's excited that he knows anything about her. That he's taken the time to ask about her.

Walking in the sand, carrying shoes and socks, she says, "So, you and Katie . . ."

He gives her a knowing look. "It's not like that."

She cocks a brow.

"We're just friends. She needed someone to talk to."

This surprises her. Katie doesn't talk much about herself. Ella knows more about her from Candy and Mandy than from Katie herself. And even then, it's not much: that Katie moved away last year and recently returned. That her parents are super-strict. That her last relationship was a mess.

"Talk to her about what?" Ella asks.

"I wouldn't be a very good friend to say so," he points out.

Ella likes that he doesn't tell her. That he won't betray a friend's trust. But maybe he's playing her. Playing them both. She doesn't think that Katie wants to be just friends.

She asks him his plans after high school. He changes the subject. She doesn't know if it's because he has no plans or because she wouldn't approve of his plans.

Whatever the case, she doubts she'll ever forget this strange day on Coney Island in the winter. She tucks the photo booth strip in her pocket.

Back on the boardwalk, the sun is nearly gone; it looks like the world in a disaster movie. She's shivering from the chill but trying to hide it. He drapes his leather jacket around her.

They walk to the subway. The area quickly morphs into an urban neighborhood. It's filled with street merchants selling their wares. There's a man across the street yelling at the sky.

Up ahead, walking toward them, a pack of boys. They seem to be harassing people. One of them knocks a ball cap off a man, laughing; another smashes an empty liquor bottle on the sidewalk.

Fear is tingling her skin. She's shivering, not sure it's from the cold. She takes his arm, gestures for him to cross the street.

He takes her hand and looks down into her eyes. His are hazel with flecks of gold.

"Don't worry," he says.

Just two words and her fear evaporates.

Then the group of boys stops laughing. They seem to be contemplating the couple.

Instead of harassing them, starting something, taunting them, they do something unexpected.

They cross to the other side of the street. Car horns blare and there's yelling as the group weaves through traffic, then hurries away into the distance.

Ella holds his hand all the way to the subway.

She's never felt so safe in her life.

CHAPTER 50
CHRIS

Chris drives down the secluded road, only the occasional streetlamp lighting his way. The sky is overcast, the moon hidden. His thoughts meander. To nights like this, before the world fell off its axis. When Vince would steal the keys to the Monte Carlo—even before he had a driver's license—and they'd escape the maelstrom of domestic life in the Whitaker home. They'd grab their rolled-up sleeping bags, always kept at the ready, and simply take off. To wait out the storm. Rusty was the eye of that tempest. But their mom had a volatile streak, and his parents brought out the worst in each other, which was always surprising since it was hard to believe that Rusty could possibly have more awfulness in him. He was a bottomless well of ugliness.

Whenever it became too much, they'd drive out to a patch of woodland near the overpass, not far from the old ship graveyard. From the outside, "the cave," as Vince called it, looked like a tangle of overgrown bushes and vines. But, across a hidden path in the weeds and through a small opening, there was a hollowed-out section, like an igloo. They weren't the only kids who knew about the cave. Sometimes they'd find empty beer cans, and once a used condom, which was gross. But on the bad nights it provided shelter and a place to sleep in peace.

Mr. Nirvana had said he'd be camping tonight at a favorite spot, so maybe . . .

The problem: Chris hasn't been there in years, and he doesn't remember how to get to the cave. He recalls a dirt road. The drone of vehicles on the overpass. Up ahead he sees headlights shimmering on the elevated highway. He'll keep driving until he recognizes something.

The thought hits him again. What if the traveler isn't Vince? And if it is Vince, why hasn't his brother reached out to him? Maybe he tried. Chris isn't easy to track down. A new last name. A new school. A new life. He doesn't use social media and has no contact with friends from before. Sure, he's inexplicably returned to the area for work. But no one remembers a kid who moved away in middle school. He's been through the old neighborhood on the still-dangerous patch of misery in Linden only once, hoping their house had been demolished. But it's still there like a ramshackle haunted house from the movies. It is haunted.

Chris opens the window and the wind whooshes inside the car. He hears trucks barreling along the overpass now, and he feels like he's getting close. Slowing, he scans each side of the road, looking for anything familiar.

Then he spots the narrow dirt road. He reduces speed, takes a sharp turn, the sound of rocks under the tires. He spots the barbed-wire fence and flashes to a memory of them scaling it, Vince helping his little brother avoid the sharp, twisted metal.

He pulls to the side of the narrow road. What is he doing? This is foolish. Yet something compels him to continue. He locks the car, then trudges through the tall grass and muck to the fence. He removes his new suit jacket, throws it over the rusty barbed wire, then carefully climbs over. He has another memory: Vince leading the way through the stand of trees ahead and over a knoll to the cave.

He follows the same route now, making his way through the thicket of trees. He hears the crack of a twig and freezes in place. It's just an animal, right? A deer or something harmless. He doesn't recall worrying about any predators back when they were kids—there was only one predator they feared.

Chris sometimes wonders what he'd do if he ran into Rusty now, and has even fantasized about giving his biological father the beating he deserves. But he's resisted the urge for two reasons: one, Clint and Ms. May wouldn't approve; and, two, he might just kill the old bastard.

The tree line comes into sight ahead. The cave is on the other side, through a path.

He picks up his pace and makes it to the opening. And there it is.

Nothing.

Absolutely nothing.

The entire area has been cleared. It's now a field marked with NO TRESPASSING signs. The cave is gone.

He imagines Vince showing up here after all these years, disappointed that the place where they'd taken refuge was no more. Chris is about to head back to the car when he spies an orange glow coming from beneath the overpass—a campfire.

He's come this far.

Soon, he stands in front of an abandoned fire.

He sees a bottle, convenience-store wine, by the looks of it. And some trash. He must have just missed whoever was there.

"Vince?" he calls out, his voice bouncing against the concrete support beams. He yells his name again, though he knows his brother isn't the camper. It's the stench—urine and filth—that gives it away. Vince is a neat freak. Cleanliness was his way of exerting control in their chaotic lives. Mr. Nirvana also values hygiene and orderliness, another clue that he's Chris's brother. The smell, the mess by the fire, that's not Vince.

"Who's Vince?" the voice says.

Chris turns, a shot of adrenaline coursing through him. A man, a teenager, actually, emerges from the pitch-black area under the bridge. The kid has a bandage covering his nose. He's holding something. Chris's pulse quickens when he realizes that it's a knife.

"Sorry," Chris says. "I didn't mean to intrude. I was just looking for someone. I'm on my way." He holds up his hands to show he's no threat.

"You'd better go, motherfucker," the kid says.

Chris keeps his hands up. The kid is just scared. Chris would be scared too.

As he starts backing out of there, the kid says, "I'll be needing your wallet . . . and that watch too." The watch Clint and May had given him for graduation.

Chris says, "Look, I don't want any trouble. I've got like twenty bucks. You can have it, and I'll be on my way."

Chris's senses are heightened now, burning. He experiences another lightning bolt in his chest when he sees movement in the shadows from behind a support beam.

More of them.

He needs to get out of there.

Then, in the weak light behind the cylindrical column, a figure appears. A teenage girl. Her cheeks are streaked in dirt-laced tears. Her eyes dart to Chris, then to the kid with the bandage, back and forth.

And then she mouths two silent but unmistakable words to Chris: *Help me*.

Chris's heart bangs hard, his mouth sandpaper.

He knows he should give the kid what he wants, then turn and run.

But he's tired of being afraid. And he's not leaving her.

When he looks back at the kid, Chris notices he's moved a few steps closer. "Okay," he says, "here's the wallet." He reaches in his back pocket, then throws his wallet toward the kid. When the kid bends down for the prize, Chris will charge.

But the kid has street smarts and doesn't take the bait.

Chris's eyes flick to the girl. Trauma and shock radiate from her.

The kid is advancing and the knife has come up.

"Give me the watch." He's only a few feet away now. "And I'll take the shirt while you're at it."

Chris can't argue with the boy's clothing needs. He's almost lathered in street grime. His face is dirty, his arms are dirty. His jeans could probably stand on their own. There's nothing clean about him except the bandage covering his nose.

Chris reaches slowly to his watch band and unclasps it. When the kid's gaze locks on the watch, Chris makes his move: he bats the knife arm aside and rams his forehead squarely into the center of his attacker's face. The bandage is his bull's-eye. He feels cartilage crunch, the kid howls.

The boy staggers backward. One hand covering his face, the other waving the knife wildly. The girl has come out of the shadows.

"Run!" Chris yells to her.

With bare feet she races past him and into the darkness. Chris suffers a wave of nausea as he realizes she's not wearing pants.

The boy continues to push toward Chris, the knife slashing the air, blood pouring from his nose.

Chris jumps back, avoiding the arc of the blade, then connects a punch on the bloody red bandage, which elicits another wail of pain. The kid's unsteady on his feet. Chris charges him, grabbing his wrist to keep the knife at bay, using his weight to knock the kid to the ground. Still holding his wrist, Chris slams the kid's hand against the earth over and over until the knife skitters away. The kid's whimpering now. Chris rolls off him and springs to his feet.

Chris stands over him. He yanks out his phone, dials 911, tells the operator his coordinates on the phone's GPS.

The kid will live. In the distance, Chris sees the silhouette of the girl still running. He feels a flood of melancholy watching her.

Then he feels something else. A new emotion washes over him: pride. And he has an epiphany. *This* is how he wants to feel in his life.

His glance turns back to the groaning kid who's still on the ground. The boy's eyes raise to meet Chris's. They widen, like he's looking at something behind Chris.

Chris turns to look, when he feels a crushing blow to the head. Instantly, he's on the ground. He sees starbursts, debilitating pain, then feels a boot in his stomach, ripping the wind out of him. His watch is torn from his wrist. He tries to speak, but can't form the words.

The figure, carrying a large branch the size of a baseball bat, walks over to the kid with the bandage. He kicks him in the ribs. Then searches his pockets. The figure drifts into the gloom. And Chris drifts away as well.

DAY 3

CHAPTER 51
KELLER

"You got a positive ID on the body yet?" Hal asks, taking a sip from his coffee mug, wincing at the awful brew. The blinds in his office are open, giving the room a gray hue from the gloomy morning outside.

"It'll take a day or two for the DNA results, but her purse was in the barrel," Keller says. "And Atticus is tracking down dental records, so we'll get confirmation soon. But it's her."

Mary Whitaker.

Wife of Rusty. Mother of Vince and Chris. The woman who reportedly ran off nearly twenty years ago, but was actually rotting inside a steel drum at a storage unit near the sewage plant.

"What's the husband say?"

"Four words: 'I want a lawyer.'"

"I guess he's not such a dumb son-of-a-bitch after all. Unless you count the years he had to get rid of the body." Hal's phone rings and he gets an annoyed look on his face as he waits for his secretary to answer the line. "The media's gonna go nuts once they learn the victim is Vince Whitaker's mother. Let me know when you get a positive ID. We'll need to release a statement."

"Will do. As for notifying the family, we obviously don't know how to reach Vince Whitaker, but he has a younger brother."

Hal releases a loud exhale. "I remember. The kid not only got to be the old man's punching bag, he believed his mom abandoned him."

"Any idea how to reach him? We're having a hard time. It looks like he was adopted. Probably changed his name."

"Let me make some calls," Hal says. "We should be able to get foster care information. He got placed with a nice couple, if I recall. Maybe they'll know how to reach him. Remind me, what's his name?"

"Christopher."

"That's right. I'll get on it." Hal sits back. "Well, Agent Badass, you've had a busy couple days in Union County. Tell Stan we appreciate the help, but I think we can take things from here."

"If you don't mind, I'd like to tie up some loose ends?"

Hal scrutinizes her. "Sure. Why not? Maybe you can find Hoffa's body while you're at it."

Keller debates whether to ask the next question. She regards Hal for a long beat, then says, "I have a question about the Blockbuster case."

Hal gazes at her from over the lip of his mug, cocks an eyebrow for her to continue.

"We met with Tony Grosso."

"Grosso? Haven't heard that name in years. How is he?"

"Very retired."

"That's how he was on the job too."

She smiles at that. "He was one of the leads on the Blockbuster case."

"I remember."

"We asked him about the file, and he said something interesting."

Hal waits.

"He said that the investigative team buried something from the official file—something that might have been embarrassing to a victim's family. He said someone on the team at the time was tight with the family."

Hal furrows his brow. "What are you asking me, Agent Keller?"

He's no longer calling her *Agent Badass* or *Sarah*, Keller notices.

"Grosso said one of the victims, Katie McKenzie, had been pregnant. Not when she was killed, but before. He said it was an open secret at the office, but left out of the file."

"And you think I was aware of the 'open secret'?"

Keller tilts her head to the side. She feels like shit, but Hal's the only prosecutor she knows who was on the task force back in the day. Pointedly, she says, "We also think that someone left out a key detail from the investigatory file: something the killer said to Ella Monroe."

Hal studies her again, frown lines appearing between his eyes. "This is why I recommended you to Stan, you know?"

Keller doesn't understand.

"You don't fuck around. I can count on one hand how many people would've had the stones to ask me that question."

"Hal, I didn't mean to—"

Hal holds up a hand. "Don't you dare back down."

His eyes remain fixed on hers. She forces herself not to look away. He seems pissed, but there's also reverence in his gaze.

"To answer your question: you're barking up the wrong tree. I didn't—I don't—know any of the families of the victims personally. And Ella Monroe never told me the perp said something to her. That's not something I would've left out of the file for any reason."

Keller feels heat in her face.

"Any other questions?"

Keller has some, but she decides they can wait. She shakes her head.

"Then it sounds like you've got some work to do. Talk to HR; they'll have records of everybody who worked here during the investigation."

"Thank you, Hal."

His phone rings again, but this time he picks it up, dismissing Keller without a word.

"Why did you threaten Madison Sawyer?" Ella asks for the third time.

The interview room in the juvenile facility is cramped, hot, and smells of cleaning products. Next to Ella are the public defenders, Henry and Julia. The other public defender, the handsome one, didn't come with them this morning. The lawyers have thus far been mere spectators, letting Ella do the questioning until Jesse warms up to them.

Across the table, Jesse's arms are folded across her chest, which seems to be her favorite pose. "I didn't threaten anyone."

"We have the prosecution file now, Jesse. We've seen the texts," Ella says. There are several angry texts. The last says: *You'll be sorry.*

One of Madison Sawyer's classmates gave the detectives screenshots. The texts don't say what the girls were fighting about.

Jesse's jaw is set. "Show me. Show me one place where I *threatened* her."

That's true enough. There's no explicit threat to the seventeen-year-old girl who died at the ice cream store along with her younger sister and their manager. But *You'll be sorry* along with Jesse's research on the Blockbuster case could be enough for a jury to convict. Not to mention that Jesse lied to the detectives about why she'd gone to the ice cream shop.

"Why were you and Madison in a fight?"

Jesse's mouth is a slit.

"Jesse, you told your lawyers you'd talk to me. So talk to me."

Henry finally says something. "We can't help you, if you won't open up, Jessica."

"Fine, I'll defend myself."

Ella lets out an exasperated breath. "You told me girls at school had been talking bad about you." She remembers Jesse's explanation when they were at Phyllis's house: *"She was talking shit about me."*

Jesse sits in silence. At last, she says, "She was telling everyone I was like a porn queen. That I slept with my teacher at my last school and let him take pictures . . ."

"Mr. Parke?" Ella asks.

Jesse's surprised. Ella can see it on her face.

"How'd you—"

"I met with him. I didn't know he had anything to do with your fight with Madison. I just wanted to understand your history a little better."

"I don't want to talk about it." Jesse glances at Henry, then at the table.

Henry seems to read the room: Jesse doesn't want to talk about it in front of him. He stands. "I'm going to get some coffee. Can I get anyone anything? Jesse, would you like some water or a Coke?"

Jesse shakes her head. She whispers "Thank you" in a barely audible tone.

After Henry is out of the room, Ella says, "I know it's hard, but we can't help you if you don't fill us in. It took me fifteen minutes to find Mr. Parke. How long do you think it will take the prosecution to find him? Or a journalist who's as skilled as you are?" Ella throws in the compliment, which tends to help draw people out.

Jesse's face is pained now. "I thought we were friends. He said I was talented, like *really* talented, and he was helping me get a job at the local newspaper. And then he . . ." She trails off.

"And then he what, Jesse? It's okay to talk about it." Ella thinks about Chad Parke's tale of a young girl obsessed, a woman scorned, setting him up, ruining his life.

"Mr. Parke asked me to come over to talk through some ideas he had on how I can dig deeper on my Blockbuster piece. He used to have pizza parties at his apartment for the whole newspaper staff, so I thought other kids would be there. But when I got there we were, like, alone."

Ella feels acid rising in her throat. "And what happened?"

"That's just it. I don't know. We had pizza and soda, and it was all fine. I just thought he wanted to work with only me since he said I was the best reporter we had on the paper. And he was fascinated with the Blockbuster case. The next thing I know, it's midnight and I've been out cold."

Ella swallows. "He drugged you?"

"I honestly don't know. He said I fell asleep and I didn't think anything had happened to me, you know, down there." She looks at her pelvis. "I thought it was weird, but then again, it was late and I was tired."

Ella's heart is breaking. Next to her at the table, Julia is stiff, tense, like she's trying not to react.

"Then Mr. Parke's fiancée sent some pictures—photos of me—to the school. She found them on his phone. Right away, the school and lawyers and counselors and everybody starts asking me questions like I did something wrong."

"And Madison found out about it?"

"She was on Snapchat with some girl from my old school. There were all kinds of rumors about me and Mr. Parke when he was put on leave. Madison started telling people I transferred to Union High because I'd seduced a teacher and made a porn video with him. Her friends started calling me 'porn queen.' I just wanted it to stop. I was mad when I sent the texts, but I didn't hurt Madison or her sister. I just wanted it to stop." Jesse is crying now. The first real emotion Ella has seen from her.

Julia reaches across the table for Jesse's hand, and Jesse doesn't pull away.

"Madison wouldn't answer my DMs, so I went to

her work. I just wanted to talk." Jesse's chest shudders. "But when I got there, I chickened out. I went into the bathroom. And when I came out . . ." Her breath is ragged now.

"It's okay, take deep breaths," Ella says. "I'm proud of you for sharing this, Jesse."

When Jesse stops crying, Ella asks, "Did you tell anyone at the school what was happening?"

Jesse nods. "I told my counselor. She said they'd look into it."

Ella makes a note. They need to talk to the counselor. The cyberbullying could help Jesse's case since it makes her sympathetic. But it also provides a motive to kill.

No one says anything for a long time.

Finally, Julia speaks. She still has a hand on Jesse's. "I need to talk about why you were researching the Blockbuster case. The prosecutors think you were doing so to make the ice cream store crime look like—"

"That's bullshit!" Jesse shouts, ripping her hand away from Julia's.

Julia appears taken aback. Ella certainly is. Jesse has gone from devastation to fury in an instant, like flipping a switch.

Julia keeps her voice calm, steady. "I'm not saying that, Jesse. But it's what we think the prosecution is going to say."

Jesse looks at the table, as if she's deciding what to share. "What is it you want to know?"

"Why were you researching the case?" Julia asks.

"I want to be a journalist. The prior reporting was crap and I wanted to find out . . . everything."

In a measured tone, Julia says, "Here's the thing. It's kind of a big coincidence, don't you agree?" She looks at Jesse. "That you were researching that case and then happened to be involved in a similar attack."

"So you think I—You believe that I—"

Julia pauses. "No, but what I think or believe doesn't matter."

Ella doesn't want to pile on, but there's something gnawing at her that she needs to ask. "Did you know who I was—at the hospital?" That Jesse had been researching the Blockbuster case was already a coincidence, as Julia pointed out. But what were the odds that Ella would be called in to help Jesse at the hospital after the attack? It's a bridge too far.

"Did you know who I was?" Ella says again.

Jesse looks at the table, nods. Quietly, she says, "I asked for you."

Ella doesn't know what to say. She'd assumed it was Mr. Steadman's idea to call her in. "Jesse, you need to explain what's going on."

Resignation, or something similar, flits across Jesse's face. "Can you get me my phone? I can show you. I hid it in your car under the—"

"I know. I found it."

"We have it," says Julia. "We're going to have to turn it over to the prosecutors soon."

Jesse looks distressed at that. "Why?"

"Because it might be evidence," Julia says.

"It *is* evidence," Jesse says.

Julia looks at the teen curiously.

"Evidence of what?" Ella asks.

Jesse stares deep into Ella's eyes. "Evidence that Vince Whitaker may be innocent."

CHAPTER 53

Henry Robinson stares across the table at Jesse. He's returned to the interview room and is removing a cell phone from a clear plastic bag. He speaks in a fatherly tone. "We've got to be careful with this device."

Ella sits next to him, nodding in agreement. Julia is recording everything on her phone to preserve the chain of evidence, including proving that the defense team and their client didn't tamper with the phone.

Henry continues, "Thanks for giving us the password. Our computer people have now cloned the device so if anything is deleted or destroyed there's still a backup of everything stored on the phone."

"I'm not going to delete anything," Jesse says.

"I know you're not, but I just want the record to be clear."

Jesse makes a *gimme* gesture with her hands, and Henry places the device in front of her. The phone is no longer in the Hello Kitty case and looks like any other iPhone. Jesse scoops up the mobile and begins thumbing the screen in that proficient way of teens.

She pulls up a folder. "Here's my research file." She turns the phone toward them.

"The prosecutors have printouts they found at your foster home. Is this the same stuff?" Henry asks.

"No, the phone has all my research. I printed a few things out at school, but this has everything."

"What is it you wanted to show us?" Henry asks.

Jesse says, "The other guy isn't here today, so I guess you already know one thing."

"Who's not here?" Henry says.

"The other lawyer, Chris Ford."

"What do you mean?" Ella says, beating Henry to the punch.

Jesse shakes her head, annoyed, like she's dealing with idiots. "You don't know, do you?" She looks at her lawyers, one at a time. "He didn't tell you."

"I'm confused, Jessica," Henry says. "Maybe you can start from the beginning."

She thumbs her phone again, then slides it to their side of the table.

It shows yearbook photos. One from Freemont Academy. Chris Ford looking serious in his high school senior picture. He's younger but it's clearly Chris. Under the photo it reads: VALEDICTORIAN.

Next to the photo is a second yearbook picture from Union Elementary School. Chris is a gawky twelve- or thirteen-year-old. His hair is uncombed, and he appears malnourished. But it's him. It's the name associated with the photo that strips all the oxygen from the room.

Christopher Whitaker.

"Wait, what?" Ella says. "Whitaker . . . you're not saying . . ."

"Chris Ford is Vince Whitaker's younger brother," Jesse says. "He was adopted, best I can tell."

Henry is stroking his goatee. He turns to Julia, raises his eyebrows into a silent question: *Did you know anything about this?* She's still recording, her phone trained on Jesse. Julia shakes her head: *Don't look at me.*

"I told him yesterday that I know who he is," Jesse says.

Ella wonders if this is why Chris didn't come to work today. She studies Jesse. If she's not guilty, she's going to make one hell of a journalist someday. Ella also has a feeling that there is much more she doesn't know about this girl. Things she may not want to know.

"If you'll excuse me," Henry says, standing. "I need to make some calls." He rushes out, probably sensing a potential shit show when the press finds out the Blockbuster murderer's brother is on Jesse's defense team.

Ella's brain is trying to work through the implications. Chris Ford is really Chris Whitaker. What's it mean? It's weird, for sure. But she can't see how it changes anything.

"You said your phone would explain why you were investigating the Blockbuster case, why you think Chris's brother isn't guilty," Ella says. "I don't see how Chris Ford, or Whitaker or whatever his name is, has anything to do with—"

"Chris isn't why I was investigating the case. He was just something I uncovered in my research."

"Why did you decide to investigate the case in the first place?" Julia asks, still filming. Julia seems wired now, probably in shock over the news about her colleague.

Jesse snatches the phone off the table.

"Whoa, take it slowly," Julia says.

Jesse moves more deliberatively. She pulls up something else on the slab of metal and plastic.

"Did you know that Katie McKenzie had been pregnant?" Jesse asks.

Ella shakes her head. She has a sudden memory: Candy and Mandy huddled in an intense conversation with Katie in the break room, the three abruptly going quiet when Ella came inside. Is that what it was about? Katie was pregnant?

Ella says, "How do you know she was pregnant when she was killed?"

"I didn't say when she was killed."

Ella doesn't understand.

Julia also looks perplexed. She's lowered her iPhone, recording the tabletop now, though it's unclear if she realizes it.

Jesse continues, "She gave the baby up for adoption— she was out for most of her sophomore year. You can check the yearbooks."

The picture is coming together. Katie had moved away for a short period, long enough to give birth.

"Who was the father?" Ella asks. It couldn't be Vince

Whitaker. Katie didn't meet Vince until she worked at the video store. Ella was at the party where they'd met.

"That's the question, what I've been trying to figure out," Jesse says.

"How do you know all this?" Ella asks. "Adoption records are sealed."

Jesse pulls up another file and hands the iPhone to Ella. The document is grainy, hard to read. Ella pulls the screen close to her face. It's a blurry PDF of some type of government record, by the looks of it. She enlarges the screen and for the second time in less than an hour she's stupefied: CERTIFICATE OF LIVE BIRTH.

As Ella puzzles out the words on the birth certificate, Jesse says it aloud:

"I know because Katie McKenzie was my birth mother."

CHAPTER 54
KELLER

After meeting with Hal, Keller finds Atticus in his small office. He has a visitor, a petite woman carrying a Tupperware container.

"I'm sorry, I didn't know you were tied up," Keller says. "I can come back."

Atticus says, "No, it's okay. This is my mom."

The woman gives a big smile that reaches her eyes—the same Bambi eyes that she passed on to her son.

"You're the FBI agent Atticus has been talking so much about," she says in a slight Indian accent.

"Mom!"

"He still gets embarrassed, just like when he was a little boy."

Keller smiles, shakes her hand. "It's a pleasure to meet you."

"You as well. Atticus has been so excited to work with you. He's always wanted to be in the FBI. He took the job here as a start, but maybe you can help him if he—"

"Really, Mom." Atticus has jumped out of his seat and is guiding his mother to the door.

Keller hides a smile. "From what I've seen so far, he'll make a fine FBI agent."

His mother beams. "I'll let you get to work." She hands Atticus the Tupperware. "I made your favorite for dinner." She looks at Keller. "If you don't mind spicy, there's plenty."

"I *love* spicy, but these two don't agree." She places a hand on her belly.

Atticus's mom releases a lovely laugh.

Her son shepherds her out the door.

From the hallway, Mrs. Singh calls out, "Nice to meet you. Keep my boy safe."

Atticus gives an exasperated shake of the head as he shuffles her away.

When he returns, he says, "Sorry about that."

"Nothing to apologize about. She's obviously very proud of you. I didn't know you were interested in the Bureau."

"Someday. But I need to stay near home. Mom's health isn't good, so it's not the right time."

"Your father isn't able to . . ."

"He died when I was in high school. He worked as a security guard at a bank, there was a robbery, and . . . I didn't mention it before because, you know, it can be awkward for people."

"I'm so sorry, Atticus."

"It's okay. But there was an FBI agent, he was kind to me. And he caught the guy, and ever since, I wanted . . . you know."

Keller nods. She pictures a young Atticus imagining he's a G-man like in the old television shows. He's a good candidate for the Bureau: he's smart, meticulous, and HQ loves Yale men. The kid could be at Quantico right now or making six figures in the business world, but instead, he chose to take care of his mom.

"Anyway," Atticus says, changing the subject, "you're heading out?"

"I'm not done with the county just yet. I'm actually going on a stakeout, of sorts—want to join?"

"Hells yeah, I do." He smiles. "What're we staking out?"

Keller recalls Hal's comment that she still has work to do. "A loose end."

CHAPTER 55
CHRIS

Chris opens his eyes to the sound of beeps, the feeling of tubes running across his body, and the look of concern on Ms. May's face.

Clint appears in the frame. "There he is." His deep voice echoes overhead.

The sound reverberates through Chris's head, a jolt of agony both piercing and dull at the same time. When it subsides, Chris tries to shake off the grog. It takes a minute, then he understands. He's in the hospital. The memories are flooding back now: The underpass. The kid with the knife. The girl mouthing *Help me*.

"Did they find her?" he says, his voice hoarse.

Ms. May smiles and pats his arm gently. "You need to take it easy, Christopher. You have a nasty concussion."

"Don't worry, she's safe," Clint says. Chris hears pride in Clint's tone. "She said you saved her."

"Who is she? What—"

"They're both runaways. He'd been abusing her.

She's safe now," Clint says. "You're lucky. They found your car, then found you out cold."

"Did they catch the kid who was hurting her?"

"He's down the hall," Clint says. "He's been arrested and they have an officer stationed at his room. He said there was another guy who whacked you on the head. They haven't caught him yet."

May shushes Clint. She pushes ice chips at Chris.

The doctor comes in and checks on him. Says he's lucky. He'll be fine, but he needs to take it easy. They'll keep him overnight for observation.

At some point—the timeline is fuzzy but it has to be afternoon, as a lunch tray rests on the bedside table—his boss, Henry, appears in the room. He asks to speak with May and Clint outside. They close the door, but if Chris cranes his neck, he can see through the glass window. The three of them are huddled close, talking in whispers.

Something's wrong. He can tell that much from the grief-stricken expression on Ms. May's face. Even Clint—who rarely breaks his stoic veneer—appears rattled. Henry comes back inside.

"How you feeling, son?"

"Better," Chris lies. He's still having trouble keeping his thoughts straight. Like shaking a table with a jigsaw puzzle on it, the pieces rattling, distorting the image.

"That's good. I heard you're quite the hero."

Chris doesn't respond. The buildup is nearly killing him. *Do they know why he was under the bridge? What's going on?*

"I've got some upsetting news. It's the worst time in

the world, but we wanted you to hear it before you saw it on TV or your phone."

"What is it?"

"Rusty Whitaker was arrested last night."

The beeping on the heart monitors accelerates. Not because Rusty's been arrested. That's good news. Rather, because there's only one reason Henry would bring this up: he knows that Rusty's his biological father. Knows that Vince is his brother.

"What'd he do now?" Chris asks, deciding it's futile to play dumb.

"Murder," Henry says.

No surprise there. It was only a matter of time. "Who'd he kill?"

Henry takes in a deep breath. "I'm sorry, son. But they think it's your mother."

Chris's head is spinning now. He's struggling to arrange his thoughts. The beeping on the monitors grows louder. His chest tight.

"What? I don't understand. My mom left when I was ten. Why would he kill her now? And how would he even find her? I tried for years."

Henry's face is pained. "They found remains at a storage unit where he works. The body had been there for . . . a long time." Henry stops, studies Chris. He looks concerned. "Are you all right? Do I need to get the doctor?"

Chris is floating now. Out of body. But he understands. And the realization nearly levels him. The woman whom he'd resented for so long, whom he'd hated for leaving him in the brutal care of Rusty Whitaker, whom he'd let go of on graduation day, hadn't abandoned him after all. A medley of guilt and grief and anger envelops him.

He sits up too quickly and releases a wail. It's partly from the pressure in his skull, but mostly the sound of devastation.

"Whoa, you need to take it easy," Henry says, guiding him back down onto the bed.

Chris feels tears on his face. His breaths are staccato. How much more can Rusty Whitaker take from him?

But with the tumult emerges a revelation. A heaviness lifted from his chest. An ugly mass removed.

She hadn't abandoned him.

"Are you okay?" Henry asks.

May and Clint are back in the room, standing at his bedside.

Chris nods, wipes away tears with his hand. "I'm going to be released tomorrow. I'd like to stay on the case."

From Henry's expression, Chris knows that isn't in the cards.

"Let's talk about that after you've recovered," Henry says. "For now, you need to rest, take some time off."

It's not a request. His short time on the Jesse Duvall case—maybe his time at the PD's office—is over. And, strangely, he thinks that might be for the best.

CHAPTER 56
ELLA

Ella's back in her office. She'd considered canceling her afternoon sessions—the meeting with Jesse was *a lot*. But she didn't want to let down Layla, the cutter. Ella thinks she's nearing a breakthrough with the sixteen-year-old, and she doesn't want to lose momentum. Besides, she needs a mental break from Blockbuster, the Dairy Creamery, Jesse Duvall—all of it.

She fluffs the pillows on the small couch. Puts the box of tissues subtly on the end table. Reviews her notes from their last session.

No matter how hard she tries, though, her thoughts return to Jesse. She still hasn't had time to digest everything Jesse told them.

The biggest bombshell: that Jesse is Katie's child. Is it true? There's no DNA test, but Ella thinks so. She sees it now. In the eyes—Jesse has Katie's eyes. Jesse's are fiercer, less timid, but they're the same almond-shaped eyes.

Ella also can't stop thinking about Chad Parke. Jesse's story about her former teacher has the ring of truth. But so did the teacher's version. Was Jesse obsessed with Parke and set him up when he rejected her? Or was she the victim of a predator who took advantage of a young girl who needed a father figure? Jesse is extremely smart and world-wise for someone her age. She also seems to be unusually manipulative. It's hard to believe Jesse could be duped by Parke in the way she describes. On the other hand, she's just a kid, a teenager. Whatever the truth, Ella needs to speak with the school counselor about the cyberbullying. Ella knows Dale Steadman—he would treat cyberbullying seriously, surely mandating that staff report all incidents to him. If the counselor failed to report it up the chain, there would be consequences.

Ella wishes she'd had time to debrief with Julia after the meeting with Jesse. But the young lawyer had gotten a call, then rushed back to the PD's office. Ella suspects there will be many meetings today at the Union County Public Defender's Office about Chris Ford, aka Christopher Whitaker.

She doesn't think Chris broke any laws by representing Jesse, though it does seem like a conflict of interest. Ella feels peculiarly angry at him. At the same time, the prism through which she's seen things has changed. If Jesse is Katie's child, then who's the father? Would that person have a motive to kill Katie and her friends? And who was Katie fighting with in the parking lot? Everyone thought it was *Him*. But maybe it wasn't. Maybe they'd seen *Him* earlier and just assumed that's who Katie was fighting with. A memory of that night floats in her head.

Ella stands at the back door to the break room. She's hugging herself from the chill. And she doesn't like him seeing her in the stupid uniform.

He's holding a flower. A sad specimen of a flower, but still.

"I want to see you tonight—celebrate the New Year together," he says.

"I'm supposed to go to a party at Brody's with Candy and the girls after work."

"Cool, I'll meet you there."

"I'm not sure . . . Katie . . ."

"You haven't told her yet?"

Ella shakes her head. "She's been upset about something."

"About what?"

"I don't know." Ella gives him a look. "Maybe that you haven't called her?"

"We hung out just a couple times. And I swear, I think her ex keyed my car. Too much drama."

"How do you know I'm not dramatic?"

"Good point, you are hiding me away from your friends."

On cue, someone comes into the break room. Ella glances behind her, and it's Stevie grabbing some paperwork. He disappears back into the store.

"Meet me tonight," he says. "Depending on my dad, I should be able to get there around eleven. Or if you're worried about your friends, it doesn't have to be at the party."

"No, I need to tell her. I'll see you there," she says, guiding him outside before anyone sees him. She leans in and their lips touch. She feels electricity through every part of her. When they pull away, he has a dopey look on his face. He inhales through his nose, like he's taking in the moment.

"Nirvana," he says quietly.

"What?"

"Never mind, I'll see you tonight."

The questions return. Did he really see Katie right after that kiss? Did they really get into an argument? Did he come back at closing and kill her, and Candy, and Mandy, and Stevie? Had Ella been spared, the only one of them with a nonfatal wound, because he liked her? It all never made sense. But they found the knife in his locker.

"Hell-o." Layla bounces into the office. Her patient's in good spirits. Layla's smile fades. "Are you okay?"

"I'm fine," Ella says, pasting on a smile.

"You look like you were crying."

"Just allergies," Ella says.

Layla narrows her gaze.

Ella doesn't like lying to this girl who's bared her soul to her.

Ella says, "You know what? That's not true. I *was* crying. This week has been a shit show."

Layla smiles. "I'm glad you said that." She plops down on the sofa. "It's exhausting, isn't it?"

"What?" Ella says.

"Pretending all the time. Faking the smiles and cheerfulness, so everyone stops worrying about you."

Ella says, "Then let's stop doing it. Fuck it."

Layla smiles, a genuine one this time. "Yeah. Fuck it."

CHAPTER 57
KELLER

"What are we waiting for?" Atticus asks.

They're in Keller's Volvo, parked down the street from the McKenzie home. Far enough away not to draw attention, close enough to see the comings and goings of the McKenzies. The sky remains gunmetal gray—the sun hasn't appeared in three days.

"I'm hoping to get Katie's mother alone." Keller shifts in her seat. She feels pain in her pelvis. An uncomfortable feeling, but not uncommon during her pregnancy. She's not due for a few weeks, so it's nothing.

"You okay?" Atticus asks, seeing her discomfort.

"Yeah, it'll pass," she says, taking in a deep breath. She's certainly not having twins in her pre-owned Swedish automobile, much less having them delivered by Atticus Singh.

"Maybe we should go to the door," Atticus says.

"You know what happened last time. We need to get her away from her husband or we'll just get the door slammed in our faces again."

Atticus looks uncertain, but he doesn't say anything.

An hour passes. She's got to pee and is starting to think that maybe Atticus was right—they should just go pound on the door. The thought is interrupted when Atticus says, "At last."

Ms. McKenzie walks down the front steps to her car. She's carrying what looks like a sheet cake. She puts the cake on the passenger seat, gets in the car, then pulls out.

They follow at a discreet distance.

Ms. McKenzie is a cautious driver, never exceeding the speed limit. In light traffic, it's a struggle to keep a safe distance to avoid Ms. McKenzie spotting them.

Atticus points to a sign for a church. "Maybe someone's birthday or some kind of celebration."

But Ms. McKenzie's car passes the church. They follow her through the business district, across the railroad tracks to a rougher patch of town, a sea of check-cashing shops, liquor stores, and fast-food joints.

"What the hell?" Atticus says as he watches Ms. McKenzie pull up to a throng of men huddled in front of a bodega. A young man breaks from the group and heads to Ms. McKenzie's car. He hunches over, says something, then reaches inside the vehicle. There's an exchange.

"Never judge a book by its cover," Keller says.

"I get that," Atticus says. "But the Church Lady doing a drug deal? *Damn*."

They follow Ms. McKenzie as she backtracks toward her home. And, sure enough, she stops at the church.

She parks and carries the sheet cake inside.

Keller thinks about going in after her, putting the pressure on, grilling her in front of the congregation. She decides against it. This woman knows more than she's saying, and she may be a secret drug user, but her daughter was murdered. If anyone deserves a break . . .

A half hour later, Ms. McKenzie emerges from the church.

Keller climbs out of her car, Atticus following after her.

"Ms. McKenzie," Keller calls out.

The woman turns, offers a plastic smile. It takes a moment for her to recognize them and the smile disappears.

"My husband already told you that we have nothing to—"

"Does your husband know about your trips over to the bodega?"

Ms. McKenzie swallows hard.

Keller continues, "I'll bet if we search your car, he won't like having to bail you out."

Ms. McKenzie's head snaps back and forth, looking around the lot. "What do you want?"

"We have a few questions. Answer them, and I'm inclined not to take this further."

Ms. McKenzie's lip quivers. She nods for Keller to continue.

"We know about Katie's pregnancy."

Ms. McKenzie tears up now. She doesn't reply. She doesn't need to.

"I understand why you wanted it kept confidential. I do."

A car pulls into the lot and two churchgoers get out. They're holding strings with latex balloons that say CONGRATULATIONS! on them.

Ms. McKenzie's demeanor changes. She pulls herself together, smiles and waves, like she's chatting with friends. The couple waves back, the balloons bobbing behind them in the breeze.

"Do you know who the father was?"

Ms. McKenzie shakes her head. In a soft voice she says, "We knew she was seeing someone. She wouldn't tell us his name. We assumed it was him."

"Vince Whitaker?"

Ms. McKenzie nods. "We made arrangements for Katie to stay with a family, to give the baby up."

"The pregnancy isn't mentioned in the investigation file."

Ms. McKenzie nods again. "A friend of ours works for Union County." She looks sadder now, rather than the panic from before. "He helped keep it confidential."

Detective Grosso was right. "Who's the friend?"

"My big brother's best friend from high school. My brother died over in Iraq and his friend kind of took over, you know? He never had kids of his own, and he doted on my Katie."

"Who, Ms. McKenzie?"

"I don't want to get him in trouble."

Keller lets out a breath. "That's probably better than the alternative." She glances inside the woman's car.

Ms. McKenzie remains quiet.

"It won't take me long to find out on my own," Keller

says. That's true. HR is pulling the records for Keller; they said they'd have them by the end of the day.

"Joe was just trying to help. To spare our family the—"

"Joe who?" Keller asks, her pulse pounding in her ears.

Ms. McKenzie looks desperately to Atticus, then back at Keller.

Then she says it: "Joe Arpeggio."

CHAPTER 58

"I say we put Joe Arpeggio's ass in the box and grill him," Atticus says, staring at his crime wall back at the office. He's still amped up from the stakeout. He writes "J.A." on a Post-it Note and sticks it on the board next to Katie McKenzie's photograph.

Keller smiles in spite of herself. "We can't rush. It's probably nothing more than what we already know: a friend trying to protect a victim's family from more pain." She walks up to the crime board. "And if there is something to it, we need to do the legwork. Bulls in china shops get nothing but broken dishes." Oh god, she sounds like her father.

"What do you need me to do?" Atticus is eager, ready to roll up his sleeves.

"We know Arpeggio's connection to Katie McKenzie." Keller puts a finger on the Post-it Note on the crime wall, then traces a line to the photos of the ice cream store victims on the other half of the board. "We need to see if he's connected to any of the new victims."

Atticus nods. "On it. We just got the rest of the records from the cell phone companies. I'll start there."

"Look for unusual patterns, things out of the ordinary. If he has a connection to one of the vics, it's not going to be obvious. There's only one thing sneakier than criminals."

"What's that?"

"Teenage girls."

Atticus smiles.

"What else do we know about Arpeggio? What's he do outside the office? What's he do for fun?"

"Fun?" Atticus says. "I can't imagine him having fun."

"We don't have enough for a warrant into his phone or computer, but we have every agent's best investigative tool."

Atticus waits for her to reveal the secret.

Keller holds up her phone: "Google."

Hal appears at the door of Atticus's office. "The original Starsky and Hutch," he says. "No wait, that's sexist: Cagney and Lacey."

"Not sexist," Keller says, "just extraordinarily out of date."

Hal shrugs. "I got a name," he says.

They look at him, unclear what he's talking about.

"For the little brother, Chris Whitaker," Hal says. "He goes by Chris Ford. Get this: he works as a Union County public defender."

Keller thinks about this. Given where Chris Whitaker came from, that's impressive. Rusty Whitaker's spawn seemed destined for the penitentiary.

"It gets even more interesting," Hal continues. "I

called over to the PD's office. The head PD is an old friend. Turns out Chris Ford is in the hospital. He was attacked last night."

By late afternoon, Keller's at the hospital. Chris Ford is awake and seems slightly agitated.

"That was brave, what you did to save that girl," Keller says.

"So I've heard."

Chris is banged up. He has scrapes on his face, his hair's a mess, and he looks out of it. For the first time she sees the resemblance, the angular features like his brother's. There's even some of his father in his eyes.

"I'm sorry about your mom," Keller says.

"I assume the FBI doesn't send agents to extend thoughts and prayers, so what can I do for you, Special Agent Keller?"

"Please, call me Sarah," she says. "I have some questions if you're up for it?"

Chris nods for her to continue.

"I know it's been a long time, but I want to talk about the last time you saw your mom."

He looks away, stares at the muted television mounted on the wall, and nods again.

"Tell me about the last time you saw her."

"*Air Bud.*"

"Pardon?"

"We watched the movie *Air Bud.* It's about a dog who can play basketball." Chris continues looking at the television.

"When was that?"

"I was ten, so 1997."

"Is there a reason you remember it so clearly?"

"Yeah, because I went to school the next day and never saw her again," he says, a little edge in his tone.

Fair enough. It was a stupid question.

"Actually," Chris says, his voice softer, "I remember because I had a big math test the next day and was I worried about it. She told me that relaxing, doing something fun, before a test would help way more than cramming."

"Good advice."

"It got me through law school."

"That's the last time you saw her?"

He nods. "The next day, I rushed home to show her the A I got on the test, and she was gone."

"Where did you think she went?"

"He told me she'd run off with someone. It wasn't hard to believe if you've met my biological father."

Keller nods. "I arrested him."

Chris nods like he knows this already.

"How about your brother? When's the last time you saw him?"

"Ah, the real reason for your visit."

Keller makes no reply.

Chris starts to say something but seems to change his mind. "The last time I saw Vince was the day they released him for insufficient probable cause."

"And what do you remember?"

"It was late. I'd already gone to bed. But I heard

voices in the living room, so I got up, hoping it was him. He'd been arrested and I didn't understand what was going on."

"And what happened?"

"I remember coming out of my room, but he had some customers there. He sold pot. He was small-time, dime bags, mostly to high school kids. Anyway, he was stern with me, told me to go to bed."

"Was he always like that with you?"

"No, almost never. You may not believe it, but he's a gentle guy."

Keller tries to keep her expression neutral, like she might believe him, might not.

"But that night," Chris continues, "my dad was there, so the customers were probably friends of his. And one of the customers, an older guy, was acting weird, twitchy. I'm guessing Vince didn't want me exposed to that crowd. So I went to bed."

"That's the last time you saw him?"

"When I got up in the morning he was gone."

"Have you had any contact with your brother since then?"

"None."

She gives him a skeptical look.

"Trust me, I'd love to talk to him."

"Why's that?"

"Because I'm a lawyer and I can help him now."

Keller offers a compassionate smile. This young man has been through a lot.

Chris adds, "They let him go for insufficient evidence. Even now, the only evidence they have is an anonymous tip and a knife conveniently found in his locker after his release. My brother may have been a lot of things, but he wasn't stupid. He never would've left a murder weapon in his own locker."

They also have Vince's fingerprint placing him at the scene, but Keller doesn't say that. And Chris is right, the case against his brother has some holes. One of Keller's instructors at Quantico always said that MOM is the key to any criminal investigation—motive, opportunity, and means. Atticus has questioned the "opportunity" since there's evidence that Vince Whitaker was home at ten when the video store closed and that his father had the car that night. For Keller, though, it's the "motive" that's troubling her. Why kill all of the employees?

"You have any idea where he is?" she asks.

Chris hesitates. "I don't know where he is currently."

Keller notes the careful wording, holds his gaze. "But you have an idea?"

Chris searches her face, as if trying to read what she knows.

"I'm not feeling so well. The concussion and all."

"Chris . . ."

"I think I need to rest, Agent Keller."

Keller considers pushing him, but decides against it. He saved a young girl last night and just learned his mother was murdered. Some of her colleagues at the Bureau would've pushed, would've scolded her for allowing compassion to interfere with an interrogation. But Keller doesn't see things that way. She's learned that the best way to get someone to open up, and for her to sleep at night, is to follow her instincts. If a reluctant witness or suspect trusts her now, they're more likely to confide in her later.

"If you do learn his whereabouts, I trust you'll let me know." She hands him a business card.

Chris doesn't respond. He puts his head back like he's not feeling well.

Before she leaves the hospital room, she says, "I'm sorry for your loss, Chris. I am."

On her way to the car, her phone rings. The caller ID says UCPO, so she thinks it's Atticus with an update on his research into Joe Arpeggio.

"Agent Keller, it's Joe."

Speak of the devil.

"Hi, Joe." She tries to sound friendly, nonchalant, but she wonders whether Katie McKenzie's mother has called him.

"I just got word that Rusty Whitaker wants a deal. Says he's got information we'll be interested in. Hal thought you should be there." A proffer. A night in the clink can do wonders.

"That was fast."

"They want us there now. Can you make it?"

"On my way."

CHAPTER 59
CHRIS

Chris needs to get out of there.

Beyond the visits from his boss and the FBI, the medical staff won't leave him alone. They're constantly coming in and poking and prodding him, giving him periodic neuro tests to make sure he doesn't have a brain bleed or his mental state isn't deteriorating. Chris presses the doctor on whether he *really* needs to stay the night, and after some browbeating the guy begrudgingly says he can give Chris an AMA discharge. He makes clear, probably for legal reasons, that AMA stands for Against Medical Advice.

After signing the forms, Chris finds his clothes in a plastic bag in the closet, then rips off the backless blue gown, and gets dressed.

He's still hazy. Maybe this isn't the best idea in the world, but he feels some inner force, some instinct, maybe, pushing him to flee.

It's ironic because his dreary apartment isn't much better than the hospital. Clare is already in the process of ghosting him, so he can't go to her place. Henry told him to stay away from the office. And soon, the media will be swarming his parents' house, seeking a peek at Vince Whitaker's kid brother, who's been assigned to defend another accused mass killer. On top of that, he has no money since his wallet isn't in his effects. The guy who clocked him on the head probably has it.

You know what he needs? He needs a drink. A stiff drink. He beats back a depressing thought: *Like father, like son.*

He considers going to Corky's. That's too visible. No, there's only one option. Somewhere no self-respecting reporter or law-enforcement agent would venture. Somewhere they'll let him run a tab.

On his way out, he bumps into Julia, who's holding a vase of flowers she must've picked up in the hospital gift shop.

"They've released you?" she asks, giving him the once-over, concern on her face.

"Yeah."

Julia narrows her eyes, skeptical. "Chris, are you sure you should—"

"Can you give me a ride?"

Julia purses her lips, deciding what to do. She nods.

Soon, she's parked in front of a dreary establishment on the outskirts of the county known as Clyde's Bar, neither of them having spoken during the drive.

Julia examines the dismal exterior, trash bags piled at the curb out front. "You sure it's safe to go in there? I hear that place is bad news."

"I'll be fine."

"You shouldn't be drinking. You have a concussion and, no offense, but you look like shit."

Chris makes no response.

"Let me take you home, you can relax, watch some TV, recover."

"I appreciate you coming to the hospital, Julia," he says, "and for the ride." He considers asking her if he can borrow twenty bucks, but thinks better of it. He opens the car door.

"Chris, seriously, let me take you home."

He hobbles out of the car and goes inside the bar.

It's early evening and Clyde's is nearly empty. The place picks up around midnight. An old man crouches over his beer at the over-glossed bar, looking like he's in the mess hall of a prison guarding his meal. At a booth in the back, an older woman wearing heavy makeup and torn fishnet stockings taps on her phone. A hard-looking man in a leather jacket sits at a table on the other side of the place staring out at nothing. It's a place for people who don't want to talk about their problems. Don't want to socialize. Don't want a cocktail. They want to sit and drink bottom-shelf booze and mind their own damned business.

Chris tended bar at Clyde's during his summers home from college. Clint happened to have gone to high school with Clyde, who at that moment is behind the bar, looking a thousand years old. He pours a drink into Chris's glass.

"Been a long time, college boy."

Chris smiles.

"Why you slummin'?" Clyde doesn't ask about the

scrapes on his face or the hospital bracelet. He sees worse on a nightly basis.

"Slummin'? You should see my office. Or worse, my apartment."

Clyde lets out a laugh that sounds like the inside of a pack of Winston's. Chris thinks back to his bartender training when he was twenty. Clyde saying, *"These fools barely have a pot to piss in and the only time they tip is if you laugh at their jokes."*

"How's the old man?" Clyde asks, meaning Clint.

"He's hangin' in there."

"Toughest dude I ever met. I ever tell you about when we was in high school and some fool called me a—let's just say, it wasn't politically correct."

Chris smiles again. Another memory from his training: *"Tell them a story. That'll keep 'em drinking."*

For the next hour, Chris half-listens to tales of Clint and Clyde back in the day. He has a hard time imagining Clint as the bellicose brawler Clyde remembers. But men change over the years. Some men, anyway. Rusty Whitaker never changed. And the one bit of good news this week, no, this year, is that Rusty would finally rot in a cell like he deserves.

Clyde looks over Chris's shoulder, his face wrinkles. "Someone's *lost*," he says.

Chris glances in the reflection in the mirror behind the bar. An attractive woman, a professional, elegant, has come into the place. He twists around to confirm, and it's her all right: Ella Monroe.

She must've talked to Julia.

Spotting him, Ella charges over. She doesn't look happy.

"Hi," Chris says, his voice thick with ironic cheerfulness or something close to it. The alcohol combined with the head injury have made him punchy.

She glowers at him, but says nothing.

Clyde senses the tension and disappears into the background. Another thing he'd taught Chris, *If the customers are fightin', stay the hell out of it.*

"You're here to commend my heroism?" Chris asks.

She's having none of it. "You're his brother. You knew what happened to me, and you still . . ." She stops, her breathing is ragged.

"I'm sorry," he says. "But what did you want me to say? 'Hi, I'm the brother of the guy who allegedly tried to kill you'?"

"Allegedly." She grabs onto the word.

"I'm sorry," he repeats. "I am. I know what you think. But I don't believe Vince—"

"The evidence says otherwise," she interrupts.

"It does for Jesse too. But do you think she did it?"

Ella doesn't answer.

Chris takes a gulp, then stares ahead at the lines of bottles.

Ella takes the barstool next to him. There's a long stretch of silence.

Eventually, Chris says, "Ever since I was in middle school, I've wanted only one thing: Vince to come home so I could help prove . . . Sorry, I get it, you don't want to hear this."

She turns to him. She doesn't look angry anymore. It's something else. Sadness? Curiosity? Pity?

"Try me," she says.

Chris signals to Clyde to fill his glass. Clyde approaches, asks Ella if she wants anything.

"I'll have what he's having."

Clyde fills two glasses, and Ella takes a big drink.

"That night, what time did you close the video store?" Chris asks her.

"Ten."

"And you were—" He stops himself from saying it. "It happened shortly after closing?"

She nods.

"That's the point. Vince was at home. Cooking my piece-of-garbage father dinner. I remember because Vince got there just before ten—I was watching the clock, worried he wouldn't get home before Dad. It's impossible that he was at the video store."

"Someone saw his car there at closing," Ella says.

"An anonymous tip supposedly given to detectives who were under pressure to make an arrest. There's no record of that call. And even if it was a real tip, not one made up by the cops, no one has ever come forward as the witness. No one's been able to test the person who claimed they saw our car. And the customer who saw Katie McKenzie arguing with someone in the lot only heard a male's voice and never got a look at who she was arguing with."

"But he *was* at the store that night. I saw him earlier."

"Yes, *earlier*." Chris turns to her. "He told me he'd visited a girl. He was crazy about her. He'd walked all the way to the Blockbuster just to see her. If that was Katie McKenzie, then why would he kill her? Why would he kill all of them?"

Ella looks like she's going to say something, then stops herself. After a moment, she says, "Then why run?"

Chris contemplates the glass of brown liquid. He has no answer. He drains the glass, taps the rim, signaling Clyde for another. The bar owner gives him a look, like, *You sure that's a good idea?* Chris taps the rim again, and Clyde obliges.

Ella takes another swig of her own drink, emptying her glass without even a wince. She gestures to Clyde, who by now appears amused at the two of them for some reason. He fills her glass.

"Julia told me about your mother," she says. "I'm sorry."

Chris gives a clipped nod. He doesn't want to get into it all.

Ella seems to sense this. They drink in silence again.

Then: "What did Vince say about the girl?"

"Pardon?" Chris says.

"That night. You said Vince was talking about a girl. What did he say?"

Instantly, Chris is back in his kitchen before Rusty got home, the smell of Hamburger Helper in the air. His brother euphoric.

"He said she was special. She smelled different."

"Smelled?"

He nods. "Vince always said we'd get out. Escape from our dad. Our world would smell different too."

Ella swallows. Her eyes are wet.

"He had a name for it." Chris takes a pull of his drink. He's about to say it, when Ella does it for him.

"Nirvana," she says.

Chris is taken aback. How in the hell does she know that? And then his phone pings. An alert. The vlogger. But it isn't a video this time. It's another livestream. He pushes back his stool from the bar, stands up.

"What is it?" Ella asks.

"I'm going to put a fucking end to this question once and for all."

"What question?"

"Whether my brother is back. Whether he's a killer." He asks Clyde to put the drinks on a tab, then starts to leave.

"Christopher."

He turns to find Ella staring at him.

"Can I come with you?"

CHAPTER 60
KELLER

In a meeting room at the Union County jail, Rusty Whitaker sits next to his lawyer, a middle-aged woman with short hair and an exasperated expression. It's crowded on Keller's side of the table: the AUSA prosecuting the federal charges against Rusty for the cigarette counterfeiting ring, as well as Hal Kowalski and Joe Arpeggio, who are running point on the state murder charges.

"For the record," Rusty's lawyer says, "this meeting is against my advice. I was just assigned to the case. The Union County Public Defender's Office has some type of conflict, so the judge appointed me to represent Mr. Whitaker on the state charges. I'm not clear about the federal charges. A federal defender may be involved. In any event, I need time to assess the case." She gives Rusty the side-eye. "I've told Mr. Whitaker that until I'm up to speed, he should exercise his right to shut the hell up."

"You understand what your lawyer is telling you?"

Keller asks. Because it was her collar, etiquette dictates that she starts the questioning.

Rusty nods.

"Please say it out loud for the recording." Keller looks back at the camera mounted to the ceiling.

"Yeah, I understand. I already signed the damn Miranda form."

"And you've requested this meeting, and you're speaking to us of your own free will—against the advice of your counsel."

"Yeah."

Keller looks to the AUSA, who nods. Hal also concurs. The prosecutors have what they need in the event Rusty later claims he was unlawfully coerced.

"I'm Agent Sarah Keller with the FBI, and I think you've been introduced to everyone else."

"I remember you," Rusty says with disdain.

"We understand you want to make a proffer."

"I don't know what that means, but I want a deal. A good one."

"A deal for what?" Arpeggio joins in, sounding impatient.

"I got some information you'll want." Rusty turns his gaze back to Keller. "That you'll both want." He smiles, his teeth gray and jagged. He still makes her skin crawl.

Arpeggio says, "I gotta tell you, Rusty, we don't need a deal. You're the last person to see your wife. Her body's at your place of work. Your prints are on the barrel. And once the test results come back, I imagine your DNA will put the final nails in the coffin."

Rusty scowls, bunches his fists. His cuffs are anchored

to a steel bar on the table. Keller imagines him using those callused meat hooks on his wife, on his sons.

"I got a bigger fish," he spits out.

Arpeggio shakes his head. "It's dinnertime, Rusty. Start talking or we're out of here."

Keller isn't sure it's the right play, but it works.

"I can give you Vince."

Arpeggio goes still for a moment. "Explain," he says.

"You get me a deal, and I promise, I know where he is."

"You can lead us to Vince Whitaker?" Arpeggio asks, his tone skeptical.

"Get me the deal and I can."

Keller says, "I won't speak for Union County, but on the federal side, you'll have to forgive me for being skeptical. It'll take more than a promise if you want us to go up the chain on this."

The AUSA concurs: "Yeah, we need more than just your word for me to—"

"I don't give one shit about your silly cigarette charges," says Rusty. He turns to Arpeggio and Hal. "I want a deal on the murder."

"Mr. Whitaker," his lawyer says, "I'm going to advise you that you shouldn't say more until I—"

"Shut up," Rusty tells his lawyer. "Go talk to whoever you gotta talk to," he says to the group across the table. "But you want to find Vince, you'd better do it soon." He lowers his head, scratches his chin on the back of his hand, his shackles clanking. "You ain't getting anything until you give me a deal and put it in writing. You can make it conditioned on you finding Vince, if you want."

"We need to talk about it," Arpeggio says.

"Don't take too long," Rusty says, "the offer expires tonight."

"What do you think?" Arpeggio asks the group in the corridor outside the interview room.

"I don't trust him," Keller says. "At the same time, he's willing to make the deal conditional on us finding his son."

Arpeggio looks at Hal.

Hal says, "A dilemma. Trade one killer for another."

"I think we should make a deal," Arpeggio says. "For the families. It's been fifteen years and we can give them some closure."

Hal looks to the AUSA. "If we make a deal conditioned on capturing Vince Whitaker, will you all throw in the cigarette charges to sweeten the deal?"

The AUSA shrugs. "I'll have to confirm that the Secret Service is okay with it, but probably."

Keller frowns. But she understands. If the state wants a deal badly enough to take a plea on a slam-dunk murder charge, the Feds will likely extend a professional courtesy.

Keller thinks about Rusty. He seems so certain he knows where to find his son. It's odd because Rusty would be the last person she imagines Vince would reach out to.

Keller thinks back through Chris's description of seeing his brother for the last time. Rusty and a group of drug fiends, a twitchy, threatening man. It's then she has a thought, a theory.

"Do me a favor?" she says to Hal and Arpeggio.

Arpeggio gives her a noncommittal look, but Hal nods.

"Talk to me before you make any deal. I have an idea."

"What is it?" Arpeggio asks.

"A hunch. But one that may allow us to have our cake and eat it too."

CHAPTER 61

Keller is irritable, but she isn't sure if that's because she's just been in close quarters with Rusty Whitaker or because she and her twins are ravenously hungry. She should pull over, eat dinner, but she wants to run down her hunch first. On the drive she calls Atticus.

"How's it going? Any luck?" she says on the Volvo's speakerphone.

Atticus's voice comes from the overhead speakers: "I haven't found any connection between Arpeggio and the Dairy Creamery victims. I've started going through cell records. Madison Sawyer and her sister made no calls or texts to Arpeggio or a burner phone. I just got through all the logs for the last month on Madison's cell, and I've skimmed through her texts—Mintz downloaded them to the evidence portal. I'm about to go through her little sister's call logs and texts."

"Nothing?"

"Not yet. I'll tell you, though, from the texts, Madison wasn't the nicest girl. I hate to speak ill of the dead and all . . ."

"Teenage girls can be mean as shit."

"One interesting thing: the sisters were in a fight about something. Madison said she was going to tell their mom about it."

"What?"

"It's not clear. They talk in code. I've googled all the weird abbreviations they use but haven't cracked it. How was the meeting with Rusty Whitaker?"

Keller debriefs him on the proffer.

"Is Hal going to make the deal?" Atticus asks. "And what about you all on the federal charges?"

"Not if I can help it. Did you see my text about getting me the address?"

"Yeah, just sent it. What's up?"

"A long shot. I'll keep you posted. Let me know if you find anything in the cell records or a connection between the girls and Arpeggio."

Keller disconnects the line and follows the GPS link Atticus sent her, pulling into the driveway of a home in Elizabeth ten minutes later.

She bangs on the front door.

It opens tentatively. "I told you I have nothing to—"

"We've arrested Rusty Whitaker. He's about to sing. Once he does, any deal for you is over. It's now or never. And I know . . ."

There's a long pause. The man hesitates, cricks his neck, then opens the door for Keller to come inside.

CHAPTER 62
ELLA

Ella glances at Chris, who's staring at his phone. They're bouncing around in the back of a cab, which just hit the exit to Forty-Second Street in Manhattan.

"He's somewhere in Central Park," Chris says.

That's a stroke of luck. Ella's family has an apartment on the park. She spent many weekends there as a kid, knows the terrain. On breaks from college, she'd stay there to avoid Phyllis. It made her popular with the kids in the dorm, a free place to crash on the Upper West Side. She's kept in touch with none of them.

"Comments in the feed say his fans are already giving chase," Chris adds.

Ella asks Chris for the phone. She examines the screen. It's too dark to recognize anything. Mr. Nirvana's in a dark area of the park. It's dead quiet.

The traveler walks in silence as the screen moves down a path that soon turns black except for the light from the camera. There's bramble on either side. The camera zooms in on a rat next to a trash bin. It doesn't scurry away despite the light.

The traveler walks up the ominous path.

"I'd be lying if I said I wasn't scared," Mr. Nirvana says, narrating the live feed.

A voice bellows from the woods. "Can you turn that fucking light off?"

The traveler turns out the light and fast-walks, the sound of wind brushing into the microphone.

The camera turns off, then back on. The traveler shines the light on a lamppost. The camera's focus resolves on a placard with a number on it: 7802.

"If you know anything about the park, that's a clue where I am," he says. The camera pans the area. It's crowded, but no one seems to be focusing on him.

Ella says, "He's at East Seventy-Eighth."

"How do you know that?"

"The lampposts have numbers. My dad taught me. The first two numbers are the street. If it's an odd number you're on the west side; even, you're on the east side."

Chris nods, impressed.

Ella says, "Seventy-Eighth. That's near the Shakespeare Garden."

That's confirmed when the camera focuses on a small plaque surrounded by beautiful flowers and featuring a quote from *The Winter's Tale*.

"How far away are we?" asks Chris.

Ella stares out the window looking for street signs. "Five minutes."

In the stop-start traffic, her mind goes to her childhood, watching Shakespeare in the Park with her father and big brother. Renting remote-control boats at the pond, Shane standing too close to the water's edge, even then flirting with danger. The two of them climbing the rocks, Dad calling after them to be careful.

The cab pulls up at Seventy-Second and Central Park West. Ella pays the driver and they vault out of the car.

She looks about. Another image comes to her. During breaks from college, trolling the park after midnight. A perilous endeavor, even in the much safer era of NYC. Essentially, tempting someone to try it. She'd find the darkest sections—the Ramble, the North Woods, the ruins—and walk alone. Pepper spray at the ready, she'd think: *go ahead, just you try.* It was her way to take back control, but it never eradicated the fear in her bones.

She stands close to Chris, examining the phone, then walks ahead of him.

On the screen, Mr. Nirvana is talking again: "This is the Whisper Bench, one of twelve secrets of the park I'll cover in the next twelve hours. All night in Central Park!"

The vlogger places the camera at one end of the curved stone bench then goes to the far end, his back to the camera. In a soft voice, he says, "The secret here is that if you whisper on this end, you can hear it all the way over there where my camera is. Can you hear me?"

"This way." Ella yanks Chris toward the Whisper Bench, just west of Belvedere Castle, which she marveled at as a girl.

As they run, Chris looks down at the screen, then up at their surroundings, then down again. They're not the only ones tracking Nirvana. They need to find him before his fans chase him off.

"There!"

Chris points at a figure. The man is holding up a camera that has a light mounted to it, shining like a spotlight in the darkness.

The man is about twenty yards away. They're getting closer. Chris stops unexpectedly, seemingly lost in thought. Like this is a moment he's dreamed about, and it's about to happen.

The light disappears; the vlogger either turned it off or rounded the corner. The livestream has a slight delay. Ella looks up from the screen to Chris.

"He's just around the corner ahead. You ready?"

Chris drags a hand slowly over his face. Ella is concerned. He's still looking ashen, slightly out of it. He's concussed and the exertion might even be dangerous.

"I'm ready," he says. "Are you?"

It's a good question, one she doesn't know the answer to. What will she do if this is *Him*? And what if he *is* the killer—isn't approaching him dangerous? It's dawned on her that Mr. Nirvana is in the U.S. at the same time as the ice cream murders. A dreadful coincidence or something else?

Chris is searching her face. Her nerves are on fire, she's almost sick with unease. She decides that it's time to confront her fears. She starts by saying *His* name for the first time in fifteen years: "Vince Whitaker."

Chris looks at her, confused.

Ella grabs his arm and they run toward the man.

CHAPTER 63
CHRIS

The moment of truth.

Mr. Nirvana is holding up his camera, narrating, his back turned to them. So close now.

Chris looks at Ella. Behind her steely resolve, he sees trepidation. He realizes that for him, this could be a reunion with a long-lost family member, a fabled hero in his story. For her, it's something else entirely. A reunion, of sorts, yes. But with someone she's long believed shattered her life.

He takes her hand, squeezes it. "You don't have to come."

She catches his gaze. "No, I do."

They face one another and, with a mutual nod, walk hand-in-hand toward Mr. Nirvana.

His back is still to them, the camera aimed at a castle-like structure. He's saying something to his viewers, his fans. Chris sees a few park dwellers up ahead pointing to Mr. Nirvana as well. They're not the only people who've found him.

"Vince," Chris calls out.

The man doesn't respond, but Chris swears there's a nearly indiscernible reaction, a hitch in the man's step.

They near the vlogger, who continues narrating his livestream. He has the same build as Vince. His voice sounds familiar, but it has been so long.

"Vince!" Chris says, louder. He feels Ella's grip on his hand tighten.

The man spins around. "Sorry, bro. I don't know who you're looking for, but I'm in the middle of filming."

After so many years, longing for this moment, practicing what he would say, how he would say it, how he would manage to hold back the tears and the pain and the loss, and embrace the brother who kept him safe, the older sibling who insisted that Chris work hard to find a way out, to find nirvana.

At last, that day is here.

But it's not Vince.

CHAPTER 64

Chris and Ella walk in silence through the park, hung-over from the booze and raw emotion. Disappointment swells in Chris's chest. Ella paces trancelike next to him. Neither has said anything in a long time.

Ella's phone chimes. She examines the caller ID, hesitates like she's considering ignoring the call. "It's my mother," she tells Chris. "She *never* calls, so I'd better take this." She puts the phone to her ear.

Chris watches as her face tightens with concern.

"Right now?"

An ambulance, siren blaring, barrels by. Ella puts a finger in her ear, anxious to hear whatever her mother's saying. Her tone becomes more panicked. "What's going on? Is something— Yes. I'm in the city." She listens. "Okay, I'll meet him at the apartment." She clicks off.

"Everything okay?"

"I'm not sure. I've never heard my mom sound so frantic. She needs me to come home. She's having a car pick me up at our apartment."

Ella and Chris arrive at her mother's estate in Summit at nine-thirty. Chris stares at the grounds, taken aback for a moment. Amid the grandeur, there's a fleet of law-enforcement vehicles. A loud rattle of generators powering portable floodlights fills the night air.

Ella lowers the limo's privacy barrier. "What the hell's going on, Charles?" she asks the driver.

"You should talk to your mother," the driver says.

Ella looks at Chris. She appears rattled, disoriented. Chris decides he should take charge of the situation, which is crazy because he remains rattled and disoriented, himself, not to mention concussed.

"Let's go see what's going on," he says.

They walk up the steps to the porticoed entrance and are stopped at the front doors by an agent wearing a blue windbreaker.

"I'm sorry, Miss, but I'm not permitted to let anyone—"

"The hell you aren't," says an older woman from behind the agent, Ella's mother, Chris presumes.

Behind her are two men in expensive suits—lawyers, Chris is certain. The gray-haired attorney puts a hand on Ella's mother's shoulder but she shrugs it off.

The lawyer addresses the agent. "The warrant is for the exterior only." He says it with the calm confidence of the powerful. A lawyer of some stature, though Chris doesn't recognize him. "There's no reason to bar my client's daughter from the house. They can stay on the main level, out of the way, like Ms. Monroe."

Chris realizes that the agents are executing a search warrant. What the hell? He peers out over the estate grounds. The lights are clustered in a section that's fronted by what looks like lattices for a rose garden.

The young agent makes a call, then motions for Ella to go inside.

"Who're you?" the agent asks Chris.

Ella says, "He's my lawyer."

The agent relents and waves Chris along with her.

Inside the mansion, Ella's mother, a distinguished and commanding figure, gives Chris a dismissive once-over, then turns to her lawyers. "I need a moment with my daughter." Without waiting for assent, she pushes through the imposing door to what looks like a library. Ella follows her in and the door bangs shut.

Chris turns to the two lawyers. "What's all this? A search warrant? What are they looking for?"

In a hushed tone, the older lawyer says, "They're looking for trouble." He hands Chris a sheaf of papers. The warrant and supporting affidavit. "And I'm afraid they just may find it."

CHAPTER 65
ELLA

"What the hell's going on, Mom?"

"Sit," Phyllis says, motioning to the leather chair. The library is softly lit, but tonight it has the eerie feel of an old Hitchcock movie.

Ella lacks the energy to fight. She collapses into her father's favorite chair.

Phyllis walks over to the bar and pours them both a drink. She seems to be searching for the words, which by itself worries Ella. It's not like Phyllis to be at a loss for words. Her wealth has given her the confidence, no, the sense of entitlement, to say whatever comes to mind, without filter.

"They're digging up the garden," she says.

"Dad's garden? What in the world . . . ?"

Phyllis sits, takes a deep breath. "New Year's Eve. I should've been there for you."

Ella's confused. This isn't the time for belated apologies. Federal agents have raided the grounds.

"After what happened with your brother," Phyllis continues, "I shut down. But your father, he got angry."

Ella never saw him that way. Yes, Dad was different after what happened to Shane. More assertive with her mother, more independent from her. It seemed he'd finally gotten out from under Phyllis's heavy thumb. But Ella never saw him as angry. Sad, yes. A man who cried in the dark in this very chair. And in the garden.

She has an immediate sense of dread. *In the garden.*

"What are they looking for?"

"He loved you so much," Phyllis says, avoiding the question.

"What are they *looking* for?" Ella repeats, more urgently.

Phyllis hesitates for a moment. "When they released that boy from jail—it released something in your father. I'd never seen him like that. You were still recovering and it was just too much for your father to take."

"What are they looking for?" Ella asks a third time, her voice quivering because she thinks she knows.

"That night, I heard him on the phone talking to the other fathers. The religious one always got your father fired up." Her mother coughs a laugh. "Your father didn't spend a day in church in all the years we were married, but that man with his eye-for-an-eye scripture talk . . ."

Ella braces for the devastating news she knows is coming.

"All I know is, the night before that boy supposedly ran off your father and some men were in the garden."

"What men?"

Phyllis simply looks at her. "He came inside late, covered in dirt, drenched in sweat. Like he'd been—"

"Digging." Ella's own voice sounds hollow and distant.

"I should've done more. After you left for college, your father fell into another depression. He came to me, said he was going to turn himself in," her mother says. "He couldn't live with the guilt of what they'd done."

Ella is having a hard time processing.

Her mother continues, "I told him it would devastate you, that you couldn't take any more. I begged him not to turn himself in."

"And he *didn't*," Ella says. "He took his own life."

"He did that to protect you. He must've thought it was the only way to end the pain, to protect you from knowing what he'd done."

Ella stares at her mother with disgust.

"I had no idea he would . . . I was desperate, Eloise. I didn't know what to do. I tried to get your father to talk to a psychiatrist, to talk to his brother. I even called that teacher you worshipped so much and asked him to try to talk some sense into your father. To explain what turning himself in would do to you."

Ella does a double take. "You mean Mr. Steadman? He talked to Dad about—"

There's a loud knock on the library door.

It's an agent. The pregnant woman Ella met at Corky's. Agent Keller. They've found what they were digging for. She's not smug, she looks more sad than anything.

"Ms. Monroe, I'd like to ask you some questions," the agent says to Ella's mother.

This time the lawyer interjects. "Phyllis, I strongly advise you to not answer any questions. At least right now," he adds.

"What he said," Phyllis tells the agent.

Keller nods. "How about you, Ella?"

As she asks this, Chris walks into the library. He's not looking well. His skin is ashen, beaded in sweat, and he winces at the light. But he manages to get out the words: "She has nothing to say."

The agent gazes at Chris. "I know you think you're helping, Christopher, but I don't think you're in the best position to—"

"It's my brother's body you just found in an unmarked grave, so I'm in the absolute best position to say whatever I want." He reaches out for Ella's hand, and she takes it. "We're leaving."

For a moment, Ella's back on the sidewalk near Coney Island, the last time a man took her hand in the face of a threat. But this time she's not the one being protected.

She's the protector.

CHAPTER 66
KELLER

Keller and Arpeggio stand under the artificial light outside a taped-off perimeter surrounding the dig site. The FBI's Emergency Response Team members look like space travelers in their white coveralls, orange duct tape sealing the seams between the suits and their gloves and rubber boots. Keller remembers wearing a similar getup during her forensic training in Tennessee at the Body Farm. The team has set up a grid and is slowly excavating the soil, layer by layer, sifting dirt through a large, boxlike sieve for evidence.

Skeletal remains are visible now, elevated, as the ERT slowly searches the levels below.

It's a slow process, recovering every bone fragment, every thread of clothing, every piece of trace evidence.

"I'd love to see Rusty Whitaker's face when he learns we found his son," Joe Arpeggio says. "He almost got a sweetheart deal."

Keller gives him a fleeting smile. It would be much more gratifying if the remains of a young man weren't in that hole. If she hadn't just faced the deceased's brother, who's already been through so much, or Ella, whose father was one of the men who put Vince Whitaker in that hole.

"How'd you get him to crack?" Arpeggio asks.

"Who?"

"Mandy Young's father."

After the meeting with Rusty, something had troubled Keller: how could the old man be so confident about the precise location of his son? Vince had eluded capture for fifteen years and was likely continually on the move. So how could Rusty be so sure? More to the point, why was he willing to condition a plea deal on the authorities finding Vince first? That's when it dawned on Keller. Rusty could only be that certain if he knew Vince wasn't going anywhere.

Because he was dead.

That's when the pixels from the last three days came together. Chris's account of the last night he saw his brother. Vince in his living room with a group of men, one of them twitchy and agitated. It reminded Keller of her meeting with Mandy Young's father at the insurance company. His demeanor and his instant refusal to speak with them. Katie McKenzie's father had acted the same way. Two fathers refusing to help try to catch the man accused of killing their daughters. And something Candy O'Shaughnessy's mother said came back to her. *"The fathers were all macho, you know? Like they were gonna break into the jail and beat the kid up."*

Keller had decided to cut to the chase and confront Walter Young. She'd told him that Rusty Whitaker had

turned on him, that they knew the fathers had killed
Vince, so his only chance for leniency was to come
clean. Most people don't realize that law enforcement
can lie to suspects. And Keller had no problem with this
lie. Particularly because it worked. Walter Young broke
down and told her everything. About three devastated
fathers deciding to take justice into their own hands.
They'd arrived at the house initially to give Vince a
beating. Force him to confess. But soon the young man
was in the trunk of Mr. Monroe's car, the other men following him to the estate.

They brought Vince, still alive, to the garden, where
they beat him bloody, never getting the confession they
wanted, the confession they *needed* in order to avenge
their sweet daughters. Mr. McKenzie had brought a gun.
According to Walter Young, they each took a shot, forg-
ing a union that would ensure that they'd all go down
if any of them ever revealed the secret. The only loose
end was Rusty Whitaker. He'd seen them take Vince.
Mr. Monroe had made a sizable payment to Whitaker to
keep him quiet. Keller suspects that when they dig into
Mr. Monroe's finances, they'll find more than one payment to Rusty Whitaker over the years.

"It didn't take long for him to confess," Keller says.
"Walter Young knew Rusty would turn on them. He actually seemed relieved to get it off his chest. He's been
carrying this around for fifteen years. They all carried
it. Ella's father killed himself in this very garden."

Arpeggio nods.

Keller looks around. None of the other agents are
within earshot. It's a good time to ask Arpeggio about

his relationship with the McKenzie family. She checks her phone to see if Atticus has found any connections between Arpeggio and the Dairy Creamery victims. He texted her earlier that he was chasing a lead:

Might have found something, going to check, call me when you have time.

Her calls have gone straight to Atticus's voice mail. She considers calling again now, but decides it's time to confront Arpeggio.

"They've arrested Katie McKenzie's father."

Arpeggio offers no reaction.

"How do you feel about that?" Keller asks.

Arpeggio narrows his eyes. "Feel about what?"

"Having your old friend's husband arrested for murder."

Arpeggio's jaw pulses, a nearly imperceptible twitch of his mustache. But he says nothing. Arpeggio is a skilled interrogator who understands that it's always the chatty who do themselves in. The quiet ones are the most likely to walk out of interrogation rooms of their own free will.

"I spoke with Katie's mom today," Keller says.

"I know." Arpeggio stares into the night. Past the dig site, past the tennis courts, into the darkness.

"We also talked to Tony Grosso." Keller waits again.

After another expansive silence, Arpeggio says, "The family had been through enough. They didn't need the press making Katie out to be some kind of slut. She was a sweet kid; she just made a mistake."

"And that's why you buried the pregnancy?"

"I didn't bury anything. I just asked Grosso to, you know, keep it out of the reports. I knew it would come out when they caught Vince Whitaker."

"Unless they never found him." Keller moves her eyes to the grave.

Arpeggio turns to her now, anger whitening his features.

"You were close with Katie?" Keller asks.

He sighs impatiently. "Her mom asked me to help when Katie got into trouble. I helped find the lawyer who arranged the adoption."

"Why you?"

"Have you met her father?" Arpeggio shakes his head. "I'll never know why she married that guy."

"So that's the only reason you helped hide the pregnancy?"

Arpeggio gets a confused look on his face. "Why else would I—"

"You were close with Katie . . ."

"Wait, you're not suggesting . . . that's *disgusting.* I can't believe you'd even . . ."

This time it's Keller who's quiet.

"I was a family friend, that's it."

Keller checks her phone. No new messages from Atticus. She decides to bluff.

"You were close with one of the Blockbuster victims. And we found a connection between you and the Dairy Creamery victims."

Arpeggio looks genuinely shocked. "What are you talking about? I didn't know any of them."

Keller regards him.

"Look, do what you've got to do. But I didn't know them. And Katie was basically my niece. Her mom was my best friend's sister, and she asked me to help with things. She was married to a controlling guy, rigid, emotionally abusive. I helped out. Coached Katie's Little League team. Taught her to drive when she flunked out of driving school. Stuff like that. She was a kid, for Christ's sake."

Keller stares at Arpeggio for a long time, and she reaches a singular conclusion.

She believes him.

CHAPTER 67
ELLA

Ella tears out of the garage in a 1970 Mercedes 280SL, her father's favorite car among his small fleet. It's a convertible and her hair is dancing in the wind.

Chris still seems out of it. A punch-drunk expression, his body swaying with the curves that Ella's taking too fast.

Her universe is folding. She's in another dimension. A *Twilight Zone* episode. The monster she's feared for so long was buried two hundred yards from her wing of the family home. Her father—the one who always tried the hardest to understand her—collapsed under the weight of his crime. It wasn't about her brother's death, the attack on Ella, or even his controlling wife. It was grief and shame for taking a life.

"Are you okay?" she says to Chris, whose world must also be spinning counterclockwise. In the past twenty-four hours, his mother and brother have both been found, their murdered bodies hidden for years.

Chris holds up some papers. "I read the search warrant. The fathers. They . . ." His face is colorless, expression distant, as if imagining his brother's last moments.

"How did they find out where he was?" Ella asks.

"One of the fathers confessed," Chris says. "The warrant says my father knew, wanted to cut a deal, but one of the fathers flipped. Told them where to find the body." He swallows a sob. "The last time I saw my brother, he was talking with a group of men. Your dad and the others. My father was there. I thought it was a drug deal to make some cash so he could go on the run. But it wasn't. It was an abduction. And Vince knew. In his final moments, he was trying to keep me safe."

Ella screeches around a bend in the road, imagining her father as part of the mob that kidnapped and killed a teenage boy.

"Where are we going?" Chris asks.

Ella doesn't know where she's going. She doesn't know how to process it all. She and the broken man next to her have lived their entire adult lives in the shadow of New Year's Eve 1999. They're both the children of murderers.

And they both loved Vince Whitaker.

All at once, she knows where to go. She hears Phyllis's voice: *"I tried to get your father to talk to a psychiatrist, to talk to his brother. I even called that teacher you worshipped so much and asked him to try to talk some sense into your father."*

Soon, she's in Asbury. A residential neighborhood. She pulls up in front of a modest ranch-style home.

"I need to talk to someone," she says to Chris.

He nods, unbuckles his seat belt to go with her.

"I actually need to do this alone." A man she's trusted, a mentor, her support system through it all, lied to her. Knew something devastating and did nothing. And she needs to understand why.

She hands Chris the keys to the car. "You can take it. I can Uber."

"I can wait, if that's okay?"

She nods. She's starting to worry about him. He's pale, clammy. "Are you sure you're okay?"

"I'll be fine." Chris puts his head back and closes his eyes.

Ella walks up the driveway. There's a beat-up red convertible—a two-seater that's seen better days—in the driveway. He has a guest, his girlfriend, maybe.

She knocks on the door. There's movement inside, then a delay before the door opens.

"Ella?" Mr. Steadman says. He's flustered. Maybe she interrupted him. A romantic evening, perhaps. She realizes that she's never been inside his house.

"I'm sorry to come unannounced. But I need to talk with you about something, and I—"

She stops. A wave of electricity vibrates through her. Instantly, she's drenched in panic sweat. It takes her brain a second to catch up with her eyes. There's a man behind Mr. Steadman, staggering toward the door. His suit jacket and dress shirt are steeped in red.

"Run," the man says. "Run!"

"Oh my god, what's going—"

"Oh, Ella . . ." Mr. Steadman spins around and rams a fist at the man's abdomen. When he pulls his hand away, it's covered in blood. Ella realizes that it wasn't

Mr. Steadman's fist, it was a knife. The man stiffens, takes in a sharp breath, and slumps to the floor.

Ella opens her mouth to scream but her voice box is paralyzed.

Steadman seizes her by the arm and yanks her inside.

CHAPTER 68
KELLER

Keller is back at the Union County Prosecutor's Office, which is mostly empty at this hour. Atticus hasn't returned her texts, so she imagines he's holed up in his office, immersed in his research.

She walks down the dark hallway, her footfalls echoing, her shadow conjuring the word *waddle* in her mind.

She opens his office door and slaps on the lights.

Not here. Maybe he took off for the night, though it seems out of character. The kid works really hard.

She sees the empty Tupperware container on his desk, smiles as she recalls his mom bringing him dinner.

He was here, working late. Doing some additional research, it seems. The box of yearbooks they'd taken from the school sits on the floor. On his desktop, two yearbooks lie side by side, each opened to the last pages, where local businesses run advertisements. One of the yearbooks is from 1999, the other from last year.

Glancing around for other clues, she notices that he's

removed one of the photos from his Blockbuster crime wall—the shot of the cars parked in the lot of the video store. It's on the desk next to the yearbooks, the push-pin hole dimpling the old shot. The photo has always taken her breath away. The lot empty except for the vehicles of the slain employees. Its black-and-white finish only adds to the desolation of the image. One of the cars has a STUDENT DRIVER sticker on the bumper, the last vestige of innocence lost.

Atticus left a magnifying glass next to the photo. She smiles, imagining him playing Sherlock Holmes. She holds the magnifying glass over the photo, enlarging the video store in the background. She makes out shelves of movies, and part of the Blockbuster logo, a giant movie ticket, painted on the back wall. There's no one in the frame. The store is empty.

She moves the magnifying glass to the cars. There's no one inside any of them either. *What were you looking at, Atticus?*

She hovers the glass over each car, zooming out, then back in. Then she sees it. Small lettering on the STUDENT DRIVER bumper sticker. It reads, STEADY AS THEY GO DRIVING SCHOOL.

Then Keller's attention turns back to the yearbooks, both opened to local business ad pages. And each has an ad for STEADY AS THEY GO.

It's then that Keller realizes the yearbooks aren't from the same school. One is from Union High, where most of the Blockbuster victims attended, the other from Sacred Heart Catholic School, where Katie McKenzie went to school. Then she remembers something Arpeggio said when she'd confronted him: *"I taught Katie to drive when she flunked out of driving school."*

She thumbs through some phone records Atticus was also looking at. They were for the ice cream store victims, Madison and Hannah Sawyer. Earlier, Atticus had said that the older sister, Madison, the one who'd had a dispute with Jesse Duvall, was fighting with her sister about something. She was threatening to tell their mother.

Keller flips through the pages, which are sorted by day. Atticus has dog-eared the pages for every Tuesday and Thursday. On each of those pages, he circled the times from 5 to 7 p.m. Keller doesn't understand. There was no cell activity on Hannah Sawyer's phone on those days and times—some of the only times the girl wasn't on her phone. What was Hannah doing every Tuesday and Thursday from five to seven?

Then it hits her. She quickly calls Atticus's mobile.

Right to voice mail.

She clicks on the number for Joe Arpeggio.

He answers on the first ring. "Look, I don't know if there's much more for us to—"

"It's not about that," Keller interrupts. "Hannah Sawyer. Her phone records. She didn't use her phone every Tuesday and Thursday. Do you know why?"

"I'm not sure what that—"

"It's important," she says firmly. "Can you call her parents?"

"There's just the mom, but yeah. What's—"

"Right now," Keller insists.

There's a long silence. "Sure, yeah, hang on, I'll conference her in."

Keller's pulse races as she waits to be reconnected.

When Arpeggio comes back on the line, he's on with Hannah and Madison Sawyer's mother. "I'm sorry to bother you so late," he says, "but we had a question that we hoped you could answer for us."

The woman's voice sounds tired, drained. "Whatever I can do to help."

"I have Agent Keller from the FBI on the line with me, I'll let her explain."

Silence.

"Hello, yes, just a quick question," Keller says. "On Tuesday and Thursday nights, we wondered if there's a reason Hannah wouldn't have used her cell phone. Maybe you all didn't allow screen time on those days or there was—"

"She had driver's ed on those nights," says Ms. Sawyer.

Bumps ripple down Keller's arms. "Is that through the school? Or—"

"Kind of. It's a private business. But it's run by the school's principal, Mr. Steadman."

CHAPTER 69

Keller's heart hasn't stopped thumping since she raced out of the office and sped to the home of Principal Steadman. The same words keep scrolling through her head on a loop. *I should wait for backup, I should wait for backup, I should wait for backup.*

She can only pray that Atticus didn't already make the same mistake that she's making now.

But her heart drops when she sees the car parked in Steadman's driveway: an MG convertible with a faded red paint job, soft-top repaired with duct tape.

Arpeggio's on his way. Stan's sending the troops. They should be here any minute now.

But she can't stop thinking about Atticus's mom: *"Keep my boy safe."*

She steps to the front window; the drapes are drawn. She hears a scream. A commotion.

I should wait for backup.

A jolt of fright tears through her as the garage door roars open.

She sees Steadman skulk out of the garage. His body language reads angry, frantic. Keller feels yet another spike of adrenaline as she takes in his shirt: covered in blood. She ducks behind the shrubs awkwardly and watches.

Steadman fumbles with keys and climbs into Atticus's car. He's tall and he has to adjust the seat in the compact sports vehicle. The engine rattles to life and he pulls it into the garage.

He's hiding Atticus's car. There's only one reason for that.

I should wait for backup, I should wait for backup.

She pictures Bob's face. How upset he was when she charged into the custodian's house and garnered her fifteen minutes of fame.

But if Atticus is still alive, he won't be for long. Maybe . . .

She hurries quietly to the garage door. It starts to roll down. She pulls her service weapon and holds it in front of her with both hands as she ducks under the closing door.

Steadman's eyes darken when he climbs out of the car.

"Hands in the air, don't move!" Keller shouts.

The garage door closes behind her. She sees Steadman's own car also in the confined space, its trunk open but not empty.

A muffled wail comes from the woman tied up inside the trunk. She's screaming in terror. It's Ella Monroe. Her eye is swollen, mouth covered in tape.

Steadman takes advantage of the distraction and drops low behind the car.

Keller fires a shot that misses, allowing the principal to scurry through the door leading into the house, slamming it shut behind him.

Keller races to Ella. She removes the duct tape covering her mouth.

Ella's words come in rasps. "There's a man, Mr. Steadman stabbed him." She's hyperventilating. "He lured Chris inside . . . he hit him so hard."

"Slow down," Keller says, taking an exaggerated breath through her nose and releasing it from her mouth.

Ella mirrors her. "Mr. Steadman, he's not who . . . He's been pretending . . ."

Keller yanks at the tape binding Ella's wrists. It's too tight. She looks around the garage, spots some pruning shears. She races over, scoops them up. She cuts the tape from Ella's wrists. Hands her the shears to cut the tape around her ankles. "You get free and you get out and run. Can you do that?"

Ella nods.

Keller moves away from the car, toward the door. Steadman slammed it shut, but it's open now, the interior dark. She hears a distant shuffling. Raising her weapon in a double grip she aims into the house. If she has a clear shot, so does he. The next instant she pays the price for being a second too slow. A piercing agony splits through her chest just under her shoulder. She slams against the garage wall.

Pain, excruciating pain. Her eyes move to the source of the agony. *What in the holy fuck?* An arrow is protruding from her.

Keller doesn't know why there is an arrow, or why

Steadman is so good with it, but she does know it's silent. And lethal. And the bastard was aiming for her heart.

She sees Steadman through the door, nocking in another arrow. She gets off a shot and he retreats inside the house.

The pain is coming in waves now and is threatening to overwhelm her. She grits her teeth. She won't let it happen. *I should wait for backup.* But Atticus is inside. If he's been stabbed, he could be alive. And there's Chris Whitaker . . .

She drags herself back to Ella, who looks completely paralyzed by fear.

"What are you still doing here?" Keller whispers. "You need to get out now."

"But Chris is in there."

"I'll get him. You get out. Head up to the corner, out of sight. Help is coming. Wait for them. Bring them here."

Keller helps Ella to her feet and pushes her toward the garage door.

Keller then takes the shears and cuts off the back end of the arrow with the tail feathers. She can't angle the shears around to her back to snip off the head, so that'll have to stay along with the part that's inside her, keeping her from bleeding out.

She's back at the door and inches her way into the house, gun barrel up and ready. She finds herself in the kitchen now, running on instinct, smelling blood. Too much blood.

She sweeps her gun unsteadily from left to right, her

breathing coming hard. The pain is severe. It's imping-
ing on her vision, pulsing light and dark.

"Atticus!" she cries out.

There's a noise from upstairs.

She moves to the living room. On the mantel are
photos of Steadman. He's in hunting gear. Posing with
a dead lion in one shot. A slaughtered elephant in another.

What in the . . . ? How can this be the same man
adored by his students? The support system for Ella all
those years. She thinks back to the Whitaker file, the
key evidence, the knife found in the locker at the school
where Steadman works. The phone in Jesse Duvall's
hospital room, where Steadman visited her. Katie Mc-
Kenzie, pregnant by an older guy. A controlling, obsessive older guy. Katie didn't flunk out of driving school,
she quit to get away from her instructor. She thinks of
Hannah Sawyer fighting with her big sister about a secret; a relationship with an older man. Someone who
listened, spent hours alone in a car with her, made her
feel special.

She hears movement upstairs again.

Then something terrifying happens, some *Silence of
the Lambs*–level shit.

The lights go out. The place is pitch-black.

CHAPTER 70
KATIE

"You can't do this to me—I can't go on without you."

"We've been through this, Dale. It's for the best. For both of us," Katie says. They're tucked behind the video return receptacle in the parking lot. They've been there for nearly ten minutes. She needs to get back inside. But he's acting erratically. One minute penitent, the next aggressive, raising his voice, angry.

"If this is about what happened—the baby—it's in a better place. It's better off with—"

"*She,*" Katie says, "she's not an *it*." She says this with more edge than she's ever used with him. Katie hadn't given the beautiful pink bundle a name. She hadn't earned the right to name her. But the couple had named her: Jessica Marie Duvall. Not that she'll tell him that. She remembers writing her name on the note. *Dear Jessica.* The strange feeling of writing to someone you love more than your own life, but who you'll never see again. It was a condition of the adoption, that they'd give her the note when she turned eighteen.

"Tell me this isn't about Vince Whitaker," Dale says. "I can understand you being upset about giving up the brat, but Whitaker is trash."

"It's not about him. Or anyone. It was wrong, Dale— you understand that . . ."

"What I understand is that I saw Whitaker here tonight." He twists around, points to the back of the building.

Katie doesn't understand. She hasn't seen Vince tonight. And if he's been at the store, how does Dale know that? And how long has he been out here? Just waiting for her to empty the bins. How does he even know it's her job to empty the return bins? Unless he's been out here before. Watching.

"I didn't see Vince tonight. And, anyway, I told you, we're just friends."

"Pfft."

"I need to get back inside. I'm working."

"You'll be eighteen soon, and we can find a way . . . People will understand, if we give it time, we can—"

"I don't love you. And I need you to leave me alone." There, she said it. She looks around. They're shielded by the large bin. When she'd told him about the pregnancy, he'd hit her, harder than ever before. She's worried he might lash out now.

He grabs her arm. Pulls her close. His face dark with rage.

"Everything okay?" the voice says behind her. She turns her head. Stevie. Thank God for Stevie.

Dale drops her arm. Pastes on a fake smile. He's so good at that.

"Everything's fine," Katie says, her tone forced.

"Oh, okay," Stevie says. "Ah, a customer said someone was fighting or something over here and—"

"No, we're fine," Katie says. "I'll be right in."

Stevie looks torn. "You sure?" He pushes his shoulders back on his thin frame. He looks diminutive next to Dale's broad-shouldered stance.

"Really."

He reluctantly heads back to the store.

"I need to get back," she says.

"I need you, Katie."

"I'm sorry."

Fury fills his face again. "If you think I'm just going to—"

A voice from behind cuts him off. Candy and Mandy have charged outside.

"What are you going to do, *Dale*?" Candy emphasizes his first name, like it's forbidden. He's a teacher, after all.

Dale turns white.

"Yeah," Mandy chimes in, nodding, like: *You'd better back the fuck off.* It's clear what they mean. They know everything and can ruin him.

Candy says, "So you'd best leave her the fuck alone."

Steadman glowers at her. Then: "Or what?" His face is nearly trembling.

"Or your world will be tipped upside down."

And with that, Candy laces her arm through Katie's left arm, Mandy through Katie's right, and they march her back inside the Blockbuster.

CHAPTER 71
KELLER

Keller's hand is shaking, her breathing is labored and loud. She edges forward slowly in the darkness, her gun outstretched. The pain from the arrow shoots down her left side, and up into her skull, where it explodes in bursts. Wincing, she manages to pull her phone from her pocket, and clicks on the flashlight.

She has a jolt of terror when she sees him. Steadman is several feet away, as still as a stone. Waiting for her. He's holding something. It looks like a spear. His arm is cocked. She staggers to the right as he releases the weapon, whatever it is. It glides swiftly by, slamming into the wall with a sickening thud.

Before she has time to react, something hard batters down on her arm, her gun discharges, then her head is pounded into the wall. She's disoriented, on the floor. She sees nothing, she feels around for the gun.

That's when she feels the body. It's stiff. She wipes her eyes, tries to adjust to the dark, but it's hopeless. Still, she feels the skinny tie, the buttons from the suit jacket.

Atticus.

Only terror overcomes the wave of heartbreak.

A sliver of light comes from her phone, which was knocked to the floor.

She's on her side, shirt drenched in blood from the arrow. She's going into shock. The twins seem unusually still.

She should've waited for backup. *I'm sorry,* she tells her twins. *Move, please move,* she tells them.

She feels nothing.

She can only listen now, pray for the sound of sirens.

Then she feels it. The familiar kick under her ribs. A tiny foot. Feet.

They're telling her not to give up.

She calls out. "Dale Steadman, it's over. They know about you and Katie McKenzie, about you and Hannah Sawyer."

"I don't think so," the voice says, peculiarly calm. "I came home and Ella Monroe and her boyfriend were in my house. Everyone knows she's a basket case. Your colleague arrived and they stabbed him."

A ray of light from outside crosses his face. "You came to warn me." He approaches her. He's holding a hunting knife.

Dale Steadman is delusional. His story will never hold water. But it will be too late for Keller before he understands this.

As he leans over her, she closes her eyes.

But they pop open to the sound of a roar in the dark, a man's voice, desperate and primal, and she sees a form fly across the room.

Steadman crashes to the floor.

She hears a struggle, furniture cracking, and somehow climbs to her feet, the pain nearly causing her to black out.

Headlights from a car outside fill the room. Chris Whitaker is on the floor with Steadman, bloody and battered and fighting for the knife. Before Keller can locate her gun, Chris wails in agony as the blade thrusts into his chest.

Steadman pushes him off and locks eyes with Keller. She's nearly at the gun, but the room is moving sideways. She's unsteady on her feet. She manages to scoop up the gun, her index finger sliding over the trigger. But a split second later, Steadman slams her against the wall, the pain blinding as the arrow touches the wall and pushes in deeper.

When Keller's vision returns, she's lost hold of the gun, and Steadman stands before her clasping a knife.

"It's over," he says, his dead eyes staring into hers.

But Keller isn't listening to him. She reaches behind her and pulls out the arrow. Before Steadman's mind can fathom what she's up to, she rams the arrowhead upward into the soft triangle under his chin.

He gags and topples into her.

Keller tries to push him away, but can't.

She can feel the blood gushing from her now. She feels faint.

Still pressed against her, Steadman is releasing a horrible gurgling sound. He lurches forward, puts his hands around her neck.

She's trying to gasp for air but he's squeezing too

tight. She's losing consciousness. But at once his body jerks, he releases his hold, and he crumples to the floor. Behind him, Ella still clutches the spear that is jutting from Steadman's back until she too hits the floor.

The next images come in waves, as if under a strobe light.

The room filling with figures.

Stan.

Hal.

Arpeggio.

A medic with a concerned look on her face.

Keller sees the darkened ceiling . . . she's being carried away on a stretcher. She shifts painfully to look around her.

She passes Atticus, who isn't moving . . . Chris, who isn't moving . . . Ella, who isn't moving.

And then everything goes dark.

EPILOGUE

Keller waves to Bob, who's pushing a double stroller that nearly takes up the entire sidewalk. He has an over-stuffed diaper bag slung over his shoulder. She's told him he doesn't need to do this, but he brings the twins for lunch near her office every Wednesday. It's a production, getting them seated at the diner, but he insists.

After the nightmare of folding the stroller, wiping down the table, setting up the baby seats, and having toys at the ready before one of them starts up, they finally look at their menus.

"You don't have to do this, you know," she says.

"I get an afternoon away from the moms at the park, *and* I get to see my favorite G-woman, why would I not?" He's wearing a concert T-shirt and for a moment she's taken back to their first date. Him fawning over her job, never once talking about himself, a rarity in the dating scene. He left his job shortly after the kids were born. When Keller was in the hospital that terrible night—when things were touch and go for both her and the twins—he told her he'd made a deal with God. If they got through this, all of them, then he would dedicate every second of his life to taking care of his family. He's a tad dramatic, her husband.

"I have news," Keller says.

He looks at her, waiting.

"Stan is transferring to the New York City field office. He'll still be a SAC, but they're grooming him to be the A-DIC."

"Who came up with all these acronyms? They sound like jobs on a porn set."

Keller smiles despite herself. "He wants me to come with him."

Bob thinks about this. "What do you want to do?"

"I wanted to talk with you."

"I'm a moron. Why would you want to do that?"

She smiles again, swats him with her menu. "I'm serious. It will mean more hours. A longer commute. You'll have to take on more with the kids." She gazes lovingly at the twins, who each have a fistful of Cheerios from the container Bob put in front of them.

"You didn't answer my question. What do *you* want to do?"

"Stan said I could focus on financial crimes. The cases are super-interesting. It's the best white-collar crime team at the Bureau."

"No psycho high school principals?"

She shakes her head in exasperation. "That reminds me: Jesse Duvall was on *Good Morning America* this morning. She's getting a lot of attention for that piece she wrote in the *New Yorker* about the case. She mentions me in the segment."

Bob's eyes light up. He's already on his phone, pulling up the clip. "It's a long interview, I'll watch the whole thing later, but where does she mention you?"

"Near the end."

Bob fiddles with the device, fast-forwarding, then holds the phone so they both can see the screen. The twins are watching them, seemingly fascinated.

Jesse Duvall sits on a veranda, a handsome estate in the background. She looks like a movie star.

The host says, "So the killer, he says something extraordinarily creepy to you during the attack, the same words he said fifteen years prior to the lone survivor of the Blockbuster killings?"

"That's right."

"Why do you think he did that? Or let you survive, for that matter?"

"I think he wanted to divert attention from himself. At the time, everyone thought Vince Whitaker was the Blockbuster killer, so he thought they might think Vince killed the employees of the ice cream store. But his backup plan, which was what ended up carrying the day, was that the authorities would believe that *I* committed the crime."

"Why would he think that?"

"Because he knew I was researching the Blockbuster case. He didn't know why, but I'd met with him when I was having a problem with some girls at school. We talked about my interest in journalism. I was like, 'You

were a teacher and knew all these kids from Blockbuster, tell me about them.'"

Bob pauses the clip. "Does she get into the thing about
her teacher?"

"Briefly," Keller says, "she just mentions that after
her *New Yorker* story other girls came forward and
creepy Chad Parke was finally charged and pled guilty."

Bob nods, clicks PLAY.

The host asks, "Why do you think he killed so many?
And there was a big gap in time here, what do you
think triggered him to do it again?"

Jesse seems to ponder this. "I think he killed my
mother because he was obsessed with her. If he couldn't
have her, no one could. I think he killed her friends at
the store because they knew about their relationship
and threatened to tell. I think the same thing happened
with the Sawyer sisters. Hannah wanted out of the relationship and told her older sister when he was stalking
her. Madison was going to tell their mom. He must've
been watching the ice cream store and saw me go in
there and decided to take the opportunity. As for the
time between the crimes, we'll never know."

The host says, "Do you think he knew you were his
daughter?"

"I don't think so. But I don't think it would've
changed anything if he did."

"All these years, he was a monster in plain sight."

"I struggled with that a lot. Shouldn't I have put the
pieces together sooner? Could I have prevented what

happened at the ice cream store? Then a wise FBI agent said something to me I'll never forget."

The host waits, an eager expression on her face.

"She said there's a saying, 'The sheep spends its life worried about the wolf, only to be eaten by the farmer.'"

Bob blurts, "Yeah!"

The diner goes quiet for a beat, then the murmur returns. Keller shakes her head.

Looking at the twins, she says, "I'm so happy they're too young to be embarrassed of us yet."

"Embarrassed? Are you crazy, their mama's the wisest new agent at the Manhattan field office."

Keller stares at him a long moment.

"By the way," Bob says, "did Jesse make a bunch of money from the article or something? That's a pretty impressive mansion she's at."

"That's the crazy part. Ella Monroe's mother took her in. I met that woman and, let me tell you, she's a tough one. It could be her chance to do what she should've done with her own daughter, a second chance to get things right."

Keller looks at her husband again. "You're sure about New York?"

"As sure as I am that you're a badass."

"I told you not to call me that." But she can't hold back another smile. She both hates and loves when he calls her Agent Badass.

Hates it because it reminds her of the case that nearly killed her and the twins; loves it because it's Bob's way of showing that—despite his vow, his fears—he won't let their family be defined by the trauma. She also loves it because it reminds her of how lucky they are. That she and Bob have each other. That they're blessed with the love of their lives, Michael Atticus Keller and Heather Attica Keller.

YOUTUBE EXCERPT
The Night Shift Travel Vlog
(10K views)
"Delivering Supplies via Amazon (River)"

EXT. DAYTIME—MAMUSA PORT

A blue ferryboat is docked on a mud bank.
Three wooden planks jut out of the boat to
land.

                    TRAVELER 1 (O.S.)
    We boarded our ferry on the port out-
    side of Iquitos. They let us store
    our scooter and supplies on the first
    deck, which had crates of fish on ice
    and live chickens. It's gonna be an
    adventurous twenty-four hours for
    sure.

The camera turns off, then on. The camera's
weak light captures a crowded top deck lined
with hammocks filled with other travelers.
Someone is snoring loudly.

                    TRAVELER 1 (O.S.)
    A travel tip if you're going to ven-
    ture on the Amazon River via ferry:
    bring earplugs. And bring some snacks.
    The meal service was canceled without
    any explanation tonight.

The camera flips off and on again. It's morning. The scene is of the river: coffee-colored water merging into a nearly black section.

> TRAVELER 1 (O.S.)
> We're nearly at our port. Someone said we know that because the water changed color. They served some type of chicken dish for breakfast—we just hope it wasn't one of the fellas on the lower deck. We've drifted by a few villages and seen some amazing wildlife—parrots and a bunch of different types of birds. Monkeys. We even spotted a pink river dolphin. No piranhas like in the movies, though.

The camera turns black, then on again. A motor scooter drives precariously over a wooden plank to land. The traveler maneuvers up an embankment and gets off the bike.

The camera scans a narrow path, then lands on the motor scooter, which is overloaded with oversized bags of supplies.

> TRAVELER 1 (O.S.)
> It's supposed to be three kilometers that way to the orphanage. These kids have had a rough time, so we've brought some medical supplies, some

clothes, and, of course, some toys.
It's not much, but sometimes it helps
just to show you care.

The traveler is back on the scooter. His
travel companion sits on the back, the bike
seeming like it could topple at any moment
because it's so loaded with supplies. The
camera rotates so it captures both riders in
a selfie.

> TRAVELER 1
> Until next time, fellow travelers,
> this is the Night Shift signing off.
> I'm Chris Ford.

> TRAVELER 2
> And I'm Ella Monroe.

> TRAVELER 1
> Do justice today.

The camera turns off, then back on, showing a
sea of young kids chasing after the sound of
a rattling motor scooter.

FADE TO BLACK

ACKNOWLEDGMENTS

To my wife, Trace, the love of my life and my best friend since I was sixteen years old.

To my children, Jake, Emma, and Aiden, whose mischief over the years has provided fodder for my novels, and whose kindness, empathy, and accomplishments have made their father proud.

To my agent, Lisa Erbach Vance, the best representative an author could ever hope for, one who's become a cherished friend along the way.

To my editor at St. Martin's Minotaur Books, Joe Brosnan, whose vision, talent, and support are unparalleled.

To my other editors: my private editor, Ed Stackler, who helped guide the story and kept me on schedule; my copy editor at St. Martin's, NaNá V. Stoelzle, who fixed all my mistakes; and my first reader (and daughter), Em, who never pulled any punches.

To my marketing and publicity team, Martin Quinn,

Stephen Erickson, and Kayla Janas, who expertly ensure the world knows about my books.

To my TV/film team, Joseph Veltre of the Gersh Agency and ACE Entertainment.

To my friends at Arnold & Porter for their long-standing friendship and support.

To Kimberley Howe and my friends at the International Thriller Writers for helping me and so many writers achieve their dreams.

To writer Barry Lancet for our longtime friendship and his assistance with fight scenes.

To the many professionals who assisted with my research: the FBI's Public Affairs office for advice on Bureau culture and protocol; John Thieszen, M.D., and Marc Futernick, M.D., for medical guidance; Professor R. H. Walton for investigatory insights (and for her outstanding book *Cold Case Homicides*); and former U.S. Attorney for the District of New Jersey Paul Fishman for his expertise on UFAP warrants and the Garden State. All errors are my own. As are the many liberties I took with the culture, legal world, and terrain of Union County, New Jersey.

To travel vloggers Mr. Bald and Simon Wilson, whose travels inspired the adventures of Mr. Nirvana.

To my readers, for giving me the honor of your time and for keeping reading alive.

Read on for an excerpt from

WHAT HAVE WE DONE —

the next exciting novel from Alex Finlay,
available soon in hardcover from Minotaur Books!

PROLOGUE

TWENTY-FIVE YEARS AGO

At the top of a knoll through a break in the trees, five teenagers stand at the edge of a shallow grave. A light rain falls; thunder rumbles in the night sky.

One of the boys raises the gun. It was his idea, after all; he should go first. He aims into the hole, but the gun wobbles in the half-light.

"Do it," another boy says.

But the kid with the gun stands there, arm extended, the rain beading his face, matting his hair.

At last, the only girl in the group reaches for the weapon—the .22 they bought for twenty-two bucks. She swallows, looks at the rest of them. "We agreed," she says. "We all have to." Her eyes return to the pit, and the gun clenched in her hand makes a noise like a firecracker, a faint *pop*.

The girl passes the weapon down the line. And one by one they each take a shot until the gun reaches the last boy. Lightning brightens the sky for a nanosecond. Long enough to see the tears streaming pale vertical lines down his dirty face. He's the only gentle soul at the Savior House group home.

He grips the firearm, his breaths ragged, as his best friend looms over him like the protector he is, laces his finger through the trigger guard on top of the gentle boy's, and another *pop* rends the night.

They all then fall to their knees and drive the wet dirt into the void with their bare hands.

In the dark, the gentle boy utters the words none of them will ever forget:

"What have we done?"

CHAPTER 1
JENNA

"There's my girl," Simon says in his chipper morning voice. It's one of the things Jenna adores about her husband, his unrelenting cheerfulness.

She's back from running her five miles and feeling every one of her thirty-nine years. She kisses Simon, then sits at the kitchen table across from her stepdaughter Lulu, who's eating pancakes, her shiny Mary Janes swinging under the chair. As usual, their Labrador, Peanut Butter, is at the five-year-old's feet, waiting for falling scraps.

Simon stands at the stovetop pouring batter for more flapjacks, wearing the apron that has I HAVE NO IDEA WHAT I'M DOING inscribed on the front.

"I thought you have an early meeting," Jenna says, noticing that he's still in his pajamas. He wears the button-up style like a character from a 1950s sitcom.

"I have time. I need to make sure my girls get the most important meal of the day." He pushes his glasses up on his nose. To most women, the nerdy tax lawyer wouldn't elicit the rush of whatever chemical or emotion was crowding Jenna's chest. But this boring numbers man, white-bread as they come, fills that part of Jenna that was empty for so long. She knows they're an odd match. She catches the looks, the whispers, that she must be in it for the money, the gossipers not realizing that Simon isn't exactly Bill Gates, even if he resembles him. In fact, Jenna's numbered Swiss account dwarfs their modest savings and Simon's 401(k).

Her older stepdaughter, Willow, bursts into the kitchen, backpack slung over her shoulder. She's wearing her high school uniform and customary scowl. The skirt looks shorter than regulation—Jenna's sure she's had it altered—but she's always walking a tightrope with Willow, so she doesn't say anything.

Pick your battles.

"Good morning," Jenna says with exaggerated cheeriness that would give even Simon a run for his money.

Willow mumbles something, opens the refrigerator, sighs at some unstated grocery-store failure on Jenna's part.

"Pancakes?" Simon asks, earnestly. He's immune to the seventeen-year-old's morning gloom.

"Can't. Ride's here."

Jenna says, "I can get you some fruit or something for the road."

Willow gives her a *you can't be serious* look before she leaves the kitchen with another mumble and the front door slams.

Jenna gets it. Willow lost her mother. Jenna knows

what that feels like. Maybe one day they'll be able to talk about it together.

Simon sets a plate in front of Jenna. Smiles. He doesn't ask her what's on her agenda today. He never does. They met on Match.com, a year ago—three years after the girls' biological mother succumbed to cancer. They married six months later to the consternation of Simon's family and friends. *To hell with them all*, he always says, the rare times he curses. *And Willow will come around—just give her time.*

Jenna's not so sure about that.

After breakfast, she kisses Simon goodbye, does the dishes, gathers Lulu's backpack. At the bus stop, the little girl stays on the sidelines, still too shy to join the other kids huddled on the picturesque block of their affluent village outside Washington, D.C.

Jenna understands. The other moms still haven't taken to Jenna either. Simon always jokes that they're intimidated by her looks. She doesn't think it's that, but she'll keep trying. She smiles at Karen, the perfectly named queen bee of the neighborhood moms. The gesture goes unrequited.

Jenna joins the other parents waving to the tiny windows on the yellow school bus, all seeming part saddened, part elated, at the departure of their children for a few precious hours. As the bus disappears in a trail of black exhaust, Jenna notices a woman across the street who seems to be staring at her. She's not one of the usual bus-stop parents. She has a pretty heart-shaped face, high cheekbones. Someone new in the neighborhood maybe. Too young to be a mom. An au pair? Jenna raises her hand to wave, but the woman turns away. *Not even fellow outcasts want to be friends.* Jenna watches a long moment as the woman crosses the street to avoid the other parents chatting on the sidewalk.

Back at the house, Jenna contemplates a shower. But it's SoulCycle day. She's already done her miles, so she could skip it, but they prepaid a fortune for the classes. Besides, what else does she have to do other than clean the house, which Simon already keeps immaculate? Tax lawyers, she's learned, are people of precision. Still, there's dry cleaning to pick up, a run to Whole Foods for Simon's favorite steaks, Willow's veggie burgers.

After running her errands, she again considers skipping spin class. Then a text arrives:

See you at SoulCycle!

That's weird. She's not meeting anyone at class. She doesn't really have any friends. The message is from an unfamiliar number. Maybe it's the next wave of advertising technology. They not only read your mind on your social-media feed; now it's your texts. Maybe it's the lady she met in class last week who was friendly to her, though Jenna doesn't recall giving her the number.

By noon, she's rushing into the lobby of the Soul-Cycle on Massachusetts Avenue, downtown. Though the studio is only seven miles from Jenna's house, it took forty minutes to get there. D.C. traffic is brutal, but it's still nothing compared to Shanghai or Kabul. There's a SoulCycle in Bethesda, much closer to home, but old habits from her single days are hard to break. And Emma L is her favorite instructor.

She smiles at the receptionist, signs in.

In the changing room, Jenna opens her locker. She's surprised. There's a cell phone inside. It's the cheap burner-phone variety. She examines the locker's door to make sure she's opened the right one, but it's her monthly rental. And the combination on the lock worked.

Dread courses through her.

The phone pings. The text is three words:

bathroom second stall

She scoops up the phone, shuts the tiny door to the locker, and heads to the restroom. Class is starting; she can hear music and the instructor's distorted voice coming from the studio. The restroom is empty. Lowering her head, she peers under the row of stalls. No feet.

She faces the second stall, opens the door slowly, the pulsing beat of the music still vibrating through the walls.

A jolt rips through her. Inside the stall is a woman. She's sitting on the toilet tank, her feet resting on the seat.

Another lightning bolt to the chest. It's the young woman from the bus stop. The woman steps gracefully onto the floor and shoves a duffel bag into Jenna's hands.

"I said I was done with all this," Jenna tells her. "They said I was free and they wouldn't—"

"That's above my pay grade."

"Please, I can't."

The woman shakes her head. "You'd better. For Simon, Willow, and Tallulah's sake."

The woman steps past her calmly and disappears.

Jenna's heart is banging in her chest; she feels sweat rising on her forehead. She steadies herself, then unzips the duffel. Inside, there's a pair of movie-starlet sunglasses, a wig of flowing black hair, a denim jacket, and a keycard that says: HAMILTON HOTEL. Handwritten on the sleeve, a room number: 1018.

Five minutes later, Jenna slips out of the SoulCycle studio and struts down the street in her disguise. The Hamilton's only a block away. Her gut is full of butterflies, but her training is coming back to her. Like riding a bike.

She's not this person anymore. She can't; she won't.

But her family.

Inside room 1018, she finds a rifle with a high-end scope on a tripod positioned at the window.

The phone pings again and Jenna reads the instructions.

It seems that the bald man at the outdoor table at the Capital Grille won't be making it to dessert.